WOE IS WEDNESDAY

MAGGIE FITZROY

ISBN print: 978-1-7330262-8-4

ISBN ebook: 978-1-7330262-9-1

❀ Created with Vellum

Dedicated to my father in Heaven.
He always encouraged me to write a book, even when I doubted I could.
Somehow, he knew.
He also taught me how to swim.
Thanks, Dad!

ONE

P hiladelphia, Pennsylvania
Wednesday, July 13, 1955

It was supposed to be an easy job.

Show up at a swanky party, undercover as a ditsy socialite tennis player, then secretly search the place for a missing necklace.

Never mind that I'd never held a tennis racket in my life. Or that finding the diamond and emerald pendant would be a long shot. All I had to do was try.

No problem. That is, until someone at the party ended up dead.

Which I should have seen coming, given my magnet-for-danger track record as Philly's only female private eye.

But after spending days nursing a bad ankle—which I'd injured on my not so easy last case—I needed to get back to work. I was bored. And had bills to pay.

Which was all I was thinking about when my friend and part-time receptionist, Wendy Castillo, called out to me early Wednesday morning as I limped past her open door.

"I've got a great new case for you," she said, her eyes gleaming with excitement as she came out from behind her desk. "All you need to do is find a missing piece of jewelry. Easy-peasy."

Cool. "Tell me more," I glanced over at her as I unlocked my office door.

"You know my boss, Jonathan Miller, right?" Not waiting for an answer, she followed me in.

I lowered myself behind my desk and leaned toward her. Always cheerful, Wendy was especially so today. Her dark brown hair pulled up in a ponytail, she was dressed in a cherry blossom pink dress that brought out the natural blush of her cheeks. "I've heard a lot about your boss from you," I told her. "Haven't met him yet, though."

I'd only started renting the office down the hall from Wendy two months earlier, when I'd launched my private eye business—and I'd been quite busy since. Tracking down missing persons and solving murders meant I'd not spent much time in the office.

No surprise, then, that I'd yet to cross paths with Wendy's boss, an attorney with a solo practice. "I'd like to meet him," I added, "so I can thank him for allowing you to take calls and greet clients for me when I'm out."

"Well, today's your lucky day." Wendy grinned. "The missing jewelry is a necklace belonging to his wife, Penny. He's hoping you can find it. And it will be a way for you to fulfill your part of the deal you guys made."

Oh, okay. I'd be taking this case for free. As payback for Wendy's services to me. That was the deal I'd made with her boss. She did part time work for me and I in turn had agreed to do private investigative work for him when he needed it.

This was my first opportunity to do something for him. "I'll find that missing necklace or die trying," I said, lifting my chin, trying to sound cute.

I felt my chipper, cutesy smile fading away as I realized how ridiculous that sounded. Being hired to search for a missing piece of jewelry might not be as challenging as finding someone's missing loved one, but losing something important can cause a great deal of anxiety.

I waved for Wendy to take a seat in the chair facing my desk. "I'm sorry, Penny must be distraught about losing something so valuable. I'm intrigued. Tell me more about this necklace."

"I don't know much." She pursed her lips. "Jonathan will be able to tell you more when he gets here, probably any minute." Leaning forward, she narrowed her eyes and half-whispered, "All I know is that Penny thinks her cousin stole it."

Oh. My. Family drama. "Her cousin?"

"Lily. They're close, always have been. Same age, early thirties. But, from what I understand, years ago, as teenagers, they were in love with the same boy. This boy gave Penny the necklace before enlisting in the Army after Pearl Harbor, as a promise to marry her when he returned. Lily was hurt, and jealous, but all was forgiven and forgotten when the boy never came home."

"Killed in the war?"

"Missing in action, presumed killed during the D-Day invasion. His body was never identified."

"Wow, how sad." I was getting the uneasy feeling that this freebie case was going to be more complicated than I'd anticipated. "I take it that Penny kept the necklace, as a reminder of her lost love?"

"Yes."

"Was this lost love from a wealthy family? Diamonds and emeralds —must have cost a fortune."

Wendy shrugged. "I don't know. All I know is that Lily and her husband, Arty, are going to be throwing a party at their house tonight. At their mansion, in Chestnut Hill. I think Jonathan and Penny want to bring you as their guest, get you in the door so you can slip away and snoop around. And good news, you can bring a date." Wendy wiggled her eyebrows.

Uh-oh.

I cleared my throat. "A date?"

"Yes. You can bring Steve. Of course, you'll bring Steve. Since the two of you are now an item."

My cheeks went hot. "What do you mean, we're an item?"

"Heard you spent Fourth of July at his parents' place."

"How'd you hear that?"

"Never mind. Is it true?"

I swallowed hard. "Yeah, so?"

"So ... that's a sure sign that things are getting serious. When he introduces you to his mom and dad, I hear wedding bells." She gave a saucy wink. "Be sure to give me an invite."

"Sure, Wendy, you can be my maid of honor." That came out strangled, not the flippant tone I'd been aiming for. Now my cheeks were burning up.

Steve Evans and I are friendly competitors. A successful, experienced private eye who somehow managed to involve himself in my first two cases, he's dreamboat handsome. And he claims to be in love with me. Problem is, he has a reputation for breaking women's hearts. Meaning I've been fighting hard not to fall in love with him to protect my heart.

Only I am in love with him. And he knows it.

I quickly changed the subject back to my new case. "I like the idea of going to that party. But I can't go as a detective. I'll need a cover."

"I like your attitude."

My eyes shot to the man standing in my doorway.

Wendy whirled around. "Jonathan, there you are."

"I see Wendy has been filling you in about my case." He came over to shake my hand. "Nice to meet you at last, Story Smith."

I jumped to my feet. "Likewise, Mr. Miller."

"Jonathan, please."

I nodded. He was a pleasant looking man. Average height, slim build. Reddish, sandy-colored hair, maybe close to forty.

I pointed to the only other chair in my small office, about to invite my new client to have a seat, when Wendy stood up. "I've got work to do, so I'll leave you two to talk privately. Good luck, Story." She winked. "Have fun at the party and tell Steve I said hi."

Before meeting Steve, Wendy had thought I led an exciting life. Since meeting him she has come to believe I'm the luckiest woman on the planet. I wished I could believe that. Wished I could *let* myself believe that.

Jonathan took Wendy's place in the chair in front of me.

I sat back down and shared with him what Wendy had told me about the case so far.

He nodded, then sighed. "I always knew about that necklace, but

Penny never wore it, just kept it in her jewelry case. I came along in her life years after Harry, so I never knew the guy. Wasn't threatened by him, either, because how can you be jealous of a ghost?"

"His name was Harry?"

"Harry O'Toole."

"Why didn't Penny ever wear the necklace? To spare your feelings?"

"Maybe. I never asked, and we never discussed it. I never gave the thing much thought until it went missing. It was all she had of Harry, and now she's beside herself with grief all over again over that piece of jewelry."

"Especially because she thinks her cousin stole it?"

"Yes. She and Lily grew up like sisters. Best friends. Harry drove them briefly apart and now he's doing it again."

"Through this necklace."

Jonathan's eyes flashed annoyance. "Exactly. Lily and her husband, Arty, live near us. Lily visits often. But when she came over a few days ago, she wasn't herself. Seemed nervous. Started reminiscing about Harry. Asked Penny about the necklace. Penny showed it to her, then put it back in her jewelry case. She didn't think any more about it until she noticed it was missing the next day."

"Did Penny ask Lily if she took it?"

"No. She's too embarrassed. Says Lily would deny taking it, so what would be the point? Insinuating that Lily was a thief would only create hard feelings between our families."

I cleared my throat. "So, you want me to snoop around their house during a party to try to find it? *That* wouldn't create hard feelings?"

"Not if you don't get caught. Just slip away, search the bedrooms, especially the master bedroom."

I pressed my lips together, thinking. "I can go as your guest but will have to come up with a fake identity. Maybe as a friend of Penny's?"

"Sure, that would work."

"I'm a little bruised up and I have a sprained ankle."

He shrugged. "Penny plays tennis. We can say you're a tennis friend who lunged for a ball and took a tumble."

I liked that. Liked the challenge. Pretending to be someone else for a night would be fun. Like Halloween, but better. Only ... I held Jonathan's gaze, confused. This wasn't Halloween, or any other holiday. It was an ordinary Wednesday in the middle of July.

"Why are Lily and her husband throwing a party tonight?" I asked. "On a Wednesday?"

Jonathan laughed. "I like your perceptiveness, Story Smith. It's a good question, but you'll understand once you meet Arty and Lily Duncan. They have money and they like parties. They like to throw parties. They like to throw parties that are the talk of the town. Any excuse will do."

I widened my eyes. "And this one?"

"They are calling it a WowWee It's Wednesday Party. Because why not celebrate the middle of the week? No one else is doing it. If you get an invite from Arty and Lily Duncan, you can consider yourself special. Brag about it among Philly's finest. Even if it means showing up the next day at work hungover. Well worth it."

It was batty. Crackers. I loved it. "When can I meet your wife?" I asked. "We don't have much time to get ready for this party. And Wendy said I need to bring a date."

"That would be best." He stood up and adjusted his tie. "Let's go meet Penny now, shall we? She's at home, waiting for you. Hoping you will agree to do this."

Two

My jaw dropped when we pulled up to the Miller's home on Mermaid Lane. Chestnut Hill is one of Philadelphia's most prestigious neighborhoods and the grand, two-story brown and gray stone colonial serenely tucked behind a wrought-iron gate was impressive.

Jonathan was clearly doing well for himself. Or maybe he'd married up.

So why was he renting an office in my building? It was all I could afford starting out, but rather shabby around the edges. Or to put it another way, it was on the edge of respectable. Small, one window offices with worn carpet in a low-rent district of the city.

By the looks of the Miller's opulent home, I would think he could do better. There had to be a reason, and I filed it away in my mind to ask him when I had the chance.

His wife, Penny, was clearly expecting us. When he ushered me through the front door into the marble-tiled entryway, she hurried down an elegant, white-carpeted staircase off to our right and introduced herself, reaching for my hands.

"I've heard so much about you, Miss Smith," she said with the cultured, confident tone of one raised in privilege. "I feel sure you'll be able to help me."

"Why, thank you. I'm sure I can ... I mean, I hope I can ..." I managed a smile as I held her twinkling hazel eyes, then gave her fingers a squeeze and stepped back.

Penny Miller was tall and willowy. I'm five-foot-six and she towered over me. She had light brown curly hair, a sweet, pretty face, and wore a calf-skimming, blueberry-blue dress with big white polka-dots.

I suddenly felt dowdy in my pale-yellow cotton dress, not to mention self-conscious about the fading bruises on my arms and legs.

Her eyes flicked down to my bandaged ankle. "I'm sorry to hear about your injury. Jonathan told me all about it. You were in a shootout, right? Almost got yourself killed?"

"Almost." I grimaced. "I was lucky to get away with only a sprained ankle. But—"

"But you are so brave. How old are you, anyway?"

"Twenty-six."

"Wow, so young. And you look nothing like what I'd imagined a female private detective would look like. You're so petite. A honey-blonde beauty who looks more like a magazine model than a gal with a gun who goes after bad guys."

"Uhm ... thank you ... I guess." What else could I say? That my looks were part of my toolkit?

It was time to shift the conversation away from me and onto the party. I glanced over at what appeared to be the living room just beyond the staircase, and Jonathan took the hint.

"Let's go sit down, shall we?" He led the way into the impressively decorated room. Oriental rugs. Walls dotted with paintings of fox hunts. A wide, white brick fireplace, its mantle lined with red roses in various sized vases. Real roses, that filled the air with their sweet fragrance.

He waved for me to take a seat on a blue velvet sofa next to the fireplace as he and his wife settled themselves into matching leather armchairs across from me.

"I'm sorry to hear about your missing necklace," I told Penny as I fished a notebook and pencil out of my purse, ready to take notes. "Do you happen to have a photo of it?"

She shook her head. "No. I never wore it, so it's never been photographed."

"Could you describe it, then?"

She smiled. "It's eighteen inches, alternating diamonds and emeralds, rather large stones. Fourteen carat gold."

"Sounds lovely." I wrote that down. "And quite valuable."

"Very, I'm sure. But I never thought about that." She exhaled a deep sigh. "I suppose I should have. Should have put it in a more secure place than my jewelry box. Should have at least photographed it for insurance purposes. But I never thought of it as an expensive piece of jewelry that someone would want to steal."

"I understand it was a gift," I said softly, waiting for her to tell me more.

"Yes." Her eyes welled with tears. She brushed one off her cheek.

Her husband handed her his handkerchief. She dabbed the tear and lifted her chin. "I'm okay. I need to talk about Harry without crying."

"Tell me about Harry," I said. "He was the one who gave you the necklace?"

"Yes."

"Your husband told me a little about him. That he died in the war."

"That's right. He gave me the necklace before shipping off, promising to marry me when he returned. Only he never came home."

"Where did he get the money for the necklace? Was he from a wealthy family?"

"No, the opposite, in fact. He worked summers as a lifeguard and mowing lawns and doing odd jobs around town. Saved every penny he earned."

"He sounds like a hard worker. And a dream boyfriend."

"He was," she said, twisting her husband's handkerchief in her lap.

"I understand your cousin, Lily, loved him too, and was jealous that he chose you over her?"

"Crushed. All during the war we both wrote to him, and he wrote back to both of us, sometimes together, sometimes separately. I think Lily hoped he would change his mind about marrying me and marry her instead. In the end, neither of us got him. But I was the one who got the necklace." She dabbed at a tear.

"Which she secretly coveted?"

"I never thought so. Until a few days ago. She married Arty after the war, and he's given her a marvelous life. They have twin girls and live in one of the most historic homes in Chestnut Hill, on a lovely three-acre property."

"And they like to throw parties?"

She pressed her lips together, then gave a wry smile. "Arty is a showoff. His parties allow him to flaunt his fortune. No expenses spared. Alcohol flows. Incredible music. Sometimes Dick Clark from American Bandstand shows up. And once, Bill Haley and His Comets—can you believe—"

"Bill Haley?" I squeaked. "Rock Around the Clock" is a massive hit right now."

"That's Arty Duncan," Jonathan said, waving a hand. "If you get an invite to one of his parties, you have arrived."

"Caterers float around with samples of exotic dishes, which guests can then partake of in unlimited quantities at the buffet," Penny said. "Which in summer is usually set up by the pool. It'll be quite grand."

I was suddenly eagerly looking forward to this fancy schmancy party, until I remembered the reason for my going. "Your husband tells me that you believe Lily took your necklace," I said.

She winced. "Sadly, that's true. It's gone from the jewelry box where I always kept it, and the timing of it going missing is suspicious and points to her."

"How did you happen to notice it was gone?"

She glanced at her husband, then moved watery eyes back to me. "I like to take it out and look at it. Just hold it. In the palm of my hand. Feel the warmth of it. Feel Harry's love. The love that we—"

"Penny." Jonathan's voice was sharp. "I never knew you did that. I had no idea."

By the hurt look on his face, it was clear he hadn't realized Harry's ghost was still around.

Penny whispered, "I'm sorry Jonathan."

"Why do you believe Lily took it?" I asked her.

"I can't think of any other explanation." She dabbed her eyes with Jonathan's handkerchief. "When she came over the other day, she was obsessed with talking about Harry. For the first time in years and it struck me as odd, but I humored her. Then, at her request, I let her hold the necklace for a few minutes and then put it back in my jewelry box. She watched me. She knew where I kept it."

"And you want me to come with you to the party tonight— to the WowWee It's Wednesday party—to try to find it?"

"Yes. I can't think of what else to do."

Jonathan pulled a pack of cigarettes out of his jacket pocket, lit one, and turned to me. "Do you smoke?"

I shook my head.

Inhaling, he blew out a stream of smoke and held his wife's troubled gaze through the haze. "Penny, our private eye will need a cover identity for the party. I suggested she pretend to be one of your tennis friends."

Penny blinked at me. "Alright. Do you play?"

"No. But I'll brush up on the lingo. Come up with a dramatic story about how I hurt my ankle. Then I'll make it look like I'm downing drinks to take away the pain—becoming so obnoxious people will just want me to go away. Which I will. To search for the necklace."

Penny smiled through her tears. "You're creative, Story Smith. I think this is going to work."

"I can't go by my real name, though. I'll need a different one. How does Millicent Pettigrew sound?" It had just popped into my head, and to my ears had the ring of snobby-rich. "Millicent will have delusions of becoming the next great tennis champ," I added. "Her braggadocio will add to her obnoxiousness." I grinned.

Penny returned my grin. "Perfect. But let's make it Millie for short. Easier to remember. And you'll bring a date?"

I pressed a finger to my lower lip, like I was thinking about it, although Wendy was right, of course I'd ask Steve. "I'll ask a friend who is also a P.I. He can help me."

"Wonderful," Penny said. "I think this is going to be fun."

"I think so, too," I said, standing. It was time to go. I had to find Steve and hoped he was available. "I will do everything I can to find your necklace," I said. "But tell me, what should I do if I do find it, maybe in a drawer somewhere?"

"Just put it in your pocket." With a look of cunning and determination in her eyes, Penny lifted her chin. "If Lily thinks she can just take it from me, she's got another thing coming."

———

I went back to my office and called Steve's receptionist, Alice, to see if he was in.

"Yes, dear," she said. "I'll transfer you now."

"No, wait." I didn't want to ask Steve to be my date over the phone. Asking him in person would be awkward enough. "Just tell him I have an urgent matter to discuss with him, and that I'll be right over."

Hanging up before she could say anything else, I hurried out to my car.

Steve's office is a short drive from mine. Although both of our offices are in Philadelphia, that's where the similarities end. My tiny place has one window that overlooks a parking lot. His spacious digs are on the top floor of a new high-rise, affording him a magnificent view of the Delaware River.

When I arrived, Alice greeted me with a welcome smile. A kind, doting, grandmotherly type woman, I had always admired her dedication to Steve, who was a few years older than me. It was clear she was anxious for him to find the right woman to settle down with and she seemed to like me.

She'd worked for Steve for years and had witnessed a parade of women stream through his life.

So, her liking me made me as nervous as Steve's liking me. With Steve, I had too much to lose besides my heart. Namely, my business.

"Story." He bounded out of his inner office and reached for my hands.

A rush of heat streamed through me. So much for trying to control my feelings. I sent a mental message to my blood to cool it. To no avail. My cheeks caught fire. I let go of his hands.

Okay ... so maybe asking him to be my fake date wasn't such a good idea. Only I couldn't think of anyone else. Didn't want to, either.

"I've missed you." Steve gazed deep into my eyes, then glanced down at my ankle. "What have you been up to? Are you feeling better? It's been way too long."

In truth, it had only been a little over a week since we'd spent Fourth of July at his parent's country estate outside Philly. We'd celebrated the holiday and the successful conclusion of a murder case we'd ended up investigating together.

But he was right. It had been too long.

"My ankle is healing nicely, thank you ... and I finally got back to work … today … and I have a new case already … and—I need to ask you a favor." I was babbling. Boy oh boy, was I babbling.

His eyes lit up. "Anything. For you."

I glanced over at Alice, who was trying, with little success, to pretend she wasn't listening to us. The smile playing on her lips gave her away.

"Could we go into your office?" I half-whispered. "This is kind of … you know … sensitive."

His mouth curled into an amused grin. "Sure."

Closing the door between his office and the reception area, he gestured for me to take a seat across from his desk.

I glanced over and down at the river, sparkling in the sun, then moved my eyes back to him and took a deep breath. "I need you to be my date to a party tonight."

He stared at me. Blinked, blinked again. Then burst out laughing. "You look so serious, Story. That was the last thing I was expecting you to say. Of course. Of course I'll go to a party with you. Anytime. But tonight? It's Wednesday."

I smiled. "It's a WowWee It's Wednesday Party. And don't get any ideas. It won't be a real date. I'm going undercover."

"Undercover? To a party?"

"Yes, so you won't be going with Story Smith—you'll be going with Millicent Pettigrew." I pronounced my fake name with a haughty, affected accent as I fluffed my hair.

Steve laughed again. "Smashing. So—this is part of your new case?"

"Yep."

"Intriguing. Fill me in."

I told him everything I knew, and when I finished, he was no longer laughing. "I'll be glad to stand guard while you slip in and out of rooms searching for that necklace," he said. "But are you going to wear some kind of disguise? What if someone at the party happens to know you?"

I shrugged. "I don't exactly run in Arty and Lily Duncan's social circle. But just in case, I'll ask my mother if I can borrow her wig. She has a brown one. Maybe I can scrounge up some fake glasses, too. And I won't wear any makeup. You know, try to blend in."

Steve chuckled. "You, blend in? Never happen, but it will be fun to watch you try." He drummed his fingers on the desktop. "But what about me? I should probably use my real name, right? I've been in business in this town for a while. People know me as a private eye."

"They also know you as a guy who dates a lot of women. So, no problem. You can go as you. People will just think Millicent Pettigrew is your latest conquest."

Holding my gaze with a slow grin, he rearranged his lips into a teasing frown. "But how do I know this Millicent Pettigrew is my type?"

"Ha, very funny, Steve. She'll be your type." I stood. Time to go. I had much to do to get ready.

He stood, too, then held up a hand. "Wait. What does that mean? That she'll be my type?"

I opened my mouth, shut it, opened it again. "Uhm ... We'll figure it out. You know, improvise."

He winked at me. "I like the sound of improvise. We could get creative."

Flustered, I swallowed hard. "By the way—Millicent's nickname is Millie."

I headed for the door. Steve knew where I lived. I asked him to pick me up at six.

"From there, we'll head to the Miller's," I said, "then follow them to the party."

"Can't wait, *Millie*." Steve flashed me that smile of his that had always made my heart do flips. "See you then."

THREE

I was feeling quite proud of myself when Steve knocked on my door.

Before going to answer it, I took one more peek at myself in my bedroom mirror. Which made me grin because I almost didn't recognize the woman giving me a goofy grin back.

In my mom's brown shoulder length wig, I looked ... well ... washed out.

With her spare tortoise shell glasses perched upon my nose, I looked serious. Since she was farsighted, everything was a bit blurry. Well, just a little. I could handle that.

I'd also borrowed one of my mom's dresses, a pale green party frock that was too big for me and did not nothing to flatter my complexion. Which was the point. I wanted to look shapeless, uninteresting, and most of all, forgettable. A woman who could slip away and not be missed.

Steve knocked again, harder, and I hurried to the door.

I live in a modest apartment in the Manayunk section of Philadelphia, which he'd been to a few times, although I'd never been to his place. I longed to know where he lived but had never dared asked. What if he invited me there? Then what? He and me, a single woman, alone in his place? Oh, no. That didn't bear thinking about.

I yanked the door open.

Steve gaped at me, clearly amused, then shook his head. "You've got to be kidding."

"What?" I waved him inside.

"Millicent Pettigrew is definitely *not* my type."

I lifted my chin. "That's good, right?"

"Yessss. Since Story Smith is my type and you look nothing like her."

Steve looked like Steve, only more cleaned up than usual in a dapper navy-blue blazer and white trousers. I tried to pretend he had no effect on me but I'm pretty sure I failed.

"I like Millie's shoes, though." He moved his flirty gaze to my flat white pumps. "Except for that fat bandage around your ankle—don't you think that's overdoing it?"

"I double wrapped it. I'm a tennis player with a sprain, remember?"

"I remember. But you've never really played tennis, have you?"

"No. But I know a little bit about the sport. Like the word *love* is part of the score." I chewed the inside of my cheek, suddenly more nervous than I would have liked. How *was* I going to pull this off?

Steve ran a hand over his slicked back dark brown hair. "Good thing I play tennis. Means I'll be able to cover for you. Anytime the conversation gets tennis-heavy, let me take over. You just nod."

I relaxed a little. Steve was too good to be true. He'd saved my life, and now he was saving me again. I gave him a grateful grin. "Thanks, Steve. Improvise, improvise. That'll be the name of our game. I'm going to pretend to be real, real ditsy and very quickly drunk because the sooner I can wander out of the party and start searching rooms, the better."

"And I'll be right behind you."

"Uhm... I hope nobody notices that."

A corner of Steve's mouth twitched up. "Why? I'm going to the party as your date."

I didn't like the gleam in his eye. "What? What are you thinking?"

He lifted his eyebrows and held them there.

"You have a plan, Steve. What is it? Tell me, I need to know."

"I've decided that Millie Pettigrew is my type after all."

Uh-oh. "Oh."

"Yep, I think I'm in love with her. Madly in love. So much in love that I won't be able to keep my hands off her. Or let her out of my sight."

"Oh ..."

"Which means when Millie wonders off, Steve will disappear with her. Nobody will care. They'll just figure we're off doing ... you know."

"Oh, right ..." Only something told me that would be too easy. What if somebody did care? But I couldn't think about that right now. I'd just have to improvise when and if the time came.

"You ready?" Steve reached for my arm.

"As ever, I suppose." My heart thudding in my chest, I swallowed hard. "Let's just hope I find that necklace."

———

The Duncan estate on Hartwell Lane was grand, so large and wooded that it was hard to believe we were still in Philadelphia. Pulling up to the entrance gate in Steve's car, a uniformed guard waved us through as guests of the Millers, who were just ahead of us, in Jonathan's white Chrysler New Yorker.

Steve was driving a black Mercedes-Benz—the third car I'd seen him drive in the short time I'd known him and his most impressive, by far.

It sure helped us fit in. Up ahead, more men in uniforms were directing luxury cars of all shapes and sizes onto a grass lawn beside the Duncan's sprawling red brick mansion. Two-story. Many windows. Several wings.

Just how many rooms? How many rooms would I need to search?

Steve glanced over at me. "What are you thinking, Story—I mean Millie?"

"I'm thinking I'm impressed."

"With what?"

"With the Duncan's mansion. And with this new car of yours. How many do you own anyway? Are you trying to upstage my T-Bird?"

Steve inched us forward in the line of vehicles, his eyes on the Miller's New Yorker. "I could never upstage your ragtop. Sweetest car I've ever laid eyes on."

Steve loved to drive my white 1955 Thunderbird, even though he considered it too conspicuous for a private eye. But I didn't care. With baby blue leather seats, it was an eye-catching automobile. But it was a well-earned gift, and it fit my personality. Open. Optimistic. Impulsive. And a bit wild. Just the right car for a woman who'd courageously—or crazily— left her safe, boring job for a dangerous line of work that could get her killed.

"I like your Mercedes," I told Steve. "But you have so many cars. When did you get this one?"

He shot me a lopsided grin. "A few days ago. Why? You like it?"

"How could I not?"

"It's black, so that makes it unobtrusive, unlike your T-Bird."

I ignored the jibe at my T-Bird. "Still ... it must have cost a fortune."

"So?"

I stared at Steve. His "so" said it all. He was rich. Not born rich, because he'd confided to me during my last case that he'd been adopted as an infant. A secret very few people knew. Still, he'd grown up with nothing but the best. He was lucky and he knew it.

He had his eyes on the parking attendants, who were directing the Millers to go right. Widening his grin, he muttered, "Relax, Story, you can do this. We can do this."

"Millie. It's Millie."

He parked, leaned over, planted a kiss on my cheek, then teasingly touched the tip of my nose. "Right. Girl of my dreams—how can I forget?"

Jonathan appeared at my door. He opened it and helped me out.

Steve came around and took my arm as Penny hurried over to join us. Wearing a flowered satin dress that went well with her husband's white seersucker suit, her expression was a combination of excited and nervous. "Ready?" she asked me in a hushed voice. "You look great."

Nodding, I whispered, "Millicent Pettigrew is ready. Lead the way."

Steve and I had already briefed the Millers on how we planned to carry out our mission. I'd introduced Steve to them when we'd rendezvoused at their house to follow them to the party, so we were all on board.

We trailed behind a swarm of guests to the open front door, where a petite ash-blonde with a pixie-cute face greeted everyone who entered. Her almost white hair was cut short in a bob, and she was so slender that she couldn't have weighed more than ninety pounds, soaking wet.

"Lily," Penny crooned. "You look fabulous. I hope you don't mind if Jonathan and I brought a couple of guests."

A flicker of surprise sparked in Lily's eyes as she glanced at Steve and me, quickly followed by polished, polite delight and a murmured, "Hello. Welcome."

This was Lily? I tried to hide the surprise I felt as I flashed her my best arrogant, overly confident Millie Pettigrew smile. Lily and Penny might be cousins, but they in no way resembled each other.

I'd just assumed ... So, when was I going to learn that private eyes should assume nothing?

"Why didn't you tell me you were bringing guests?" Lily asked Penny in a high-pitched little girl voice that matched her appearance. Which was enhanced by the pale peach dress she wore, which had ruffles everywhere. Ruffles around the neck, ruffles down the sleeves, ruffles around the hem.

"It was a last-minute decision. I was sure you wouldn't mind." Penny patted my arm. "This my friend, Millie Pettigrew. She's a tennis pal who recently took a tumble playing and to get her mind off her poor, sprained ankle, I asked her to come along. With her boyfriend, Steve."

Lily glanced down at my bandages. "Ouch. Poor dear. Why of course—"

"Ouch is right, and now I'm missing my chance at a spot on the Olympic team." I heaved a heavy sigh. "The psychological pain is just as bad as the physical."

"Which means ... isn't it a good thing she has me?" Steve draped an arm around my shoulder, pulling me close. I felt him trying to refrain from laughing and I knew I'd gone too far with that Olympics thing, but, hey, I was having fun.

Lily gave me a funny look, then turned to Steve. "You look familiar. Do I know you?"

He stiffened. "I don't think so."

"I know you!" A platinum blonde emerged from the crowd ahead of us and hurried over. "Steve! Steve Evans!" Beaming she reached for his free hand—the one that wasn't still draped around my shoulder—and squeezed it. "I didn't think I'd ever see you again," she squealed. "And now, here you are! Yay!"

Yay. Here we were. Hadn't even gotten in the door before running into one of Steve's former girlfriends. Who had her huge, cornflower blue eyes fixed on him, ignoring me completely.

Nice.

"Hello, Claudia," Steve said, his tone dry, with a hint of alarm. "Nice to see you again."

Claudia? Oh, no. A bell went off in my brain. Shortly after meeting Steve, my big brother Rob—also a private eye at the time—had warned me not to fall in love with him. Claimed Steve had been engaged to a woman named Claudia, then broke it off, breaking her heart. One of many, Rob said.

"Seems the two of you know each other," Jonathan, behind me, remarked, sounding none too pleased.

That was nothing compared to how I felt.

"We were engaged once." Claudia sniffed. She was slurring her words and weaving back and forth. Drunk?

Steve pulled his hand away. "Not exactly, Claudia."

"You asked me to marry you, Steve."

"Not that I remember."

"I've never gotten over you."

"Funny. You appear fully recovered to me, although slightly inebriated." Steve turned and grabbed my hands and gazed into my eyes. "Anyway, as you can see, I'm with Millie now. And I'm not even going to try to hide it—I'm madly in love."

Oh, golly. He was giving me a smile of heart-clutching adoration. A Prince Charming smile. Now, now, I had to keep my head. He'd called me Millie. I was Millie. And this was improv.

"Millie? She's your type now?" Claudia looked me up and down with a you've-got-to-be-joking smirk, then pointed to my ankle. "What happened to your foot?"

"She hurt herself playing tennis." Steve kissed my cheek. "Now, if you'll excuse us, we need to go on into the party because we're holding up the line behind us."

Gracing Claudia with my best Millie gotcha-grin, I kept a firm hold of Steve's hand as we finally made our way inside.

I tried not to show it, but I was shaken and shaking. My goal had been to keep a low profile, and I felt like I'd already failed. I had an enemy now, when I'd been hoping to remain mostly invisible.

Only ... maybe things weren't that bad. I looked around. The party was packed, the music loud. Well-dressed people milled about, drinks and cigarettes in hand. "I hope we can lose Claudia in this crowd," I murmured to Steve as we meandered into the living room.

"Don't worry about her," he whispered in my ear.

"Don't worry, I'm not." I spotted a bar at the far end of the room. "Anyway, it's time for my show to begin."

His cheek twitched. "That's my girl. What do you have in mind?"

"How about you go over to the bar and order me a drink? A gin and tonic with a slice of lime. Or, what looks like a gin and tonic. Tell the bartender to hold the gin. Because Millie's going to get fake drunk. As fast as possible."

FOUR

I couldn't just down one drink and casually meander off. Somebody might notice. No, had to play the game for a while. Socialize. Schmooze with the other guests. Act as if I wasn't anxiously longing to slip away to search for a missing necklace.

Which, with any luck, I'd find. And then be able to call it a night.

Failing to find it was not a concern. All I had to do was give it my best shot.

But failing to pull off being Millicent Pettigrew was a different kettle of fish. If I blew my cover, I'd not only look like an idiot, jeopardizing my career, I'd also compromise Penny's relationship with her cousin—while failing to find her necklace. Which wouldn't bode well for my career, either.

So, when Steve handed me my first gin-less gin and tonic, I took a sip, fixed a too-confident, obnoxious Millie-smile on my face, and hobbled over to a young couple standing beside a white baby grand piano. Time to make small talk. And, hopefully, they didn't play tennis.

Steve caught up to me and took my arm before I got to them, whispering, "Stick with me. We need to stay together, remember?"

I gulped another sip and sighed. "Right. Right. Sorry. Sorry."

"Hi," the woman greeted me. She had shiny brown shoulder-length hair and was drinking something pink and bubbly with a floating cherry on top. Waving her colorful concoction in my direction, she announced, "I'm Sheila and this is my husband, Bill. Don't believe we've met."

"I'm Millie Pettigrew and this is my boyfriend, Steve." I leaned my head on his shoulder to reinforce the boyfriend part. Sheila was ogling him. Like most women did with Steve. So, so, so annoying.

Bill, drinking what looked like whiskey on the rocks, just looked bored. With me, with Steve, with his wife.

"How do you know Lily and Arty?" Sheila plucked the cherry out of her drink and sucked on it while holding Steve's gaze. "I don't recall ever seeing you guys at one of their parties."

"I'm a tennis friend of Lily's cousin, Penny." I pointed to my ankle. "Unfortunately, I'm out of commission for a bit. Took a spill going for a ball I should have let go."

Bill snorted a laugh, coming alive, suddenly interested in the conversation. "No shame in going for the ball," he declared. "Always go for the ball. I love women who go for the ball, no matter what. What were you trying to execute? A jumping backhand?"

Great. This prematurely balding fellow sporting a bow tie was a tennis player. And I had no idea what he was talking about. What was a jumping backhand? I swallowed the rest of my drink, stalling for time, hoping Steve would answer for me.

But he didn't. His lips were twitching. Like he was having fun watching me squirm. Really? This was *not* the plan.

I nodded at Bill, flashing him a proud smile. "Yep. I was going for a jumping backhand alright." Sounded good to me, and rather daring. I liked daring. "Came down hard and twisty."

"Ouchy." Bill winked at me.

Sheila took a sip of her drink. "Where do you play?" She waved her glass at me. "I don't recall ever seeing you on the courts."

"Uh ..."

"Philadelphia Cricket Club," Steve said quickly, maybe too quickly.

"That's right." I nodded, feeling my face flush. Steve and I had discussed this. The Philadelphia Cricket Club, in the heart of Chestnut Hill, was *the* place to play tennis.

"We're members." Sheila sniffed.

Oh great. Of course, they were.

"Never saw you there." She put a hand on Steve's arm. "Nor you. I'd remember *you*."

I raised my chin and gave her a haughty smirk. "I'm almost never home. I travel the country playing tournaments. Usually win them, too, and of course Steve comes with me as my—"

Steve tightened his grip on my arm. "Millie, dear, we really should go over there and see Lily." Shooting Sheila and Bill a please-excuse-us smile, he steered me away from them and toward our hostess. Who was holding court in the middle of the room, surrounded by giggling guests.

"Didn't it occur to you that they were about to ask you which tournaments you've won? To name them?" Steve hissed in my ear. "You need to be careful, Story."

"Millie," I hissed back. "Millie."

"Millie," Lily cried out. "And Steve. So nice of you to come to my party." She turned to the man next to her. "This is my husband, Arty. Arty, meet Penny's friends."

Arty could not have appeared less impressed with Penny's friends. He flicked Steve and me a smidgen of a smile as Lily introduced us, then broke eye contact and looked around the room, as if seeking folks more interesting to spend time with.

How rude. A chill pricked the back of my neck. Who did this stocky, ruddy-faced jerk with the slicked-back blond hair and arrogant demeanor think he was?

He was so instantly dislikeable that I wondered if he could have had anything to do with the missing necklace. Given his wealth, it seemed unlikely. But I needed to at least consider it.

Lily didn't seem fazed by her husband's rudeness. And she either didn't notice, or pretended not to care, when he broke away from us without a word and headed to the bar. Where a cute redhead, who didn't look a day over eighteen, seemed to be waiting for him.

Lordy ...

My private eye instincts told me to keep watch on those two—because the teenager and much older man suddenly had eyes only for each other.

But darn it, I wasn't a private eye tonight. I was a self-absorbed tennis nut who wouldn't even notice the way Arty was rubbing the redhead's arm.

Reluctantly, I turned back to Lily, who was making small talk with Steve. Except, oddly, she wasn't looking at Steve. She was watching one of the party waiters, who was carrying a tray of stuffed mushrooms, make his way around the room.

Like the other catered helpers, he wore a crisp white uniform. Unlike the others, he had a pronounced limp.

Lily waved to him. But he didn't respond—instead, heading away from her.

She frowned, clearly disappointed, then twisted her lips into a frustrated pout.

Seriously? Did she want a mushroom that badly? They did look yummy, but still ...

As he approached the bar, he turned sharply and headed back in our direction.

Poor man. With his heavy limp, he also bore facial scars that appeared to have been smoothed over with surgery. As he came closer, I saw he'd been goodlooking once, and even now, with a thatch of jet-black hair falling over one eye, was still attractive.

Lily waved to him again. Again, he acted like he didn't see her.

"Do you want a mushroom?" I asked her. "I don't think that waiter sees you, but I can go get you one."

She blinked at me, as if startled by my offer. "Oh, no. Thank you, Millie, but I, uh ..." She bit down on her lip. "If you'll please excuse me, I need to go see about something in the kitchen."

Steve and I watched her rush off. She skirted around the waiter, acting suddenly uninterested in his mushrooms, or in him, and disappeared.

"Strange," Steve muttered. "What do you think that was all about?"

I shook my head. "I have no idea."

He nodded at my empty glass. "I'll go get you another drink."

I handed it to him. "Thanks."

He hesitated. "Come with me."

I stiffened. "Why? You don't trust me to carry on an intelligent conversation about tennis?"

He grinned. "How'd you guess?"

I grinned back. "Come on, Steve. Give me some credit. I don't need you by my side every second."

Shrugging, he waved my glass. "Okay, Millie. Be right back."

I watched him head to the bar. Then, without a drink in my hand, I felt like a stage actress who'd just lost her prop.

Spotting Penny across the room, I caught her questioning gaze. She was wondering if I'd made any progress.

Clearly not. But the evening was young. I flashed her a serene, I-know-what- I'm-doing smile, then turned away, stifling a sigh. This undercover stuff was harder than it looked.

"Well hello baby, what's a pretty lady like you doing standing here all alone?"

I turned around. A tall man with wavy brown hair and eyes the color of jade greeted me with a grin so charming it put Cary Grant to shame. His physique was equally impressive. Fit, trim, with the suggestion of rippled muscles under his navy-blue, gold-buttoned blazer.

"Hi," I said, stiffly. Men with his kind of aggressive charm tend to put me on the defensive.

Then I remembered I wasn't me. I was Millie. And I needed to lighten up. Make this fun.

"Hi doll, yourself," I cooed, summoning a smile. "I'm not alone. My boyfriend's just off getting me another drink."

"I like your glasses." He winked. "Sexy."

"Gee, thanks." I wiggled my eyebrows above my mother's most

unsexy spectacles. "Most men don't make passes at gals who wear glasses, but apparently you do."

"I do, indeed." He wiggled his eyebrows back at me. "What's your name, honey?"

"Millie. What's yours, handsome?"

"Charles Harrington." Reaching for my hand with both of his, he drew it to his mouth and planted a kiss.

He was wearing a wedding ring. Shiny gold band, hard to miss.

Great. This guy was married. So where was his wife? And what would Millie do about this flirt having a wife?

And where was Steve?

Retrieving my hand, I glanced over at the bar.

And my heart froze. Steve was talking to Claudia, with my drink in one hand and his in the other, his back up against the bar, like she was holding him hostage.

"I like you, Millie." Charles stepped closer, suddenly so near I could feel his body heat. "You're the prettiest girl at this party. What say we go find a corner and chat, since that boyfriend of yours has obviously ditched you?"

My mind whirled. What now? "Yeah, what a jerk he is," I whined, pasting a puffed-out pout on my face. Then, dropping the pout, I replaced it with a sly grin. "I like you, too, Charles. But what about your wife?"

He shrugged "What about her?"

"Is she here?"

"Yeah, somewhere."

"Won't she mind?"

"Mind what?"

"You and I having a chat in a corner somewhere."

"Not at all. She's used to it."

"Used to—?"

"She and I have an understanding about me and other women."

My jaw dropped. I was having a hard time remaining Millie. If Steve didn't get back with my drink soon … "Understanding? Other women?" I tried a sexy smile but couldn't quite pull it off.

"Hey, sugar, my wife knows I got a thing going with Lily." Charles ran a finger down my cheek. "She won't mind me and *you*."

Wait. What? "Lily?" I whispered. "You and *Lily*?"

"Matter of fact …" He gave me a slow-motion wink that told me he'd already had too much to drink. "My wife would probably rather me be with you than Lily. She thinks Lily is getting ideas about divorcing Arty and—"

"Lily?" I hissed. "Lily Duncan?" This was too much. I'd come to this party to search for a missing necklace, not to be propositioned by a horny married man who was bragging about having an affair with the hostess.

"Lily's falling in love with me." Charles sighed. "But I think I'm falling in love with you."

Oh, God …

"Millie!" Steve ran up to me and shoved my drink in my hand. "Sorry it took me so long." He eyed Charles with barely concealed distain. "Hello. Don't think we've met, old chum. Keeping my girl-friend company?"

Charles sneered at him. "While you were busy elsewhere, *chum*."

Alarmed, I cried, "Boys, boys, stop it, will you?" The last thing I needed was drama. It was time to slip away and do what I'd come to do.

I patted Charles's cheek. "You can't be in love with me, dear, because you don't even know me. Although I *am* flattered."

Then I turned to Steve and gave him a look that said let's get out of here, fast.

"Come on." I grabbed his hand. "Let's you and I go find a corner somewhere and chat."

FIVE

"Where are we really going?" Steve asked as I steered us around men and women celebrating the evening with drinks, smokes, and laughter.

"Time to get cracking," I said, slipping the contents of my drink into a potted plant by an open door that led outside.

Stepping out onto an outdoor patio, where more guests mingled, I set my glass down on a table, pulled him to a stop, and glanced around to get my bearings. "Before I get to work, I need to figure the layout of this place. This mansion's got two stories. Several wings. It's enormous."

"Sure is." Steve drained his drink, set the glass down, and waved for me to follow. "Let's go around back and scope things out."

We followed a stone pathway that led us to more partiers congregated around an enormous pool. Surrounded by tiki torches, the blue water sparkled with flickers of golden light as a small orchestra at the far end filled the air with soft music that had some couples slow dancing.

My gaze went to a second-floor balcony overlooking the pool and then to a set of stairs leading up to it. A thick velvet rope draped across the bottom step subtly declared the party ground floor only.

I smiled. That would give me privacy while searching the upstairs bedrooms.

But it also presented a challenge, as Steve and I needed to get upstairs without being observed.

Which clearly was not going to happen out here at the pool, with so many people. We needed to find another way up.

Frowning, I could tell Steve was thinking what I was thinking. He whispered in my ear, "Let's go back inside. I think I saw some stairs off the living room."

Nodding, I took his arm and let him guide me around throngs of people to where a wide hallway to the left of the front door led to several guest rooms and another set of stairs.

Where another velvet rope prevented access to the second floor.

Too bad. Glancing around to be sure no one was watching, I gingerly stepped over it and Steve followed.

I was pretty sure nobody had seen us, but even so, after we made it to the top of the stairs, I put my fingers to my lips, signaling that we needed to wait and listen.

Nothing. No one was shouting our names. We didn't hear any footsteps following us.

"Think we made it," I whispered, my heart hammering wildly in my chest. I took a deep breath to calm down. "Let's go."

"Which way?" Steve whispered back. It was growing dark and

hard to see, but fortunately I had remembered to stuff a small flashlight in the pocket of my dress.

I pulled it out and showed it to him. "Master bedroom suite. I think that's the best place to start."

Only, the second floor was massive, with wings jutting in several directions. So … which direction should we take? "Maybe the balcony overlooking the pool is part of the master bedroom," I whispered. "Follow me."

Wrong. The balcony was at the end of a hallway lined with rooms, none of which appeared to be the master bedroom, which had to be on another wing.

Tiptoeing back to the top of the stairs, we headed in the opposite direction from the balcony, found a wing that branched off another wing, and viola, there it was.

Through a partially open door I saw what was clearly a his-and-her bedroom. Floor to ceiling windows, giant matching dressers, spacious matching closets, and an immaculately made bed in the middle of the room, festooned with pillows.

I gave Steve a thumbs up. "This is it. I'm going to search the dressers, then the closets. You stand guard a little way down the hallway. Whisper loudly if you hear someone coming, try to delay them, and I'll find a place to hide."

He nodded. "Good luck."

A small lamp atop one of the dressers was turned on low, giving the room its only light, so I started there. Perfume bottles and a small jewelry box beside the lamp indicated the dresser was Lily's.

I opened the jewelry box and held my breath. No necklaces. Darn. Just a smattering of earrings and a few bracelets. I quietly closed the box, then eased the top drawer open.

Underwear. Panties, bras. I ran my hand under them and shined the flashlight in. No necklace.

I opened the next drawer down, then the next, then the next. No luck there, either. Just clothes. Slacks, sweaters, capris. If Lily had Penny's necklace, she had not hidden it in her dresser.

Darn again.

Wondering if she could she have stashed it in Arty's dresser, I tiptoed over there next and opened the top drawer. Men's underwear. Sucking in a breath, I held it as I ran my hand under boxers and socks.

Nothing. With a sigh, I opened the next drawer down, and shined the light in. I widened my eyes. A box the size of a deck of cards sat on top of some undershirts, and I was pretty sure I knew what was in it. I'd never seen condoms before, but the words "Super-Thin Transparent Prophylactics" gave me a clue.

Rattled at the intimacy of what I was staring at, I quickly closed the drawer.

Then froze. Something was happening out in the hallway.

A woman was giggling.

Giggling? My heart jumped into my throat.

Lily? Was she coming?

Panicking, confused, I wondered if I should hide. But where was Steve? Maybe he was distracting her, unable to warn me.

The overhead ceiling light flicked on.

I turned around.

Oh my God, it was Arty.

I swallowed hard. I was busted.

He blinked at me. "What the hell are you doing in here, lady?"

"I ...uh ..." Stammering, I shut my mouth. What could I say, anyway? I was standing in the man's bedroom, going through his dresser, with a flashlight in my hand. What could I possibly say that would make that okay?

The expression on his face went from confused to furious. Then it turned to fury mixed with outrage. "Answer me! What are you doing in here, miss ... miss ... What's your name again, anyway?"

"Millie. Pettigrew." My fake name squeaked out scared and shaky. I pressed my lips together in shame, my heart thudding in my chest. Where the hell was Steve?

"Millie? Penny's friend?" Arty narrowed his eyes in a threatening glare as he advanced on me. "How *dare* you come up here and go through my things? You thief, I'm going to call the police and have you arrested. I don't know how you thought you were going to get away with robbing me during my own party, but now you're not going anywhere."

Lunging at me, he reached for my arm.

Dodging his grasp, I stumbled backward.

He lunged at me again. Grabbed my arm. Dug his fingers into my flesh.

I tried to pull away. But he was too strong.

I struggled harder.

Then we heard a scream.

A loud, high-pitched, blood-freezing, heart-stopping scream. Followed by a sickening thud.

More screams followed.

Arty froze. I froze. We stared at each other, then he dropped my arm, cursed, turned, and ran out of the room.

———

I followed him out into the hallway. Haltingly, with no idea what to do. My legs were shaking so badly, I could hardly make them move. What on earth was happening?

People kept screaming. It was something bad. Maybe out by the pool. A fire? An accident? Masked gun men, robbing the place?

Steve ran up to me, appearing as if out of nowhere. Thank God. "Steve." I gaped at him, grabbed his arm. "What's going on?"

"I don't know." Breathing hard, he shook his head. "I don't know."

"Where *were* you? Arty found me going through his things. He—"

"I'm sorry, I didn't see Arty. Claudia followed us upstairs. I don't know why we didn't hear her. She was drunk and babbling on and on about wanting me back. She was going to cause a scene— so I had to lead her away, take her around a corner, promise to meet her at the bar later."

The screams continued. Everything felt like a bad dream. "Arty was threatening to have me arrested, Steve." I shook his arm. "Until ..." I jabbed a finger in the direction of the pool.

We stared at each other as loud shouts and wails replaced the screams. "Something horrible has happened," I gasped. "Whatever it is, we should go see. Maybe we can help."

"No." He shook his head. "You were about to be arrested—this is your chance to get away. Arty doesn't know your real name."

"But—"

"Don't you understand? If you get arrested, you could lose your P.I. license."

I bit down on my lip. "But we can't just leave ..."

"Yes, we can. Let's just go."

I shook my head. "No."

Steve pressed his lips together, then heaved a loud sigh. "You want to go see what's going on, don't you?"

"Yes ... and so do you."

He grunted. "Yeah. You're right. It could be important. Let's go."

Six

It was a woman.

Clearly dead. Lying face down next to the pool.

Her body was twisted into a hideous, broken, crumpled heap. I watched in horror as blood surged from her head onto the deck. Crimson streams spilled into the dark water.

Gasping, I pushed through the throng surrounding her, then pressed my hand to my mouth. In the golden, flickering light of the tiki torches I saw who she was.

"Lily," Steve gasped. "It's Lily Duncan."

Arty was on his knees beside her. "Police! Ambulance!" he yelled. "Please, somebody ... call for help ... help!"

Apparently, someone already had because police sirens wailed in the distance, getting louder and louder as they entered the property.

Moments later, officers ran onto the pool deck and pushed their way through shocked and moaning partiers as two ambulance attendants followed with a stretcher.

But Lily was clearly beyond help.

"What happened?" one of the officers shouted at the crowd.

People pointed upward, yelling in chaotic unison, "She fell ... from the balcony."

"Fell or jumped?" the officer shouted. "Who saw what happened?"

Silence. People shook their heads.

"*No one* saw what happened?" the officer called out, his tone sharp and incredulous.

"I don't think anybody was looking up at the balcony," a woman said. "It's dark up there."

"We heard her scream—the next thing we knew she was on the deck," a man said.

Murmurs of "that's right," and "this is unbelievable," and "poor Lily," followed.

"Then no one is to leave the premises," another officer shouted. "No one. Nobody leaves this party until we say they can."

———

There went my chance to slip away to avoid arrest. My only hope was that in the horrific confusion of his wife's gruesome death, Arty would be too consumed with grief to worry about me.

Numb with shock, my eyes met Steve's, then went back to watching police examine Lily.

One thing was clear: she'd either jumped or was pushed. No way could she have accidently fallen off that balcony. The stone railing was too high.

The police had obviously reached that conclusion, too.

"Everybody back, everybody—into the living room," an officer shouted as he and fellow officers began herding us like cattle off the pool deck. "We need to get statements from everybody here."

As a private eye, I wanted to question everyone, too.

But I was undercover as ditsy Millie Pettigrew. Who'd not only bragged to a bunch of people about being a champion tennis player, but who'd also been caught in the act of attempted robbery by the victim's husband.

Which made things messy. Real messy. Because being in Arty's bedroom with him during the time his wife toppled off the balcony made me a witness to his alibi—that he could not have had anything to do with her demise.

If she'd been murdered. Which my instincts told me she had. In the short time I'd been in Lily's presence, she'd not struck me as a woman who would take her life at her own party.

In the living room, Steve and I crowded onto a sofa next to Jonathan and Penny, who was sobbing.

Penny buried her face in her husband's shoulder. "What happened?" she moaned. "I don't understand what happened."

"Would Lily have jumped?" I whispered over to her.

Raising her head, she looked past Jonathan at me. "No," she whimpered, sniffing. "Of course not."

I asked softly, "Then you think someone pushed her?"

She blinked, then blinked again, looking confused, then angry. "Yes ... but why?"

"That's what the police are trying to find out," Steve muttered. "That's why no one can leave. Everybody here's a suspect." His expression grim, he glanced at me. "Everybody."

I winced at the thought of being interviewed as Millie. I'd have to confess my real identity and my reason for being at the party. Which wasn't a crime. And hopefully, when Arty learned the true reason for me going through his dresser, he would back off having me arrested.

After all, I was his alibi in a possible murder. They always suspected the husband first, so I was a valuable witness to his innocence.

Unless, of course, he'd paid someone to push Lily to her death. But why would he do that?

I couldn't just sit there. I had to do something—anything—to help solve this probable crime. For Penny's sake, if not for Lily's.

But what could I do?

Officers were moving around the room, going from person to person, conducting brief interviews, likely gathering names and addresses and phone numbers so they could follow up later.

There must have been about a hundred guests at the party, and with everyone packed into one room, it was growing hotter and more stifling by the moment. Many people sat on the floor, others stood, arms crossed, looking anxious and distraught, like they just wanted to go home.

My gaze fell on the teenage redhead who'd flirted with Arty at the bar. Slumped over on the piano bench, she held her face in her hands and appeared to be crying. I asked Penny if she knew her name.

Penny glanced in her direction and sniffed. "That's Stella Murphy. Lily and Arty's governess."

"Governess?" I stared at Penny. I had forgotten that she'd mentioned that the Duncans had children.

Penny nodded. "Stella is the new governess for Lily's twin girls." She moaned. "Oh, no, those poor, poor dears ..."

"And how old are they?" I asked.

"Eight."

"Eight?" Confused, I looked back at their governess, then again at Penny. "Where are they? Not here, I hope." I hadn't seen signs of any children when Steve and I were prowling around the second floor, but then again, maybe they'd been asleep in their beds behind one of the many doors I'd passed while searching for the master suite.

Penny wiped a tear off her cheek. "If Stella is here at the party, then they're probably staying with their grandmother tonight. Lily's mother. My Aunt Anna. She lives nearby and usually keeps them during parties. The music gets so loud, people stay so late."

"Makes sense," Steve said. "It's sure a good thing for those little girls that they're not here now."

"It seems odd that Stella would be here at the party, rather than with them," I whispered to Penny. Had anyone else noticed Stella and Arty's flirtatious behavior at the bar? Surely, I hadn't been the only one.

Penny shrugged. "Stella just started working here about a month ago. Right after she graduated from high school. She's a farm girl from Iowa. Maybe Lily and Arty wanted her to meet their friends."

And maybe there was something going on between the young governess and the master of the house. Given what had just happened to the mistress of the house, I shivered, a creepy chill running down my back.

I needed to have a chat with Miss Stella Murphy.

And with Charles Harrington, who was in the middle of the room sitting cross-legged on the floor beside a dark-haired beauty with a Snow-White-complexion. His wife?

Lily's self-confessed lover had lost his swagger. Now pale and visibly sweating, his gaze met mine before he quickly looked away.

I stared him down. What would he tell the police when it was his turn to be questioned? I would have bet every dollar I had in the bank that he wouldn't tell them he'd been having an affair with the dead woman out by the pool.

But should I tell the police that he'd bragged to me about being Lily's lover? What *was* I going to tell them when they got to me?

Minutes ticked by. The room grew hotter. I grew antsier. The officers were taking their time going from person to person, and once interviewed, people were permitted to leave.

I wanted to talk to Charles before he left. Get his address, phone number, to follow up with him later. I stood and went over to him, nonchalantly, like I just wanted to have a word with a friend.

I squatted down beside him.

He looked at me with panicky, leave-me-alone eyes, and inched away.

"Charles," I whispered. "I changed my mind about us. Can I get your phone number?"

Avoiding my gaze, he shook his head.

"Who the hell are you?" Snow White hissed at me.

Before I could answer, Charles glared at me and growled, "Go away." He looked at Snow White. "She's nobody, Renee."

"Charles, please, I'd like to keep in touch," I whispered.

"Go away and leave us alone," Renee hissed louder.

An officer hurried over to me. "What are you doing, miss? Why are you over here? We told everybody to stay put." He waved a hand at the sofa. "Weren't you just over there?"

"She's bothering us, officer," Renee whined. "And we don't even know her."

Great. Now I had the entire room's attention. Not to mention the cop's suspicion.

I stumbled to my feet. "I'm sorry, officer. I met Charles earlier this evening and I just—"

"Come with me, miss." The policeman beckoned for me to follow him. "It's your turn and clearly we need to talk."

SEVEN

He steered me back outside.

Lucky me, I was getting my own special private interview.

On my way past the sofa, I flashed Steve an I'll-be-okay grin, although the worried expression on his face told me he wasn't so sure.

Truthfully, neither was I.

The officer, an older man with a waist that lapped over his belt, gestured for me to take a seat at one of the patio tables, then lowered himself down in a chair across from me. Voices coming from the pool around back told me that other officers were still investigating the scene. Probably taking pictures, gathering evidence before transporting Lily's body to the morgue.

He and I were alone.

"Detective Salvatore Alberti, Philadelphia police." He flashed me his badge. "And your name, miss?" Eyeing me with detached coolness, he got ready to jot it down in a small notebook.

I whipped off my wig, set it down on the table, then followed suit with my mother's eye- glasses.

So much for detached coolness. His eyes widened.

"My name's Story Smith," I said, raking fingers through my sweat-drenched hair. That stupid wig was hot.

I rubbed my eyes, relieved to be able to see clearly again. "I'm a private investigator. I was hired to find a missing necklace, and I've been working undercover."

"I see." Detective Alberti's fleeting expression of surprise mixed with amusement quickly changed to one of intense curiosity and narrow-eyed suspicion. "Hired by who?"

"Penny Miller, the victim's cousin." Then I told him. Everything. Including that Arty Duncan had caught me rifling through his dresser drawer and was threatening to have me arrested when we heard the screams.

There was no point in holding anything back, even though I hated dragging Penny's name into it.

"Unfortunately, I didn't find Penny's missing necklace," I said.

"But it does sound like you and Mr. Duncan can vouch for each other's whereabouts when his wife fell to her death."

"Yes, sir."

He stood. "Then I'm going to go get Mr. Duncan now. Bring him here. Don't move, I'll be right back."

Minutes later, he returned with Arty. His eyes were red, swollen, and weepy, and he was shaking when Detective Alberti told him to have a seat across from me.

Arty didn't seem to recognize me at first. Then, when he glanced down at my wig and glasses on the table, and then back at my face, recognition dawned.

"You!" he shouted. "You're the thief who tried to rob me. Arrest this woman, officer, arrest her!"

"Not so fast." The detective sat down between us and filled Arty in about my real identity.

Instead of being grateful—which he should have been, given that I was giving him an alibi—Arty lashed out in fury. "Liar, liar! Private eye? This woman's calling herself a private eye? What a crock of horse hooey, detective. And you're buying it?"

"It's true," I said, managing to sound calmer than I felt. "I am a private investigator. And I was searching for a necklace belonging to Penny Miller that Penny believed your wife might have taken."

"Preposterous!" Arty pounded a fist on the table, his eyes shooting daggers at me. "Why would Lily steal a necklace from her cousin— who was as close to her as a sister?"

His face screwed up in pain when he heard himself referring to his wife in the past tense. He put his arms on the table and buried his face in them. "And anyway," he said, his words broken and barely audible, "Lily didn't need to steal anyone's jewelry. She had plenty of her own."

Lifting his head, he met the detective's gaze. "Lily could have had anything she wanted. Anytime she wanted it. All she had to do was ask. I loved her. Gave her the world."

Then, in a sudden burst of energy, he sat up and jabbed a finger at me. "I want this woman arrested. I don't believe she's a private detective. Women aren't detectives. She's lying."

"I'm telling the truth, and I can prove it," I said in as calm a voice as I could manage. "My undercover date for the evening, Steve Evans, who is also a private eye, will vouch for me. As will Penny Miller and her husband, Jonathan."

"Steve Evans?" The detective stood up. "Where is Mr. Evans?"

I pointed to the living room.

"Go get him," Detective Alberti told me. "And hurry back."

—————

"Steve Evans." Detective Alberti stood and reached for his hand. "I've heard of you. Quite a reputation you have in this town. One of Philly's finest private investigators, from what I hear."

"Thank you, I'm flattered." Steve nodded at Arty across the table. "I'm terribly sorry about your wife, Mr. Duncan. Story and I didn't have a chance to do more than tell her hello, but she seemed like a lovely woman."

"Oh, so not a jewel thief?" Arty's biting sarcasm made me cringe. Narrowing his eyes, mockingly holding Steve's gaze, he pointed to me. "Your girlfriend is insinuating that she was hired to search for a necklace that Lily supposedly stole from her cousin."

Steve stiffened. "Yes, that's true. I came here as Story's date to help her search for a necklace that Penny Miller believed might be in this house."

"But your girlfriend was pretending to be someone else," Arty sneered. "Wearing a wig and crazy glasses and using some other name. She came here under false pretenses."

I raised my hand. "Excuse me. Under the circumstances, I couldn't exactly come here as a private eye."

"That's because you are no such thing." Arty snapped. "Whoever heard of a female private detective? What woman in her right mind would even want to be in that business? It's dangerous."

I gritted my teeth, forcing back what I wanted to say. That he was right, it was incredibly dangerous. That there were times I questioned my own sanity. And that I really needed to buy myself another gun because I'd lost my first one in a shoot-out—where I came close to getting killed.

"I got my P.I. license in May, and I love what I do, and Steve is not my boyfriend," I said, instead. "He's a competitor and a friend who agreed to help me with this case. Which was supposed to be quick and easy. All I had to do was look for the necklace and if I didn't find it, no harm done. Lily would have never even learned that Penny suspected her."

Detective Alberti cleared his throat. "Mr. Duncan, it seems to me that Miss Smith did you a favor by being with you when your wife fell to her death. If I were you, I would drop all thoughts about having her arrested. You might need her testimony in court."

Arty gasped. "What are you talking about?"

The detective sighed. "Do you believe your wife committed suicide, Mr. Duncan?"

Arty pressed his hands to his head. "No. Of course not."

"So ... you believe someone pushed—or threw—her to her death?"

"Yes, but who?" Arty's eyes welled with tears and horror and grief.

"That's what we mean to find out," Detective Alberti said. "That's why we are questioning every guest here. And thanks to Miss Smith, we can eliminate the most obvious suspect—you."

"Me?" Arty looked sick.

"Yes, you. Because the spouse usually has the most to gain."

Arty shook his head. "No, no. I never—"

"But of course, there's still the possibility that you might have hired someone." Detective Alberti's tone was cool, impersonal, and deadly serious. "We will be checking into that."

"Outrageous!" Arty jumped to his feet. Red-faced, shaking, he looked like he wanted to run away, or throw up, or both. "Somebody murdered my wife," he shouted, "and it wasn't me, and I want the monster caught."

He shook his fist at me. "And you—I won't press charges on you. But—get out. Get out of my house now and never come back."

EIGHT

I ignored Arty's demand to leave immediately. To hell with that. I'd come to help Penny, and I wasn't going anywhere until she and Jonathan were interviewed.

I'd dragged Penny's name into things with the police, and I wasn't going to abandon her now.

Steve and I returned to the sofa, where Penny and Jonathan were huddled together, to wait.

"I had to tell the detective the truth about why I came to the party," I warned Penny, filling her in on how Arty had caught me in his room and threatened to have me arrested. "I'm sorry, so sorry. Sorry that I didn't find your necklace and sorry that Lily—"

"The necklace?" Penny's eyes were wild with grief. "Who cares about that stupid necklace now? Lily's dead. She's dead! And now I feel horrible that I ever suspected her of stealing from me. I loved her! Loved her ... don't you understand? And now she's gone!"

I reached for her hand and squeezed it. "I know. And I want to help you."

She shook her head. "Help me? How?"

"I want to find out who did this to her."

"You mean try to solve her murder?" Jonathan asked.

I shook my head eagerly. "Yes."

Steve put his hand over mine. "Story, are you sure about this? The police haven't even begun investigating. Maybe you should wait until they know more. Until we know more."

I'd never been surer of anything in my life. "Why wait?" I gave Steve a look that said he should know me better than this by now. Because waiting was not something I did well. I liked to jump into things and figure them out as I went along.

I turned back to Penny. "Before Lily fell, I happened to observe a few things at the WowWee It's Wednesday Party that now I want to check out. Strange things that may or may not be relevant to what happened to her, but I can start tomorrow."

"Turned out to be more of a Woe is Wednesday party," Steve muttered under his breath. "But leave it to you, Story ..."

"Wait a minute," Jonathan said. "Investigating a possible murder is a much more complicated undertaking than investigating the possible theft of a necklace. We'll need to pay you, discuss a fee."

"By all means, Jonathan," Penny said, with a glint of hope in her eyes. "Let's hire Story. I have faith in her. If anyone can get justice for my Lily, she can."

———

Arty caught me in his living room.

Just my luck.

Livid with rage, he exploded when he found me on the sofa with Steve, Penny, and Jonathan. He must have insisted on sitting in on Detective Alberti's interview with the Millers—no doubt to confront Penny about why she'd hired me.

But when Arty saw me, he forgot all about Penny.

"I thought I told you to get out." He stormed toward me, shaking a fist.

Jumping to his feet, Steve stared him down, daring him to come closer.

"Don't worry, Arty, I was just leaving," I said, rising. "Penny and Jonathan, we can discuss our plans more tomorrow."

"What plans?" Arty snapped. "Penny, are you still worried about that stupid necklace?"

"Mr. Duncan ..." Detective Alberti cleared his throat. "Let me ask the questions, please."

"Jonathan and I have hired Story to investigate Lily's death," Penny declared. "I don't care about that necklace anymore, Arty. But I do believe my dear cousin was murdered, and—"

"And you're hiring *this woman*?" Arty jerked a finger at me "This phony, wig-wearing idiot? That's crazy."

"Stay out of our business, Arty," Jonathan said.

"My wife's murder is my business, you fool," Arty shouted.

"Mr. Duncan ..." Detective Alberti eyed him sternly. "Please calm down and let me do my job. We don't know yet what happened to your wife. We've just begun to investigate."

"And, as I said, I was just leaving," I declared smoothy, stepping around Steve.

"Not without me." Steve put his hand out to stop me. "I drove you here, remember?" He turned to Detective Alberti. "Do you have any more questions for me, or am I free to go?"

"You're free to go, Mr. Evans. If I need to speak to you further, I'll call your office."

"Wait!" Arty shouted at Steve. "Wait just a minute."

Steve frowned at him. "Yes? What?"

"Did I hear Detective Alberti say you're one of the best private eyes in Philly?"

A corner of Steve's lips twitched up. He shrugged. "Yes. Why?"

"Well then, I want to hire *you*."

"Me?" Steve tilted his head. "Hire me for what?"

"To investigate the death of my wife." Now it was Arty's turn to stare Steve down, as if daring him to say no.

"But ..." Obviously confused, Steve glanced at me, then at Detective Alberti, then turned back to Arty. "I don't understand. Why do you want to hire me?"

"Money's no object," Arty smiled slyly. "Name your price."

"But you haven't answered my question." Steve pointed to Detective Alberti. "As the detective here said, the police are just beginning—"

"I don't care." Arty flicked a hostile gaze at me. "If the Millers think it's necessary to hire their own personal private eye, then I want my own. Only I'm not going to hire a *woman* to do a *man's* job. I want a man."

NINE

Arty got his man.

Steve agreed to work for him, not that I could blame Steve. The money would be good, and it was a juicy case. Still ... it was also *my* case.

"I don't know whether to be insulted, angry, or amused," I told Steve when he dropped me off at my apartment well after midnight. It had been a long day, an even longer evening, and a tense ride home.

"Insulted?" Steve flicked me a wry grin. "You have a right to feel insulted. The man doesn't like women who work, and he personally bashed you. And angry? Sure—you have every right to be angry. He questioned your competence just because you're a woman. But amused?"

I returned his grin. "We're working the same case, Steve. Which kind of makes us rivals."

"So that's funny?"

I gave a loud sigh. "No, not really. What matters is uncovering the truth about Lily's death. Arty has no faith in me. The Millers do. And may the best P.I. win."

Opening my car door to get out, I stopped and turned to face him. "Thanks for coming with me tonight, I really appreciate it."

"Hey, you're not angry at me for taking Arty on as a client, are you?" He suddenly looked worried.

"Well maybe a little," I said with a smile to hide the hurt that I had no right to feel. Life with Steve was getting complicated.

"Accepting Arty's case was purely a business decision," he said, "nothing more. No reflection on you or your abilities."

"I know."

"If I'd turned him down, he would have just hired another man."

"I know." I blew out a breath. "I guess being rivals doesn't mean we can't still be friends."

"Wait ..." Steve hopped out of the car and hurried around to me. He reached for my hand and helped me out.

He didn't let go. I didn't let go. My head told me to pull away. My heart told me to stay.

"I wonder how this evening would have ended if Lily Duncan had not toppled off that balcony?" Steve's voice was husky. In the light of a streetlamp, his eyes probed mine.

"Maybe we'd be celebrating me finding Penny's necklace?" I managed a trembling smile.

"Maybe."

I pressed my lips together and let the soft evening breeze cool my cheeks. "Sadly, that's not what happened, Steve."

He squeezed my hand. "I was hoping our fake date might have turned into a real date."

"Guess we'll never know." I heard my voice catch in my throat.

"And now we're rivals ... again."

"Yes, we are."

"And now we both have a lot of work to do."

"Yes, we do."

He let go of my hand and slowly backed away. "Good night, Story."

"Good night, Steve."

———

No surprise that I did not have a good night.

Steve and I rivals again? I could not believe it.

On my very first case, when I'd been hired to find a woman who'd gone missing under perplexing, mysterious circumstances, Steve had been working as a bodyguard for the only witness. That's how we'd met and ended up working together.

On my next case, Steve had been hired by an insurance company to investigate the gruesome murder of a woman whose husband had taken out a hefty life insurance policy on her. I'd been hired by the victim's daughter to prove her father was innocent. Things quickly grew complicated and bloody with that one.

Now, visions of Lily Duncan's bloody, broken body bleeding out into the pool kept me awake.

For hours.

Finally, when morning dawned, I gave up on the idea of getting enough sleep and got up. I took a shower, downed two cups of coffee and then drove to my office.

Jonathan Miller got there before me—and his receptionist, Wendy —because it turned out he couldn't sleep either. Ushering me into his inner office, we quickly came to an agreement on my daily fee, plus expenses. "For as long as it takes to find Lily's killer," he said, handing me an advance check. "Do what you need to do."

"Thank you." I gave him a grateful smile. "I'll keep you informed with a daily report."

"Where will you start?" he asked as he walked me down the hall to my office. "You said you'd noticed some things at the party that struck you as odd?"

"Several. Including with the governess. I'd like to begin with her."

I unlocked my door and went in. Jonathan followed and sat down in the chair in front of my desk. "Stella Murphy?" He leaned forward. "What struck you as strange about her?"

"How well do you know her?"

"Not well. The nanny before her quit with no warning, just as school was letting out for the summer. Lily was happy to get Stella, even with no experience beyond babysitting."

"And Arty? How does he feel about Stella?"

Jonathan rubbed his chin. "I'm not sure what you mean."

"Stella is quite pretty ..." I waved a hand, palm up, hoping he'd take the hint.

Jonathan squinted at me. "What are you insinuating?"

I didn't want to start rumors, so had to be careful. "I'm not insinuating anything, just something I observed between Arty and Stella at the party. It might mean nothing, and I hope for that young girl's sake it was nothing. But I would like to speak to her. Would you happen to know where she is now, or could you find out?"

He nodded. "Sure, I'll find out."

"They're most likely with Lily's mom," I said.

He nodded again. "Makes sense. Her name is Anna Ash. Lily's maiden name was Ash."

"Thank you. I think the twins must be with Mrs. Ash because I don't think the police have cleared the crime scene and this must be a traumatic time for the children. It would make sense for Stella to be with them."

Since Arty had forbidden me from stepping foot on his property again, I sure hoped Stella was not at his house. And I needed to talk to her before she moved back.

"I know Anna's address and can give it to you now," Jonathan said.

I handed him a piece of paper and a pencil and he wrote it down. "Anna lives a short distance from Lily, who was her only child. She doted on her. I can't imagine what the poor woman is going through right now. She might even be sedated."

"I would like to speak to Anna, too, but not today," I said. "I think I'll just drive over there now and pay Stella a surprise visit. Take a chance that she's there. I've discovered that sometimes that's the best way to get people to talk candidly."

Jonathan stood. "I'm looking forward to working with you, Story. I like your go-get-em style."

"Thanks. But I have a question that is sort of off the topic but has been bugging me."

"Shoot," he said.

"I'm wondering why your law office is in my building. I mean, it might be none of my business, but our building is nothing to brag about. It's the opposite of impressive. Oh, let's be honest, it's low rent. Your Chestnut Hill home, on the other hand, is in one of the wealthiest neighborhoods in Philadelphia. It seems to me that you'd want a better law office since you clearly could afford it."

Jonathan stared at me. Had I overstepped? Was I being too nosey? I pressed my lips together, waiting for his answer.

Then he chuckled. "I'm impressed by your curiosity. It's the sign of a good detective."

"Thank you."

"And your question is a good one." He hesitated. "Although there's a simple explanation."

"Okay."

"I used to work for a large law firm and grew to absolutely hate it and longed to go out on my own. I'm a frugal man who happened to marry into money, and I had too much pride to use my wife's money to set up my own office."

I smiled. "I see. So you're making a go of it on your own. I can relate to that."

"I bet you can," he said. "And our office building isn't so bad. It's a place to start, at least."

"I like your optimism," I said, reaching for my purse. "And now I'm off to find Stella Murphy. No time to waste—I'm heading out."

TEN

Forty minutes later, I pulled up to Anna Ash's residence, a stately brick colonial mansion surrounded by mature shade trees. As Jonathan had said, it was a short walk to the Duncan home.

I was feeling pretty good about beating Steve to the punch with Stella. As far as I knew, he had not noticed Stella and Arty together at the party and we hadn't discussed it.

A middle-aged maid dressed in a starched white uniform answered the door. She looked me up and down with an air of detachment even stiffer than her uniform. "May I help you?"

"I would like to speak to Stella Murphy." I arranged a smile on my face that I hoped projected friendliness laced with subdued sorrow. "Is she here?"

My smile did nothing to defrost the maid's thin-lipped, beady-eyed stare. "She is. Who may I say is calling?"

Bingo. Stella was here. A good start. Now all I had to do was get invited inside. I took a deep breath. "My name is Story Smith, and I'm a friend of the family, and—"

"Miss Murphy is not family." The maid looked annoyed that I didn't know that.

"I know. I'm sorry." I rushed the words out of my mouth before she could close the door in my face. "But she is the family's governess. And I would like to speak to her. On behalf of Penny—"

"Who's there?"

An elderly woman with pure white hair arranged in a prim bun appeared at the door, and the maid quickly moved to the side. "A woman who wants to speak to Stella, Miss Anna," the maid said. "She says she's here on behalf of Miss Penny."

"Penny?" Miss Anna gave me a polite, puzzled frown. "You're here on behalf of my niece to speak to my grandchildren's nanny? I don't understand."

Anna Ash's sudden appearance took me by surprise, and for a moment, knocked me off my game. She was tiny, like her daughter, Lily, short and slim, with the body of a twelve-year old girl.

Her eyes were pink and puffy, like she'd been crying for hours.

She wore a long black dress with a knitted black shawl over her bony shoulders, clearly in mourning.

But she was also obviously not sedated. Her eyes were sharp and aware. They glinted as she looked me up and down, waiting for me to explain myself.

Only the truth would do for this intelligent matriarch, if I had any chance of earning her trust. "My name is Story Smith and I'm a private investigator," I said, fishing my business card out of my hand-bag. "Your niece, Penny, and her husband, Jonathan, have hired me to investigate the tragic death of your daughter, Lily."

She took my card with shaky fingers, and I held my breath as she read it, bracing myself for what might come next.

"I'm so sorry about what happened to Lily, I truly am," I said to break the awkward silence that seemed to go on and on. "I happened to be at the party and—"

"And you're a private investigator? A *woman*? In a *man's* business? Doing a *man's* job?"

I pressed my lips together and nodded, expecting to be sent packing.

But she laughed. This woman, who'd clearly been crying her eyes out, laughed. Not in a mocking way, but in a way that lit up her face and for a moment took away her sorrow. "Delightful," she held my gaze. "I love it."

I swallowed hard and smiled. "You do?"

"Yes, I do. Nice to meet you, Story Smith. And please, call me Anna, everyone does."

"Why, thank you."

"But I'm puzzled," she added, "about why you want to speak to the family governess. Why her?"

It was an excellent question, and I hesitated before answering. "She was at the party. And I plan to interview people who were there, who knew Lily well, and may have noticed something that they may or may not have mentioned to police and ..." I bit down on my lip. "And I thought I'd start with Stella."

"I see, very well, then." Anna opened the door all the way and ushered me inside.

The maid had disappeared, and the elderly woman beckoned for me to follow her into her tastefully furnished living room, where a portrait of Lily hung over the fireplace. Lily appeared to be about twenty in the painting, and I admired how well the artist had captured her unique beauty as she strolled, with a wisp of a smile, through a field of daisies.

"Lovely painting," I murmured as I took a seat on a leather sofa overlooking the fireplace.

"Thank you," she said, lowering herself down beside me. She turned and looked deep into my eyes. "I think I know why you want to speak to Stella."

"You do?"

"Level with me—it's because she looked out of place at that shindig."

That was one way of putting it. Teenage Stella's flirtatious behavior with her much older, married boss had certainly caught my attention. "What do you mean?" I asked. "Because she's so young?"

"That silly twit should have never been at that party." Anna certainly didn't mince words. I liked that. I liked her.

"What do you mean?" I glanced around, hoping we could not be overheard.

"Stella can't hear us, if that's what you're worried about." She patted my knee. "She's upstairs, in the third-floor nursery with my granddaughters, Jane and Jean. Where she should be. Where she should have been instead of at that ridiculous party."

"So, why was she at the party, then?"

"Because Arty insisted she go."

Aha. "Arty?" I struggled to keep my voice cool. "What about Lily?"

"Lily just went along with whatever Arty wanted," she said in a way that told me she disapproved of that, and of Arty, too.

"So ... you don't think Stella should have gone to the party?"

"Her place was *here*, helping me with the twins."

"I see." I glanced up at the portrait of Lily, then back at her grief-stricken mother. "Why do you think Arty wanted Stella to attend the party? It seems to me he should have respected your wishes."

"Arty never cared a fig about my wishes. And I assume he invited Stella to the party because she begged him to go. Of course, being the pretty young thing she is, she got her way." Her tone was bitter.

"So, Stella and Arty get along well, do they?" I kept my tone light and casual, biting back a satisfied grin. This interview was going much better than I could have hoped.

"Arty has a thing for pretty young things." She glanced at me out of the corner of her eye. "Which you noticed, too, didn't you? That's why you're here."

This woman would have made an excellent private investigator. I shrugged, not wanting to give too much away at this point. "Maybe."

"I thought so ... I'm so glad Penny and her husband hired you."

"But what about Lily?" I asked. "Did she and Stella get along?"

"Well enough." Anna gave a dismissive sniff. "Lily was just happy to find a nanny at short notice. After that silly goose Louisa packed up and quit with no warning. Louisa was the nanny before Stella. She'd been with the girls since they were born, and we all thought she was devoted to them, but apparently not."

How odd. And potentially suspicious. I made a mental note to follow that up, then asked, "Was Louisa a pretty young thing?"

Anna narrowed her eyes at me. "Not as young and pretty as Stella —but you came here to interview Stella, so I'll take you to her now."

She stood and pointed to a staircase across the room. "This way. I'll introduce you as my friend, then take Jeannie and Janey off for a snack or to play in the garden. I don't want to upset the twins any more than necessary."

"Of course not. They must be overcome with grief."

"They are, and my home is open to them as long as they need it," she said as we reached the third floor. "Their father is busy with his work—as usual—as well as dealing with the police ... and ... planning my daughter's funeral ..." Her voice trembled and one of the tears she'd been holding back so bravely slid down her cheek.

I reached for her hand. She took it, lifted her chin, and walked me to a door at the end of the hall.

We entered a room filled with toys. Dolls, games, blocks, books. Everything a child could want. The two little motherless girls sat reading books in a corner while Stella, seated in a rocking chair, looked on.

"Miss Anna ..." Stella stood up when she saw us. "Hi." She glanced at me, clearly puzzled. "Hello."

Anna dropped my hand. "Stella, this is my friend, Story. She would like to speak to you privately for a few moments."

The girls stood up and silently ran to their grandmother, wrapping their arms around her waist. "This is Jeannie." Anna fondly ruffled the hair of the child on her right, then the other. "And this is Janey."

Both girls turned and looked at me, then pressed their faces back into their grandmother's waist. Dressed alike in shorts and T-shirts, they were identical in every way. Blonde hair, in braids. Sweet pixie faces, like their mother. Pretty blue eyes. Incredibly sad blue eyes.

"Come girls, let's go get some cookies, then maybe we can go to the garden and pick some flowers." Anna took their hands, then instructed Stella to answer all my questions. "It's important, and I expect you to be completely open and honest," she said. "Nothing else will do."

Stella and I stared at each other as we waited for the sound of the threesome's footsteps to fade away.

Then Stella backed up and plopped herself back down in one of the rockers. Oversized, there were two, I assumed one for each twin. "Huh ... this is awkward," she said, obviously not thrilled about talking to me. "Who are you, really? You're not Miss Anna's friend."

I went over and sat in the other rocker and positioned it to face her. "What makes you say that, Stella?"

She blinked at me. "You're way too young to be her friend."

I smiled. "Very perceptive of you. And you're right. I'm a private investigator."

She frowned. She looked different today, the way I imagined a governess in charge of young children should look. She wore a plain blue cotton dress, with her red hair in braids, like her charges.

"You're a private eye?" She pursed her lips. Unlike Miss Anna, that did not seem to delight her. "Okay. What do you want with me?"

This girl was already getting on my nerves. She had something to hide or was certainly acting that way. I would have bet my P.I. license that she didn't plan on being completely open or honest with me. Just a hunch.

"I was at the party," I said. "The WowWee It's Wednesday Party."

"Oh." She stared at me. "The cops already asked me a bunch of questions. I told them I didn't see anything. That I didn't see what happened to Miss Lily. I was nowhere near the pool when she fell, if that's what you're asking."

I raised my eyebrows. "Then where were you?"

She started rocking. Back and forth, back and forth. "Inside. At the bar."

"With Mr. Arty?" I knew the answer, of course, since he'd been with me, but I wanted to see her reaction.

She stopped rocking and gave me a hostile glare. "With Mr. Arty? No. Why are you asking that?"

"Just wondering, since I noticed the two of you at the bar earlier."

Her jaw dropped. A spot of pink bloomed on her cheeks. "What are you talking about?"

"You know what I'm talking about, Stella. He was rubbing your arm. Not exactly something a middle-aged man should be doing with his teenage governess."

She didn't say anything. Clenching her jaw, she looked away.

I began rocking back and forth, back and forth.

She jumped to her feet. "I don't have to put up with your ridiculous questions, lady."

"Oh, but you *do*." I stopped rocking. "That is, if you don't want me to go to the police with what I noticed going on between you and Mr. Arty. And— if you want to keep your job. Because Miss Anna ordered you to cooperate with me."

She lowered herself back in the rocker, then huffed an annoyed sigh. "Okay, lady, what do you want to know?"

"I want to know if there is something going on between you and Mr. Arty."

She rolled her eyes. "Nope. Next question."

"Then why was he rubbing your arm, and why were you gazing into each other's eyes?"

She slapped her forehead. "Nope. Didn't happen. Next question."

"Who do you think pushed Miss Lily off the balcony?"

That got her. She blinked at me. The color drained from her face.

She swallowed hard. "I don't know," she said in a ragged whisper. Her face screwed up in pain. "I really, really, really don't know. Please, believe me. I don't know."

I believed her. If she was lying, she was a hell of an actress. "But you do believe *someone* pushed Miss Lily off the balcony? Right? That she didn't jump?"

Stella closed her eyes. She opened them again. "No," she said softly. "I don't think she jumped."

"Why?"

"Because she was a happy person."

"Did you like her, Stella?"

"Of course. She was good to me. She was a wonderful mother."

I inched my rocker closer to hers. "Then help me, Stella. Please. I need your help solving what looks like a monstrous murder. I need you to think. Think back to how Miss Lily appeared to you lately. Was there anything different about her? Had anything changed? Had she started acting differently in any way?"

Stella went still. She closed her eyes again. "Yes," she said, finally. "I did notice something."

"What?"

She opened her eyes and looked at me. "Miss Lily had started reading the Bible. A lot."

"The Bible?"

"Yes."

"Was that unusual?"

"Yes."

"When did she start reading it?"

"About a week ago."

"Where? In her room?"

"No, at the kitchen table."

"Did you notice anything about her while she was reading it?"

"Yes. She seemed upset—maybe like she was praying to God."

My heart jumped. This could be significant. I leaned forward. "Stella, think, did you notice anything else?"

She pressed her lips together and nodded. "There was a letter. In the Bible. Tucked in the pages."

"A letter? In an envelope?"

"Yes. Plain white, nothing fancy."

My heart started to race. "Stella, have you mentioned this to anyone else? To the police?"

She shook her head, holding my gaze. "No. Only you. I didn't think about it. It didn't seem important."

It could very well be important. Maybe Lily really *had* been fooling around with Charles Harrington. Maybe she had broken it off. Maybe he'd broken it off with her. Maybe she was being black-mailed. So many possibilities ...

I needed to get my hands on that Bible.

"Stella, do you know where Lily kept the Bible? In the kitchen?"

She tugged on one of her pigtails. "I don't think in the kitchen. Maybe in the living room, maybe in the library, maybe in her room?"

"Someplace private?"

"I guess ..."

I wanted to press her more, but I'd already said enough. I didn't want her to think Lily's Bible was that important. I didn't want her to go searching for the holy book herself. Or, heaven forbid, mention it to Arty, who might mention it to Steve.

Steve and I were working the same case as rivals, and this poten-tially valuable tip was mine.

ELEVEN

Next on my list—Charles Harrington. I needed to speak to him pronto, but I'd failed to get his address at the party and had no idea where he lived.

I thought about calling Penny to see if she knew his address. Or of heading to police headquarters to try and get a look at the police report. Instead, I went with the easiest way to find a person's address. Look it up in the phonebook.

He lived in Overbrook, not a far drive from Chestnut Hill. I put my T-Bird's top down and headed there, fingers crossed he'd talk to me.

Maybe the letter in the Bible had something to do with him. Maybe he and Lily really did have an affair. Maybe she was afraid of burning in Hell for her sins and broke up with him.

Then, outraged, maybe he'd pushed her to her death.

Or ... maybe he had ended it with her, and in despair, she'd jumped off the balcony.

Or ... maybe that letter had nothing to do with him.

I needed to get my hands on that letter. But talking to Charles came first.

He lived in a large house on a leafy street that screamed money. No surprise. I parked, put my top up, and tried to figure out what I was going to say as I strolled up the front walk.

It would depend on who opened the door.

It was the middle of a workday, so chances were good that Charles was at the office. If a maid answered, I'd try to get that address. If Renee answered, I'd need to get more creative. I hoped it wasn't Renee.

Fortunately, Charles answered the door, dressed in golf attire. So, okay, maybe he didn't have an office. Probably had a trust fund.

"Hello," I flashed him a charming smile. "Remember me?"

Narrowing his eyes, he looked me up and down. "Uhm ... not really, though you do look familiar."

I cocked my head. "Silly ... it's Millie Pettigrew ... you know ... from the party ..."

A frown wiped the flirtatious grin off his pretty face. "Oh, so now you're a blonde?"

I winked. "Always was. I was wearing a wig, and my real name is Story Smith, and I'm a private eye."

Now he looked confused, which is where I wanted him. Off balance. And vulnerable. He tightened his grip on the door. "I don't get it. What do you want with me?"

"I've been hired to track down the person who murdered Lily, and I'd like to speak to you. Seeing as you guys were having an affair, and all. Can I come in?"

"Are you crazy?" he whispered. "Go away."

"I only need a few minutes of your time."

"No," he hissed. "Go away."

"Don't make me go to the police."

"With *what*?"

"With information that you and the deceased were having an affair."

Wincing, he raked his fingers through his hair. "I lied. I don't know why I told you that. It wasn't true. I was drunk."

"I'll let the police decide if it's true or not." Raising my eyebrows, I waited a beat. "Or you could let me in."

With a loud sigh, he opened the door and waved me inside, then closed it with a quiet click. "Just make this quick. I don't want my wife to hear us."

I could tell he wasn't going to invite me in beyond the vestibule. Fine. "Just tell me the truth," I whispered loudly. "Was Lily your mistress?"

His face flushed. "Look ... I exaggerated. Lily and I might have hopped in the sack a few times. But that was it. No big deal. I certainly didn't kill her—if that's what you're getting at."

"Was she in love with you?"

He scoffed. "No."

"Were you in love with her?"

He rolled his eyes. "No. What we had was pure lust."

"Did Arty know?"

"No. We were careful."

"Do you think she had other lovers?"

He gave an annoyed shrug. "I don't know. Didn't care because I wasn't in love with her." Tensing up, he asked, "Are we done here?"

"Almost. One more question—did you and Lily write letters to each other?"

"Letters? No. Why?"

"I have reason to believe—"

"Charles, who's there?"

It was Renee. She ran up to her husband and shoved him aside. Great. Just who I did not want to see.

She recognized me immediately and was none too happy to find me in her house. "You!" She screeched. "What are you doing here, you hussy? You can't have Charles. He's married to me."

Sheesh. Such drama. Such jealousy. Now I suddenly did want to speak to her. Had this jealous wife known about Lily? And if so, who knew what she was capable of? "What makes you think I'm after Charles?" I taunted, all sing song and innocent.

"Don't play games with me, lady." She glared at me, her Snow-White-complexion growing redder by the moment. "I know why you're here. My husband's an outrageous flirt. He propositioned you at the party, didn't he?"

I turned to him, faking shock. "Oh no, Charles, is that what you were doing? And here I just thought you were being friendly."

Renee stepped toward me. "Get. Out. Of. My. House. Now. Or I'll throw you out."

I inched away from her. "Look, you've got it all wrong, Renee. I'm not here to hook up with Charles. I'm here to inquire about poor Lily."

"Lily?"

"Yes, I'm a private investigator—hired to find out the truth about her death."

Renee's eyes went big. She opened her mouth, then shut it and stared at me. "What are you talking about? You know how Lily died. You were there."

"I know she fell to her death. But did she jump, or was she pushed? And if she was pushed, who pushed her? It's possible she died because she was in love with your husband."

Renee went still, then color rose in her face as she launched herself at Charles. She grabbed his shoulders and shook him. "You idiot. What did you tell this woman?"

Charles swatted her away. "Calm down, Renee. I told her nothing."

"Just that he and Lily had a thing going," I said. "Which is not exactly nothing."

Renee advanced on me.

I stepped back, out of reach of her long, painted nails.

"Lily was a fool." Renee said. "I'm glad she's dead."

I gasped. "So ... you killed her?"

"Of course not." She stared at me like I was the crazy one. Then grabbing the doorknob, she yanked the door open and shouted, "Now get out of here, Miss Private Eye. Or else!"

———

I didn't want to find out what Renee meant by "or else," so I beat it out of there.

Although, making my hasty get-away from the Harrington residence, I did feel rather pleased with myself for what I'd accomplished so far that day.

Not only had I successfully escaped Renee's claws, I'd come up with some promising leads. Driving to my office, I went over in my mind.

I'd discovered that Lily's mother had no love for her son-in-law, Arty.

I'd confirmed that Lily had been having an affair—and that her lover's wife knew about it and was unhinged enough to be capable of murder.

I'd also learned that Lily had recently seemed greatly troubled. That she'd taken to praying and reading the Bible. And that the Bible might contain an important letter. Which I needed to get my hands on.

Problem was that Arty had forbidden me from ever entering his house again. And I needed to get in there to search for that Bible. Finding Penny's necklace while I was at it would be a nice plus.

I'd just have to find a way to sneak in.

But how?

Then it hit me. Steve. Arty was Steve's client. Steve could sneak me in.

"Are you nuts?" Steve asked when I found him waiting for me in my office and popped the question before thinking it through. "You want me to go against my client's wishes and sneak you into his house?"

"Well ... when you put it that way ..." Taking a seat behind my desk, I eyed him sitting in the chair across from me. He was certainly making himself at home. Wearing a serene smile, cradling his arms behind his head, he looked like a tourist sunning himself on the deck of a cruise ship. An extremely handsome tourist.

"Wait a minute." I leaned toward him. "What are you doing here, and how'd you get in?"

"Wendy let me in."

"Oh, I forgot I gave her a key."

"She had to take dictation from her boss, so she said it would be okay if I waited for you here." He flashed me a lazy grin. "I just stopped by to see how you did today. Any good leads?"

That adorable grin almost had me. Almost. "You're my competition." I flashed him a nice-try smile. "I can't tell you anything."

"Aha. So you have had a good day. I'm sensing a very good day."

"And, like I said ..."

"Come on Story." Steve leaned across the desk toward me, seriously impairing my defenses with his closeness. "Tell me about your day and I'll tell you about mine."

"But we're not partners," I protested.

"Maybe not. But we are soulmates." He winked, making me tingle all over.

"Soulmates?" I rasped, tingling in places of my body that should not have been tingling.

"Yeah, you know ..." A corner of his lips twitched up and I couldn't tell if he was serious or just enjoying the moment. "Two souls connected in eternity. Forever destined to be united."

I laughed. "Great pickup line, Steve. I bet that has worked well for you with other women."

He put a hand to his heart, then sat back, his lips turning down into a wounded frown. "I have never said those words to any other woman, Story. When are you going to believe me when I say you're the one?"

Believing him was tempting, but I couldn't jeopardize my career. Soulmate or no soulmate.

Still, if Steve was my soulmate, maybe he'd be willing to sneak me into Arty's house. "Where did you come up with this soulmate stuff?" I asked, genuinely curious.

He smiled. "Victor Bravo."

"Victor Bravo?" Victor Bravo was a psychic medium I had met on my last case and had introduced to Steve. "Victor Bravo never called us soulmates."

"But he did predict we'd get married one day." Steve wagged his eyebrows up and down. "Same thing."

Not the same thing at all, and while Victor was eerily convincing, and sure looked the part—complete with turban and exotic clothes—I still wasn't convinced his powers were real. That he could predict the future or talk to dead people.

"I'm not going to marry you," I said, "because I'm never going to get married. And I don't think I should share what I've discovered today with my competition."

He shrugged. "Then I won't sneak you into Arty's house."

He stood up and headed for the door. "I thought maybe we could help each other with this case, Story, but I guess I was mistaken. Oh, and I'll be sure to tell Victor you said hi."

"Wait." I came around my desk and grabbed his arm. "You're going to go see Victor Bravo?"

He grinned. "Why not? He might be able to help me with this case. Can't hurt."

"But he's *my* psychic medium. You're stealing my psychic medium."

Too late, I realized how silly that sounded.

I still had my hand on Steve's arm. He hadn't pulled away. Gazing into his eyes, I swallowed hard. "Never mind. Come sit down. Let's talk."

"Let's." He sat back down.

I sat back down.

I'd have to trust him. But that didn't mean I had to tell him every-thing I'd learned that day. Only about the mysterious letter that Stella had seen Lily tuck in her Bible.

"So, you want to search for that Bible?" Steve asked.

"Yes."

"Why not let me look for it?"

"Because I want to find it myself. I'm the one who wrangled the story out of Stella, and I want to be the one to find the Bible. And the letter."

Steve ran a hand over his chin. "You're asking me to risk my repu-tation and my career to help you."

I smiled and met his gaze. "I guess I am."

"You're asking me to put you ahead of my business."

I bit down on my lip. "I guess I am."

"If we get caught, Arty might sue me. I could lose my license."

I whispered, "You might."

Steve stood up. "Then we won't get caught."

My heart did a flip. "That means you'll help me?"

"I will." Steve grinned. "As long as you let me read that letter."

Twelve

I was able to sneak into the Duncan mansion the next afternoon.

Steve learned that Arty was headed to the undertakers to finalize plans for Lily's funeral, so he picked me up at my office to drive me to Arty's house in case the grieving widower came home earlier than expected. It wouldn't do for Arty to discover my T-Bird in his driveway.

"Lily's funeral will take place tomorrow," Steve told me when I hopped in his car. "Arty doesn't see the point in prolonging things, for his sake and the children's."

That surprised me. "The poor woman hasn't even been dead for three days," I said.

Steve turned to me and nodded. "I know."

"The police haven't even ruled whether her death was a suicide or a murder."

Steve nodded again.

"I bet he wants the press attention to go away," I said. "Her death's been in the news nonstop."

"I suspect you're right." Steve shot me a grim grin. "In any case, Arty told me he expected to be gone for about an hour."

Which meant I had that much time to search the huge mansion.

When we got there, Steve volunteered to stand guard near the front door.

Slipping in behind him, I headed straight to the kitchen.

It was one of the largest kitchens I'd ever seen. Maybe the biggest. There were many drawers and cabinets but no shelves for books. A vase adorned with yellow roses sat on top of a table next to a window overlooking the garden. I could picture Stella reading the Bible there, but now, aside from the flowers, the tabletop was clear.

I opened a cabinet. China dishes. I opened another. Glasses of various sizes. I opened another. Bowls and coffee cups.

After searching every cabinet and drawer in the room, I slipped into the adjacent dining room, but had no luck there, either.

My heart began to race because the clock was ticking. I tackled the living room next, then a downstairs bathroom, then a small first floor office that was clearly Arty's.

But no Bible.

It was time to head upstairs.

On the second floor, I headed straight to the master bedroom. Fortunately, I knew exactly where it was, and at least this time I had daylight.

But no Bible in Lily's dresser. Nothing in Arty's dresser. Nothing in the closet. Nothing under the bed.

Then I spotted a trunk in a corner of the room. An old-fashioned trunk with a rounded top. I opened it. It was filled with sheets and blankets. I ran my hand under the top blanket and my fingers brushed something that felt like a book.

Smiling, I pulled it out. Yes! A Bible. A large black Bible. And—just as Stella had described—an envelope was tucked inside.

Backing up to the bed, I sat down, pulled a one-page, handwritten letter out of the envelope, and began to read the small, tight print:

Dear Lily,

I know you are not going to believe this is real, but it is. I am alive! And SHHH, keep this a secret for now, but I survived the war! I was horribly wounded and rescued by a farmer in France and was in a coma for many months. When I finally woke up, the farmer's daughter, Sophie, nursed me back to health. She was kind and very pretty and I married her. But I never, ever stopped thinking about you. I didn't think I would ever see you again—which I thought was best because of my limp and scars. I didn't want anyone from America to see me. I believed it was better that they thought I was dead because I don't look anything like I used to. Sophie loved me. She didn't think I looked broken and ugly, even though I felt that way. But Sophie died a few months ago. And I had to come home. To you, Lily. To see you. I know now that you married my friend Arty. But I still want to see you. Just you. Please don't tell anyone else about this letter. Not even Penny. If you want to meet me, I will be sitting in a rocking chair on the porch of the Congress Hall hotel in Cape May, New Jersey every day for the next week between noon and one. I hope you will come. Love, Harry.

Love, Harry?

Gripping the letter, I read it again, just to be sure my eyes weren't playing tricks on me. Was it possible that Harry—the man who'd given Penny the now-missing necklace—was *alive*?

The letter bore no date. But the postmark on the envelope showed it had been mailed two and a half weeks ago.

Had Lily gone to see Harry? She must have. How could she *not* go? Probably in secret, as he'd requested. But did meeting him have anything to do with her death?

Tucking the letter back in the envelope, I slipped it into the pocket of my shorts and hurried to find Steve.

He was in the kitchen.

"Good news." I beamed.

His eyes lit up. "You found it?"

I patted my pocket. "Sure did. Now let's get out of here."

———

I read the letter out loud to Steve as we drove back to my office.

"Incredible," he said when I finished. Tightening his grip on the steering wheel, he glanced over at me. "Good work, Story. This could be the key to the whole case."

"I know. To solving Lily's murder and to finding Penny's missing necklace. It can't be a coincidence that the necklace went missing at the exact same time that Harry returned from the dead."

Then I remembered. At the party. The waiter handing out stuffed mushrooms. He had a limp. And facial scars. And Lily kept trying to get his attention. I'd assumed she'd just wanted a mushroom. But what if that wasn't it? What if that man had been Harry?

But ... if he was Harry ...?

"Story?" Steve glanced back over at me with a frown. "You're so quiet. What are you thinking about?"

"Uh ..." I blinked at him, then looked out my window and then back at him. Part of me wanted to tell him. And part of me didn't want to tell him. He'd helped me find the letter, but did I owe him anything else? We were still competitors.

I cleared my throat. "Uhm ... I was just wondering what we should do next. Do you want the letter? Do you owe it to your client to tell him about the letter?"

"That's what you were thinking?" Steve shot me a dubious smile. "As you know, Arty is still a suspect in the eyes of the police. You keep the letter for now. I should hold off letting him know about this. For now."

I nodded. "Makes sense."

"What about you?" Steve glanced over at me. "Are you going to let *your clients* know about the letter?"

"I think I should keep it to myself for now as well. Investigate this quietly until I learn more."

He nodded. "Makes sense."

"It's our secret then," I said. "For now."

"Until we figure out what to do next, Story. You and I. Separately or together."

I sighed. "Yes. And may the best P.I. win."

Thirteen

Lily's funeral the next day at St. James Presbyterian Church in Chestnut Hill was as grand an affair as her legendary parties must have been. Or as I *imagined* they must have been, given that the only one I had attended ended in tragedy.

It was Saturday. And since her service was taking place on a weekend, when many people had off from work, it likely drew an even larger crowd than it would have otherwise, despite dark clouds that threatened rain.

Hundreds of onlookers surrounded the church when I arrived, dressed in a plain black dress, plain black pumps, my blonde hair pinned up under a wide brimmed black hat.

I wanted to blend in so I could observe possible suspects without being noticed. Especially by Arty. He could forbid me from entering his house, but he couldn't forbid me from entering the church—and I was counting on him not thinking about me at all.

Slipping into the sanctuary, I took a seat in a back pew and watched people stream past me. Some I recognized from the party, including Charles and Renee Harrington.

Jonathan and Penny nodded to me when they came in, then continued to the front and took seats in the row behind Arty, his daughters, and his mother-in-law, Anna.

I wondered where Stella was and then saw her sitting to Arty's left. The teenage governess—who had only joined the family a few weeks earlier—had a prominent seat with the family and she was sitting extremely close to Arty.

I was itching to interview Arty and felt frustrated that I couldn't —just because we'd gotten off on a bad foot.

I knew Arty didn't push his wife off the balcony, but Stella could have. She and Arty could have planned it, or Stella could have pushed Lily in a fit of rage. Maybe Lily had confronted her about her flirtatious behavior with Arty and they'd argued.

Steve could interview Arty because Arty was his client. Steve was a pro. If anybody could get the truth out of Arty about his relationship with the nanny, Steve could.

But where was Steve? I looked around but didn't see him. People continued to pour into the church, and I watched them file past me, hoping Steve was among them.

Then saw I him.

Not Steve. The waiter from the party. With the scarred face and the limp.

Keeping his head down as he limped past me, he squeezed into the end of a pew a few rows ahead.

My heart leapt into my throat. It was him. Had to be him.

A rustling noise behind me made me turn. Two police officers were closing the sanctuary doors, signaling the service was about to begin.

And that one else would be allowed in.

This was no ordinary funeral—that was unmistakenly the message. And while police had yet to determine a cause of death, there was a good chance that the woman in the closed casket at the altar had been murdered.

Did my Mystery Waiter know anything about that?

I was betting he did.

And as soon as the service ended, I was going to talk to him.

———

The service was long and sad, and I kept my eye on Mystery Waiter the whole time.

But when it ended, he disappeared.

Like a ghost.

I couldn't believe it. I'd done everything I could to keep him in sight, but he was as elusive as he had been at the party. The last mourner to enter the church—and clearly not wanting to be seen—he took advantage of the way the memorial service ended.

Lily's casket came down the aisle first, with police officers throwing the church doors open for her pallbearers to pass through.

Arty, family, and friends followed and then the church emptied out from front to the back, making me one of the last to leave.

By the time I passed the police officers and stepped out of the church into pouring rain, Mystery Waiter was nowhere to be seen.

The smart people had umbrellas, but I wasn't one of them. I looked anxiously around. But didn't see him.

Anywhere.

It was hard to see much of anything because the rain was pelting me, drenching me to the bone, streaming down my hat and into my face.

An umbrella appeared over my head.

"Looking for me?" Steve's giant black umbrella was big enough for two.

I flashed him a grateful smile. "Uhm. Actually ... yes."

"Liar." His tone was teasing, but his grin said he had me.

"What do you mean?" Swiping water out of my eyes, I took off my hat. "I *was* looking for you. Where were you sitting?"

"Up front. I wanted Arty to see that I was on the job."

"I was in the back. Because I didn't want Arty to see that I was on the job."

Huddled under the umbrella, our faces inches apart, Steve's gaze held mine and I could feel my cheeks heating up. "Who were you really looking for out here?" he asked. "You looked panicked, like you had someone in your sights and then lost them."

Darn. Steve sure was observant. Nothing got past him. No wonder he was such a good P.I. "No one." I smiled sweetly. "No one but you."

"I still don't believe you. But I'm willing to let it go for now."

"Golly, gee, thanks."

"You headed to the cemetery, Story? I'll give you a ride."

I was already soaking wet. Standing out in the rain watching Lily's casket being lowered into the ground would probably give me pneumonia. But Mystery Waiter might be there. "Sure, Steve, since you've offered, and you have this giant umbrella. I didn't come prepared."

"A good P.I. always comes prepared."

"I know. But I do have a plan."

He raised his eyebrows. "Care to share it with me?"

"I need to talk to Penny about Harry O'Toole. Get some background on him. Without revealing that he may be alive. I want to search for him quietly, without him knowing. Don't want to tip him off. He was clear in his letter that he only wanted to meet with Lily. There must be a reason for that."

Steve stamped his feet, which like mine were getting wetter the longer we stood there. "Sounds good," he said, "but you don't need to go to the cemetery to talk to Penny. There will be a reception back here in the church's community hall after the burial. That might be a better time."

He had a point. But something told me I shouldn't skip the burial service. "I'll take that ride to the cemetery, anyway," I said. "Any private eye worth her salt can't be afraid of getting wet."

Fourteen

There's something about watching a casket being lowered into the ground during a rainstorm.

It feels like heaven is crying, too.

Lily's burial was like that. Scores of people made their way to historic Ivy Hill Cemetery to bid her goodbye, shedding copious tears under somber-black umbrellas as the minister uttered final prayers.

Huddled next to Steve under his umbrella, I didn't see Mystery Waiter among them, though. Disappointing, but not a surprise.

I was also not surprised to see Stella sharing an umbrella with Arty as Anna Ash stood under another one with the twins.

"What do you think of that?" I whispered to Steve, nodding in Arty's direction.

"Odd and disturbing behavior for a man who doesn't want to look like the prime suspect in the murder of his wife," Steve murmured. "I noticed the two of them in the church, too. I obviously need to have a talk with my client."

"Good. I was hoping you'd say—"

I swallowed the rest of my words. Because off in the distance, standing in a grove of trees, a lone man with an umbrella caught my eye. He was too far away to hear anything, but he was watching the proceedings with intense interest.

"Story?" Steve whispered. "What are you looking at?"

I shook my head. Didn't move. Narrowed my eyes and kept watching the man. He was Mystery Waiter. I was sure of it.

Then he seemed to notice me watching him and my suspicion was confirmed. Because when he turned around and quickly walked away, he limped.

I watched him go. What else could I do? If I ran after him, everyone at the graveside would have noticed. And I'd probably reinjure my ankle to boot.

No matter. I was glad I'd braved the rain to attend the burial.

Because now I was nearly convinced that Mystery Waiter was Harry O'Toole.

———

"Tell me everything you can about Harry O'Toole," I whispered to Penny at the reception following the burial.

Steve and I had gone in opposite directions after walking in together, and Penny and I were scooping red punch out of a large cut glass bowl. Ignoring her puzzled look, I took her arm and led her to a table in a corner so we could be alone.

"Harry?" Taking a seat, Penny shook her head. "I told you I don't care about finding that necklace anymore. I'm ashamed I even suspected poor Lily took it." She took a sip of her punch. "There is nothing I can tell you about Harry that will help you find Lily's killer. He's long dead."

I sipped my punch and held her gaze, then set my cup down and gave her a pained, please-humor-me smile. "I know Harry died in the war, but he was obviously an important person in Lily's early life. And the more I know about Lily, the better chance I have of finding her killer." I took another sip. "Who knows, maybe I'll find your necklace in the process."

Penny took a deep breath and slowly let it out, squinting into the distance, like she was seeing into the past. "Lily and I met Harry the summer before our sophomore year in high school." Her lips formed a dreamy smile. "I guess we were fifteen."

"Where?" I asked. "Where did you meet him?"

"In Cape May, on the beach. Our families summered there every year. Lily's father, Peter Ash, and my father, Paul Ash, were brothers. Our families bought beachfront cottages next to each other when Lily and I were babies." She deepened her smile. "Such lucky girls, we were, and didn't we know it. Those were wonderful days."

"And Harry?"

"Did I tell you that he was a lifeguard? Yes, he was, and so handsome. All the lifeguards were handsome. But there was something about Harry."

"What? What about Harry?"

Penny moved her eyes back to me. "He had charm. And a special kind of swagger that exuded confidence. I guess you could call it charisma. All the girls were in love with him."

"But you said he wasn't from a wealthy family, right?"

"No. He and his dad were year-round Cape May residents. I think his father was a construction worker. I don't think Harry ever knew his mother. She died when he was very young." Penny ran a finger around the edge of her cup. "What else do you want to know? I don't know how any of this is helping you, really."

Ignoring the impatience in her voice, I asked, "What about Harry's friends? He must have had a lot of friends. Some of them also lifeguards?"

Penny shrugged. "Arty was his best friend. He was a lifeguard, too."

I had my cup to my lips and almost choked on the ghastly-sweet drink. "Arty? Arty Duncan was Harry's *best friend*?"

Penny pursed her lips. "Sorry. I thought I told you that."

"Did Arty's family have money?"

"No. They were even poorer than Harry's. Harry and Arty had been best buddies from childhood. Just like me and Lily. They were inseparable."

"But you and Lily came from a completely different social class than those boys. I'm betting you and Lily went to private school in Philadelphia?"

She nodded. "We did."

"And Arty and Harry?"

"They graduated from Cape May High School. So ...?"

So that explained Anna Ash's dislike for Arty. He came from the wrong side of the tracks. And here I'd been thinking it was his personality.

"So ... what did your families think of you and Lily having crushes on local Cape May kids?" I asked.

Penny blinked at me. "They didn't like it."

"But Lily married Arty. Who is now what you would call the opposite of poor."

Penny sighed. "After the war, Arty came home a war hero. And quickly turned himself into a successful businessman by investing in real estate. Started slowly at first but it wasn't long before he owned much of Philadelphia."

"Really?" I didn't try to hide my surprise at that impressive rags to riches tale.

Penny waved a hand. "I'm exaggerating, but not by much. Anyway, when Harry didn't come home, Lily married his best friend. The next best thing, I suppose."

Her tone was bitter, and tears filled her eyes as she looked deep into mine. "This reminiscing has been fun, but I still don't see how it's helping you. Because Harry is …"

"Dead." I gave a deep sigh. "Yes. I know."

I wanted to tell her. But the time wasn't right.

Harry's letter to Lily was starting to make more sense. And now my job was to find Harry.

But where?

FIFTEEN

Cape May.

Harry O'Toole had told Lily to meet him at Congress Hall, one of the oldest oceanfront hotels in the historic seaside resort.

So, I'd start there.

Cape May, at the very southern tip of New Jersey, had been a bustling Victorian shore town during the mid to late 1800s. Since eclipsed by Atlantic City, and other coastal towns to the north, Cape May struck me as a place frozen in time—with most of its stately gingerbread cottages and mansions still standing, although many in need of paint and repair.

Penny had told me that her father's side of the family had spent summers in Cape May for generations and had seen no reason to join the riffraff who flocked to those newer, upstart beach towns.

Now both widows, Penny said her mother and her Aunt Anna

still owned their homes on Beach Avenue, visiting during summer months whenever the mood struck.

I set out for Cape May early the next morning. A hot and sunny Sunday, the hundred-mile trip was a two-hour drive from Philly, which I drove with the top down on my ragtop T-Bird—only occasionally feeling guilty that I hadn't asked Steve to come along.

He would have, of course. And I would have enjoyed his company. But I had no idea where he was in his investigation. He'd read the letter and for all I knew, he had already been to Congress Hall. He also had access to Arty. If Lily had recently taken a trip to Cape May, there was a good chance Arty would have known.

Working solo was frustrating, but it's what I had chosen for myself. And I was going to make the best of it. And succeed.

I had one advantage over Steve—I knew about Mystery Waiter. Knew he existed. Knew what he looked like. And I would know him if I saw him again.

Rolling into Cape May mid-morning, I decided my first move would be to locate Harry O'Toole's childhood home. According to Penny, he'd been an only child, but maybe his father was still alive, and maybe he still lived there.

Only, where might Harry's childhood home be?

Pulling into town, I took a longshot chance and stopped at The Lobster House, a dockside seafood restaurant overlooking Cape May Harbor. I'd been to Cape May many times, and knew the popular family-owned restaurant had been there for years, meaning there was a good chance someone there had known Harry O'Toole, the war hero who'd never come home.

Fortunately, someone did. "He lived on Jackson Street, near the hardware store," a waiter who said he'd gone to school with Harry told me. "Not sure the exact address, but when you get to the hardware store, it's three houses down. Place is falling apart—so I don't think you can miss it."

Turned out, he was right.

Unlike the other homes surrounding it, the house I was looking for was unkempt and appeared to be abandoned. A one-story wooden bungalow with peeling faded blue paint, the pillars holding up the front porch looked in danger of collapsing. The front door was so grimy that it was hard to tell what color it had been. And the windows, while miraculously all intact, were so dirty it was impossible to see inside.

I walked up onto the porch and knocked anyway. Just in case.

"Nobody's lived there for years," a voice called from the sidewalk. "Who're you looking for?"

I turned around to see an older woman watching me with an expression of curiosity and concern. "Be careful none of those floorboards give way," she called, shielding her eyes with her hands. "They look awful rotten. And watch out for those spiders."

Spiders!? I glanced up at the porch ceiling, stifled a scream, and ran down the crumbling brick porch steps onto the weedy lawn.

"Thanks," I told the woman, pressing a hand to my chest to slow my racing heart. I gave her a rueful smile. "I'm terrified of spiders."

"I can see that." She cocked her head. "Are you looking for old man O'Toole?"

I nodded.

"He's dead."

I wasn't surprised, although I was disappointed. "When did he die?"

"A couple years after the war. Died of a broken heart, they say, after he found out his son was killed in the war."

"Harry?"

"Yes. When old John learned that his boy was never coming home, he didn't care about nothing anymore. Just let the house go and then up and died. Word is that he left the house to a cousin somewhere out West."

The woman jerked a finger, pointing down the street. "I live a few doors that-a-way. Have for years. Never saw that cousin. But if he exists, he obviously doesn't care a damn bit about his inheritance."

"That's sad," I said. "And about Harry, too. Did you know him?"

She gave a nod. "Sure. But he wasn't around much. When he wasn't in school, he was working some job or another. Come summertime, he was at the lifeguard station. He was a lifeguard, you know. That was one of his jobs."

"Popular with the girls, too, I understand."

A small smile touched her lips. "He sure was." She narrowed her eyes. "Who are you, dear, and why are here?"

I told her my name and handed her my business card. "I'm just trying to track down information about Harry O'Toole, and I was hoping his father was still alive."

She studied my card and looked me up and down. "A lady private eye. Good for you. Sorry I can't help you, though."

"Maybe you can," I said. "Have you noticed anyone hanging around this house in the past few days or weeks?"

"Like, who?"

"Anyone. Anyone who looked out of place?"

Like a man with a limp or a doomed, pretty, blonde socialite or a handsome private eye named Steve Evans.

"No," she said. "Nobody but you, dear. I'm sorry."

I was sorry, too. I told her to keep my card and contact me if she saw anyone snooping around the rundown place. "In the meantime," I said, "I think I'll head over to the lifeguard station."

"Good idea," she agreed. "Harry was a hero there. He saved people's lives. I think they even gave him an award once."

———

On the way to Cape May Beach Patrol headquarters, I stopped at Congress Hall, a few blocks away on Beach Avenue.

I didn't expect to find Harry O'Toole on the hotel's porch, sunning himself in one of its many elegant white rocking chairs, but why not look? Anyway, if Harry had been there recently, maybe someone on staff, or a guest, would remember seeing a young, dark-haired man with a pronounced limp hanging around.

Unfortunately, I couldn't find anyone who had seen a man matching Harry's description, and no one by his name had checked into the hotel that summer.

I had better luck at Beach Patrol headquarters, where at least a few of the older lifeguards remembered him.

"Harry? Pretty sure he got the lifeguard of the year award in 1940," a muscular blond guard with a deep tan, who looked to be around thirty, told me. Deep Tan was in the office on break and was eager to talk about Harry after I introduced myself and told him why I was there. "Harry was pretty much a legend in his day," he said.

"Did you know him well?"

"Not really. He was a few years older than me. I was a newbie. He was experienced—and a big deal."

"How so? Because he won lifeguard of the year?"

"That, yes. He saved lives. But he also acted like he *thought* he was a big deal—like he was God's gift to women."

"I've heard that," I said. "Do you remember any of the girls he went out with?"

Deep Tan chuckled. "You mean *made out* with?"

"Whatever."

Deep Tan shrugged. "He liked the rich ones. A lot of girls think lifeguards are cool—and we are. Hey, we work out and we're handsome and we save people—what could be better than that?"

"But Harry liked the rich girls best?"

"Best I can remember ..." Deep Tan rubbed a hand across his chin. "You know what? Carl might be able to tell you more." He pointed toward the beach. "He's on duty right now. On the stand right out there. Carl knew Harry, too. Maybe better than me."

"What can I tell you, doll? Harry was a great guy." Carl flicked a quick glance down at me from his perch on the red lifeguard tower chair, then went back to watching the water.

Carl appeared to be around the same age as Deep Tan, maybe slightly older, but with dark brown hair and a sunburned nose. Swimmers of all ages frolicked in the waves. He blew a whistle and beckoned one who'd ventured out too far to come back in.

"Was Harry a friend of yours?" I asked.

He didn't take his eyes off the people in the water. "Guess you could say that. Harry had a lot of friends."

"And girlfriends?"

He glanced back at me. "Sure."

"Any you remember in particular?"

He blew his whistle at another swimmer. "Not really."

"Do you know if he was ever in love?"

Carl dropped his jaw and turned to stare at me. "You say you're a private eye?"

"That's right."

"Then why are you asking about Harry? He never came back from the war, poor guy. What difference does it make if he was ever in love?"

I squinted up at him. "I have my reasons for asking."

Carl turned back to watching the frolickers in the water and didn't say anything.

I waited.

Kids riding rafts screamed with joy. Teenage boys tossed a football to each other between breaking waves. Two mothers at the water's edge watched their toddlers play with little toy sailboats.

Carl looked back down at me. "Do your reasons have anything to do with those rumors?"

My heart jumped. "Rumors? What rumors?"

"Guess not."

"Tell me," I said. "Please."

Carl put his elbows on his knees and leaned forward, keeping an eye on the water as he spoke. "There was a string of home robberies in Cape May back before the war. A lot of wealthy homes were broken into. The thief, or thieves, took money and jewelry. And they were never caught."

"Oh ..." I stared out at the water as the implications of what Carl was saying swirled around my brain. "They were never caught?"

"Nope."

"Are you saying that people thought Harry O'Toole was maybe the thief?"

"Harry, and his buddy, Arty Duncan. Yep."

"And the police?"

"Rumors had it that the cops suspected Harry and Arty, too. But then the war came. And that was that."

"The robberies stopped?"

"Yep. And both boys shipped off to war."

"And Harry never returned."

"Nope."

"And Arty came back a hero."

"Yep."

"So the jewelry was never recovered—and Arty was never arrested. Because too much time had passed and there was no proof."

Carl gifted me with a quick grin. "You got it, doll. Not sure what you're going to do with it, but you got it."

I had it and I was pretty sure Steve didn't. I was feeling mighty proud of myself. "I guess this was in the papers at the time," I said. "I mean, the robberies, not the rumors."

"You bet. Big news. Probably made all the Philly papers."

I clapped my hands together, too excited to hold back my feelings. This lead could be significant. "Gee, thanks, Carl," I said. "You've been a big help. Now I just need to get my hands on some of those old newspapers."

Sixteen

It was dinnertime by the time I got back to Philly, so I stopped at my parents' house to say hi, hopefully get a good meal, and to ask my father if he could help me access the archives of The *Philadelphia Inquirer*, the city's morning paper.

My dad, Ralph, is an editor at the *Inquirer*—before that a reporter—and he was the one who'd talked my mother into naming me Story when I was born.

I'd never minded being the only girl in school with that unusual name, and Story Smith was a great byline during my short career as a journalist, before I left my reporter job to become a private eye.

I was confident Dad would help me find news stories about a string of robberies that had taken place in Cape May during the late nineteen-thirties and early nineteen-forties—and with any luck, maybe he'd even remember them.

My mother must have heard me drive up because she greeted me at the door with a warm smile. "Story, why didn't you tell us you'd be coming by? Good thing I have extra spaghetti and meatballs."

"My favorite." I gave her a hug. "I would have called, but I just came from Cape May." I followed her into the dining room, where my father was finishing his dessert, blueberry pie with a scoop of vanilla ice cream.

"Looks yummy," I said. Having a sweet tooth runs in the family.

"Story says she just came from Cape May." My mom eyed my T-shirt, shorts, sandals, and convertible-top-down-windblown hair. "But she didn't say why she was there."

"For my latest case," I said. "And before you ask if I went alone— yes, I did."

Taking a seat next to my father, I told him, "But now I need your help."

My father smiled. "Sure thing."

My mother frowned.

My mother isn't keen on me being a private eye. She thinks I should have kept my reporter job, even though as a woman I'd been relegated to writing articles about the latest upcoming fashions, top secret tips on keeping your house cleaner than your neighbors', and how to whip up gourmet dinners that are sure to make your husband swoon.

Fortunately, Dad thinks what I do now is cool.

Not that I'm the first P.I. in the family because my brother, Rob, was in the business until he recently took a job as an agent with the F.B.I.

No, Dad thinks what I do now is cool because I'm daring to be different. As a woman. No husband, no kids, no secretarial job, no teaching job.

Facing down danger for a living instead.

I brought him and my mom up to date on my case so far, including what Carl the lifeguard had told me about the string of jewelry thefts and the rumors about Harry.

"The Prince of Pearls," my father said, his eyes lighting up at the memory of those news stories. "That's what they called that brazen thief who never got caught. Or thieves. Could have been more than one."

"Strange they were never caught," I said.

"The thefts went on for four years, maybe more. Most took place during the summer but not all. The press called them the Cape May Capers. And none of the jewelry was ever recovered."

"Sounds like dangerous criminals were involved," my mother said. With a loud sigh, she went into the kitchen, then came back with a plate of spaghetti and set it in front of me.

Starving, I put a napkin on my lap and dug in.

"Clever criminal or criminals for sure." My father watched me chew a meatball. "As I recall, they climbed trees to gain access to a house, crawled across roofs, hid in closets. Robbed people while they were out. And sometimes when they were home asleep."

I put my fork down. "Nobody ever woke up and confronted them?"

"When they did, they got a bright flashlight shined in their eyes, temporarily blinding them. Long enough for the thief to get away."

"Hmmm." I picked my fork up and resumed eating.

My father scraped the last pie crumbs off his plate. "This is Sunday night, so we can't get our hands on any old papers now. Our archivist will be in tomorrow morning. Come to work with me and I'll introduce you to her. She'll dig up stories for you."

I gave him a grateful smile. "Sounds great."

"Wait," My mom slid a piece of pie in front of me. "Didn't I hear you say that that cute private detective who's practically your boyfriend helped you find that secret letter in the Bible? Shouldn't you return the favor?"

I swallowed a forkful of spaghetti and wiped my mouth with my napkin. "I let him read the letter. And he's not my boyfriend."

My mother put her hands on her hips. "Well, didn't you spend Fourth of July at his parents' farm?"

"Well ... yeah."

She sniffed. "Sounds like a boyfriend."

"Even if he's not, I agree with Mom." Dad grinned. "Bring him along tomorrow. We'll meet here first for breakfast."

———

Even though it was growing late, I stopped at my office on the way home to type up daily reports from the weekend. I wanted to get down on paper all I'd learned at the funeral and in Cape May.

Darn my parents, though, because when I sat down to write, I couldn't concentrate.

They were right about Steve. He *had* snuck me into the Duncan mansion when I had no other way of getting in. I had not wanted to admit it to myself, but I wasn't being fair to him. He'd risked a lot for me. Not only his case, but his business, his reputation.

The least I could do was bring him along with me to the *Philadelphia Inquirer* archives.

But invite him to breakfast at my parent's house first?

Holy cow, that gave me the heebie-jeebies.

My mother could be counted on to embarrass me in so many ways. I'd never be able to look Steve in the eye again.

I took a deep breath. Placed my fingers firmly back on the typewriter keys. Then hesitated and sat back in my chair.

I looked at my phone. Call Steve and invite him? Or not?

I picked up the receiver.

"Yoo-hoo!"

Yikes. I dopped the receiver back in its cradle as Steve sauntered into my office. "Oh, Hi," I said.

He cocked his head. "Calling somebody important?"

I gave him a weak smile. "Just you."

He stepped toward me. "Thought so."

Damn him.

"Why were you calling me?" Wearing his signature heart-grabbing grin, he headed toward my desk.

Wait. I stared at him. "What's going on?" I asked. "How did you get in here?"

He sat down on a corner of my desk and widened his grin. "I feel like you're always asking me that question."

"Answer it. Wendy's not here. It's Sunday night. I'm the only one in the building."

Steve leaned toward me and whispered, "You left the front door to the building unlocked. Your car is out front. I figured you'd be here."

I groaned. "I can't believe I forgot to lock it behind me. I need to be more careful. Got a lot on my mind."

"Which means you've been busy. That's my girl." Steve patted the phone. "So, why were you calling me?"

I chewed on a nail. "I've been thinking ..."

"And?"

"I haven't been fair to you."

He tilted his head. "Interesting. I'm intrigued. How so?"

I told him about my trip to Cape May. Finding Harry O'Toole's childhood home. Checking to see if anyone had seen Harry or Lily at Congress Hall. Interviewing the lifeguards.

I kept Mystery Waiter to myself. Because I didn't want to tell him *everything*.

"You're taking that letter seriously." Pressing his lips together, he held my gaze.

"Aren't you?"

"Want to know what I've been up to?"

I grinned. "Yes. Please tell me."

"I tracked down Charles Harrington, that jerk from the party."

I chuckled. "Good move."

"You beat me to him, Story."

"That's right. So?"

"He admitted that he and Lily were lovers."

"Right. So maybe he killed her. Or maybe his wife did. That woman's downright dangerous."

"Renee?" Steve laughed. "She was a pussycat with me. Flirtatious to the point of being embarrassing since she was coming on to me in front of her husband."

I made a face. "Figures. Me, she tried to attack. Flew at me with those claws of hers so fast, I had to get out of there. I could see her pushing Lily off that balcony, no problem. What I can't see is how she could have lured Lily up there. That doesn't fit."

Steve shrugged. "Good work so far. So, what's next?"

"My dad is going to take me to meet the archivist at the *Philadelphia Inquirer* tomorrow and I'm inviting you to come along. I want to pull stories about the Prince of Pearls. It's possible that Harry O'Toole was the prince, and that the necklace he gave Penny was one he'd stolen."

"A long, long, long shot." Steve smiled. "But okay, thanks, I'd love to join you."

"And my mother wants to meet you. So you're invited for breakfast at my parent's house first." Swallowing hard, the blood rushed to my cheeks as I waited for Steve's response, which seemed to take forever.

The grin on his face grew wider and wider. He was savoring the moment and my discomfort. Damn him.

"Hot dang," he finally said. "Meet your parents?" His eyes gleamed. "Can't wait."

SEVENTEEN

Introducing Steve to my parents was nerve wracking enough.

But then my big brother, Rob, and his wife, Piper, showed up for breakfast, too.

Really? Seven o'clock on a Monday morning with my entire family? Was this necessary? I just wanted to get to work.

My mother, on the other hand, was treating the occasion like it was Thanksgiving. Without the turkey, but with every kind of breakfast food imaginable. Scrambled eggs, bacon, sausage, home fries, porridge, French toast, coffee, orange juice, grapefruit juice.

Everything was ready and spread out on the buffet in the dining room when Steve and I arrived. I introduced Steve to my parents, and to Piper, but Rob needed no introduction. Steve and Rob had known each other for years as rival private eyes.

"Evans. Good to see you again, buddy," Rob said. "How's business?"

"Great," Steve said. "How's the FBI agent job going?"

"Love it." Rob smiled stiffly. "I can't believe you're here. Working with my sister."

Oh, great. Rob and Steve had never been friends. "We're on opposite sides of the same case," I blurted out. "Or ... maybe not *exactly* opposite sides."

"*Hmmm*," Rob said.

Steve just smiled.

We were all standing around the table, which I now wanted to crawl under.

My mother couldn't take admiring eyes off Steve.

My father was staring hungrily at the food, which was getting cold.

My brother seemed to be trying to figure Steve out.

And Steve just continued to smile. Good move.

"Well, let's eat, shall we?" Piper said in a nervous, high-pitched chipper tone as she headed over to the buffet.

Bless Piper's heart. I wanted to hug my sweet sister-in-law, newly married to my brother. My brother was a great guy, but he didn't trust Steve and always feared he would hurt me.

Everyone piled food on their plates and sat down at the table, Steve next to me.

"We've been hearing so much about you, Steve." My mother eyed him from across the table.

"Good things, I hope," Steve said.

"Oh, very." My mother beamed. "I think you are very good for Story."

I had a forkful of eggs headed to my mouth and put the fork down. "Mom, please ..."

"I warned Story about you, Evans." Rob picked up his coffee. "She obviously didn't listen."

"I'm aware." Steve turned to me and smiled. "I'm glad she didn't listen."

"Steve and I work great together when we work together," I said. "And that's what we're doing today—*working* together. Stop worrying about me, Rob."

"I never stop worrying about you," my mom told me.

"June, please," my father raised his eyebrows at her. "Don't embarrass Story."

"I just want my daughter to have a good life." My mother took a sip of orange juice. "And that includes getting married someday and having children and having a loving husband who takes care of her. Is that so wrong?"

My face on fire from embarrassment, I looked down at my plate. Moved the eggs around with my fork. Managed a bite.

I felt sorry for Steve. But watching him from the corner of my eye, I was proud of him. He didn't seem the slightest embarrassed or defensive. Which is more than I could say for myself.

"Story is a proving to be a great private eye." Steve smiled at my mother. "She's a natural. I don't think you have anything to worry about, Mrs. Smith."

"Thank you," I whispered.

"I feel better with you at her side," my mother returned Steve's smile. "It makes me less worried, somehow."

"But why do you always seem to be at her side, Evans?" Rob wanted to know. "Aren't you two competitors?"

"I guess you could say I'm Story's mentor." Steve shrugged. "Right now, I guess that's the best way to describe our relationship."

Yes. Right now. Mentor was good. I could handle that.

"Mentor. I like that," I said, horribly aware of how hot my face felt. "Steve has been teaching me a lot. And I'm grateful for that." I looked at everyone around the table. "But right now, I just want to eat. Because Steve, Dad, and I need to get going. We have a lot of old newspaper stories to dig up."

———

The *Philadelphia Inquirer* archives room was in the newspaper's basement.

The archivist, Rebecca Stanley, greeted us warmly and assured my father that she could help us find what we needed.

Reassuring, because the room was massive, with shelves and shelves of newspapers stored by date, going back decades. The room also had an unusual odor. Musty, with a tinge of the smokey scent of ink on aging paper.

Cubicles along one wall also held microfiche machines for reading copies of papers on microfilm, which I hoped we would not need to do. I told Mrs. Stanley I would rather search through actual papers.

"Of course, dear," she said. "We'll do our best."

Mrs. Stanley wore her graying hair in a bun and reading glasses on a gold chain around her neck. She had a kind face, and her eager smile told me she was excited to be helping private eyes track down stories from the past.

"The Prince of Pearls, you say?" She tapped a finger to her chin. "I seem to remember those articles. Robberies that took place in Cape May. Not much Cape May news makes our paper, but those crimes were newsworthy. They just kept happening. And I seem to remember nobody was ever caught."

"That's right, and no jewelry was ever recovered," Steve said. "Story and I are looking for details about the crimes. Where the robberies occurred, what was taken."

I asked, "Could we please can start with the summer of 1938?"

Nodding, Mrs. Stanley led us over to the shelf labeled that year and then to the June issues.

Oh boy. Thirty days in June. And then we had July and August and the rest of that year to search through. And then 1939 and 1940 and 1941. I suddenly realized this could take a while.

Good thing I'd brought Steve along.

Fortunately, with Mrs. Stanley's help, we finished in a little over three hours. By which time it was lunchtime, and I was famished and silently thanking my mother for that giant breakfast.

Unfortunately, the dozen or so articles we did find about the Cape May Capers didn't provide much information we didn't already know.

They did provide some addresses, which I planned to visit. And descriptions of some of the missing rings, bracelets, watches, and necklaces. But nothing specifically matching Penny's missing pendant.

The first article, dated June 16, 1938, painted a picture of a brazen heist that shocked a wealthy young man and his distraught wife, along with the entire town, including the police.

The headline read: "No Suspects in Cape May Robbery, Thousands Worth of Jewelry Stolen in Dead of Night."

Short and to the point, it ran on page three:

Police are investigating a robbery that took place in the three hundred block of Beach Avenue in Cape May, New Jersey last night that occurred while the residents were out. Franklin Cunningham and his wife, Violet, left to attend a banquet in Atlantic City around five p.m. Returning a little after midnight, they discovered someone had broken into their mansion through a ground floor window, and that Mrs. Cunningham's jewelry box containing necklaces, bracelets, and earrings was missing, along with an undisclosed amount of cash from their smashed open bedroom safe.

"I can't imagine who would do such a thing," said Mr. Cunningham.

"Those jewels are family heirlooms," Mrs. Cunningham said. "They can never be replaced."

A spokesman with the Cape May Police Department said neighbors did not see or hear anything, and that police are continuing to investigate.

Subsequent articles described more robberies that summer in Cape May, each one referring to the first. All made page one, as did the stories about the string of home break-ins that took place through August 21, 1941.

"That seems to be the last one," Mrs. Stanley said. "Or at least that's the last story I can find about the thefts. I wonder why they stopped and why no one was ever arrested and what happened to all that jewelry?"

"That's what we are trying to find out," I said, then thanked her for her time.

I'd jotted down every address mentioned in the articles. Where they might lead, I had no idea, but they were a start.

Steve wasn't so sure. Nor nearly as enthusiastic as I was about what long unsolved jewel heists had to do with Lily Duncan's death.

Then again, he didn't know about Mystery Waiter.

And I wasn't going to tell him.

"Let me buy you lunch," Steve said as we walked out of the *Inquirer*. "It's the least I can do since you provided breakfast. After that, I'm going to have a serious talk with Arty. Not sure if I'm going to tell him about Lily's letter from Harry, but I do need to find out if he knew anything about Lily taking a recent trip to Cape May. And, oh, yeah, if he knew anything about her having an affair."

I smiled. "Lucky you, that Arty will talk to you. Maybe you can let me know what he says."

Steve winked at me. "Maybe I will."

His wink made me go warm all over. But I wasn't going to wait around and wait for him to call.

Nope. I was going back to Cape May. Solo.

EIGHTEEN

After a enjoying a quick lunch at a café with Steve, I went home, changed into shorts and a T-shirt, packed some clothes in a small suitcase, then hit the road for Cape May.

Getting a late start, I wanted to be prepared for an overnight stay because I had a strong hunch that I was on to something with the Cape May Capers, and I didn't want to be rushed.

It didn't take me long to confirm that the Prince of Pearls had known what he was doing. Cleary clever and clearly gutsy, he—or she—had not wasted time breaking into the average home.

No, cruising around town, I saw all the burglarized homes were huge, multi-story mansions belonging to its the wealthiest residents. Unlike some of the other houses around town, most of them were well cared for and faced the ocean along Beach Avenue.

By late afternoon, I'd seen them all. But now what? Harry O'Toole was dead as far as the world was concerned, and I had no proof he was Mystery Waiter anyway. Adding to my creeping sense of uneasiness, I was beginning to wonder if I was wasting time chasing a ghost.

Any one of the many guests at the WowWee It's Wednesday party could have pushed Lily off that balcony, if indeed she had been pushed.

With no idea what to do next, I drove to Congress Hall and parked. I put my top up and wandered down to the beach and then headed north toward the lifeguard station, where I found Carl in the office.

Super-duper. Just the guy I needed to see. He'd been helpful before, tipping me off about the rumors linking Harry and the jewelry heists.

But he had not answered my question about Harry's love life. If Harry had so many chicks, maybe Lily wasn't the only one he'd reconnected with.

"Well, if it's not Miss Private Eye again." Carl greeted me from behind the office desk, where he was filling out paperwork. He appeared far more relaxed than he had up on the lifeguard tower.

Which was good. And since we were alone in the office, I had his full attention.

"I'm so glad you're here." I wandered over to the desk. "I've been researching those robberies you told me about. Very interesting. But I can't stop wondering about Harry O'Toole's love life."

Carl rolled his eyes, but before he could wave me off, I said, "Wait. I know he's long dead. But you said he was popular with the ladies. Could you at least give me the names of any of them?"

Carl leaned back and folded his arms, looking genuinely confused but also suspicious. "Why?" he asked, narrowing his eyes at me. "Why do you keep asking all these questions about Harry?"

"I'm investigating a murder, and his name has come up."

What else could I say? It sounded vague even to me—but to Carl's credit, he wanted more. "A murder that happened *when*?" He shook his head. "You're going to have to tell me more if you want me to tell you more."

I held his gaze and sighed. "The murder happened recently ... but a valuable necklace is involved." I chewed the side of my lip. Stating my suspicions aloud made them sound even more farfetched.

"A necklace?" Carl squinted at me. "Go on ..."

"Harry gave the necklace to one of his girlfriends before shipping off to war," I said. "It may or may not be connected to the murder I'm investigating. It's a long shot, and I can't tell you more, but I need to know the names of Harry's girlfriends. You told me before that he had quite a few."

Carl's expression turned to one of amusement. "Did I say that?"

"You said that he liked to make out."

Carl chuckled. "That he did. Or at least he liked to brag to us guys that he did."

"Did he have a favorite girl he liked to make out with?"

I held my breath, half expecting that he'd name Penny or Lily, in which case I'd have to keep pressing.

He smiled slyly. "He did have one favorite. Not the type of girl he would have given a necklace to, though. She was okay to look at. No classy chassis, just so-so, if you know what I mean. Not too bright, didn't come from money."

"But she was a favorite ... why?"

Carl scoffed. "Why else? She was fast. Stacked. Put out easily and often, if you know what I mean."

I blinked at him. "I think I do know what you mean. But can you be more specific?"

"Carl and this girl used to get together on a boat that was docked in the marina by The Lobster House. A sailboat. It was old, but big enough to have a cabin, which gave them lots of privacy. Harry used to brag to us guys about what they did aboard." His lips jerked up in a smirk at the memory.

"Oh." I stared at Carl. Obviously, this favorite girl of Harry's couldn't have been Penny. She was pretty and bright, and her family had money.

Poor Penny. For years she'd mourned the loss of a man she had believed was a saint, who she'd expected to marry. Turns out he was really a cad who'd fooled around with other women—girls—while still in high school.

Even worse, he might have been a criminal mastermind.

"Do you remember the name of the boat?" I asked.

"Yes. Sweet Sailing. Always thought that was a clever name."

"Who owned it?"

"Harry and his buddy, Arty. They bragged about that, too. How they pooled their money together to buy it. Matter of fact, sometimes they'd rent it out. For a few hours, not to take it out sailing. A couple of bucks would get you a place to take your gal. If you know—"

"I do know what you mean." If he said that one more time I was going to scream. "Could you tell me her name?" I asked.

"Who?"

"Harry's sailboat floozy."

"Oh. Yeah." He graced me with a sly grin. "Gladys Jones. Her name was Gladys Jones."

Wonderful. I had a name. "Do you know if she still lives in Cape May?"

He shrugged. "As a matter of fact, she does."

"Do you happen to know where she lives?"

He arched a brow. "Why? Are you going to go see her? Because if you do, don't tell her I sent you. I don't want to get involved in this."

"I understand." I smiled. "I won't breathe a word about you."

He leaned toward me. "Don't know where she lives but she should be easy to find. She works as a maid at The Admiral Hotel."

———

The Admiral Hotel. I knew about the Admiral. It was one of the town's largest hotels, if not the largest, and it wasn't far. Just a little north on Beach Avenue.

"Gee, thanks," I told Carl. "Appreciate the tip."

He nodded. "Place is huge. Over three hundred rooms. It's possible Gladys is working now."

I went to go. Then stopped and turned back to him. "I'm just curious," I said. "How do you know where Gladys works? Have you kept in touch with her all these years?"

He gave a one-shoulder shrug. "Let's just say Cape May is a small town for those of us who live here year-round. But remember, don't tell Gladys I sent you. I don't want people to think I'm a gossip."

I assured him I had no intention of revealing him as my source, thanked him, and set out for my car.

It was possible that I was on some kind of crazy wild goose chase that would lead me nowhere. But if Harry had truly survived the war, and had gotten in touch with Lily, it wasn't beyond the realm of possibility that he had sought out Gladys, too.

Pulling up to the U-shaped, eight-story Admiral Hotel, I turned my T-Bird over to a uniformed valet, told him I wouldn't be long, and then walked up stately steps, passing under a columned portico that ran the length of the building.

Inside, the two-story lobby took my breath away. Marble walls. Mosaic tile floor. Soaring Tiffany-style glass dome overhead, along with a grand entrance staircase leading to the upper floors.

A plaque just inside the front door bragged to visitors that the hotel, built in the early 1900s as the Hotel Cape May, had 330 rooms, a ballroom, swimming pool, bowling alley—and that Henry Ford and Louis Chevrolet had once raced their automobiles up and down the beachfront.

Not a bad place to work, I mused as I headed to the front desk to ask if Gladys Jones might be on duty.

"Gladys Jones?" the young dark-haired desk clerk gawked at me as he pushed his bushy eyebrows together in haughty confusion. "One of our maids?"

"Yes, sir." I smiled. When his stony silence made me realize he required an explanation, I added, "I've just come from Philadelphia and a mutual friend asked me to look her up. I just want to say hello."

"Oh. Alright. Let me check with her supervisor." Frowning, the clerk picked up the phone, dialed, murmured something that included Gladys's name, then hung up. "She's working the third floor right now," he said, then warned, "she won't have much time to talk to you because this is our busy season."

"I won't need much time," I said, giving him a grateful smile that did nothing to warm his frown, then headed to the staircase before he could change his mind.

Once on the third floor, though, it occurred to me that I had no idea what Gladys looked like. Other than "so-so." Which, according to Carl, she'd been in high school.

But how many maids did the hotel have working the third floor in the middle of the afternoon? The hallway was cavernous and silent. My sandals sunk into plush green carpet as I walked past closed doors, occasionally hearing murmured conversations on the other side of them, but no sounds of vacuuming that would have led me to a maid.

Then one came out of a room ahead of me and closed the door. She was pushing a cart full of cleaning supplies and stopped when she saw me. "Can I help you?" she asked.

"I hope so," I said with a smile. She had straight, unevenly cropped hair that could only be described as mousy brown. Her light blue uniform fit her snuggly, as if she'd gained weight around her middle. And the lines around her eyes and the smudges under them made her look sad and tired.

"Are you Gladys Jones?" I asked.

"Yes." She stared at me, fear creeping into her eyes. "Is something wrong with your room? You haven't come to tell me something is wrong with your room, have you?" Her voice rose in pitch with every word. "If it's more towels you need—"

"Oh, no, no." I waved a hand. "I'm not staying here."

"Oh." The fear left her eyes, replaced by confusion. "Okay. I got scared because you knew my name."

"I'm looking for someone and I was told you might be able to help me," I said.

"Who?"

"Harry O'Toole." I braced myself, prepared for the usual response to that name. That he was dead, God rest his war-hero soul.

I did not get the usual response.

Instead, the color left her exhausted face, and she gaped at me like I was a ghost. "Harry?" she whispered. "Why are you looking for Harry?"

"Have you seen him?" I asked, playing along like we were talking about a living person. "Because I really need to talk to him."

"Harry O'Toole?" She spoke his name again in a strangled whisper. "I don't understand."

"I just need a few minutes of his time," I said breezily. "If you could just tell me where he's staying now, or where he's living, I'd really appreciate it."

For a second, I thought Gladys was going to faint. Her hands tightened on the supply cart and she shook her head back and forth, back and forth as she stared at me unblinking and slack jawed.

"Gladys?" I spoke her name loud enough to startle her. "Please, please, help me. I really need to find Harry."

She started to push the cart around me. "No. Go away."

I put out a hand and stopped the cart. "Please. It's important."

She shook her head and yanked the cart from my grasp.

"Do you know Lily Duncan?" I blurted, desperate to stop her.

She froze. "Lily?"

"Yes. I think Lily Ash was her name when you knew her. As a teenager. She and her cousin Penny came to Cape May every summer and hung out with the lifeguards. Like you and your friends. Remember?"

"Lily?" Her eyes went big. "What about Lily?"

"She's dead. Murdered." I took a deep breath. "And I think Harry might know who murdered her."

"Harry?" Gladys froze. She did not say that was impossible because Harry had died in the war. She did not say Harry couldn't possibly know anything about Lily. She did not say that she had no idea where Harry could be.

Clearly rattled, she didn't say anything at all, just gaped at me with a stricken look on her face.

Then, after what seemed like forever, but was probably less than a minute, she whispered, "Let's talk. Except, I can't right now. I need to get back to work."

I nodded eagerly. "Okay."

"Meet me at the hotel pool tomorrow morning at seven. It overlooks the ocean. We'll have time to talk then before I go to work."

"Great," I smiled. "That sounds great."

"Don't be late," she warned. "I won't be able to wait around for you."

"Oh, don't worry," I said. "I'll be early."

———

It was a good thing I'd packed an overnight bag. As I walked back to my car, I silently congratulated myself for having that foresight, although I was a bit worried about finding a place to stay that I could afford. Not The Admiral and not Congress Hall. Both of those fine establishments were well out of my price range.

My best bet was to find a rooming house, but in the peak of summer season I'd be lucky to find a vacancy.

I knew I should start looking before it got dark, but I wanted to explore the marinas around The Lobster House, so I headed there first. Harry might be living aboard a boat.

The Lobster House at Schellenger's Landing is where boats enter Cape May Harbor, so I parked there and walked over to the marina next door.

I didn't really expect to find an old sailboat named Sweet Sailing there, but I didn't see any harm in looking.

The marina was small. Meandering up and down the docks, I saw that most of the boats—motorboats and sailboats—were new and well kept.

Disappointed but not surprised, I kept walking and came upon a larger marina, which appeared to have more slips, with larger and newer looking vessels.

An old boat once owned by two teenage guys would have looked out of place there, and attracted unwanted attention, but I walked up and down the piers anyway, reading the names of all the vessels.

Then, I stopped at the end of one of the piers. Shocked, I just stood there and stared.

Not at a sailboat. At a bright white motor yacht. A huge motor yacht. With a spacious cabin and what looked like a powerful motor.

Its name, scrawled across the back in huge cursive letters—Sweet Sailing Two.

Could it be? I shook my head. No ... This was not a sailboat. This was a motorboat. And for all I knew, Sweet Sailing was a popular boat name.

Still ... I leaned closer and tried to see into the partially curtained windows. No one appeared to be aboard.

Was it silly to think Harry O'Toole might be living on it? Yes. I didn't see how that was possible.

But Arty? Maybe it wasn't so silly to think this might be Arty's boat. I wouldn't put it past Arty to name his new yacht after an old sailboat from his youth.

Still, what did it matter if this was Arty's boat? It wasn't getting me any closer to finding out who'd murdered his wife. Although I planned to ask Gladys what she might know about it.

I walked back to The Lobster House and treated myself to a yummy flounder dinner with a baked potato and coleslaw. Then I asked my young waitress if she knew of any boarding houses nearby.

"Browne Cottage, on Howard Street," she said. "Rooms are two dollars a night."

I dabbed my mouth with my napkin and smiled. "I can afford that. But do you think they have any vacancies?"

"Let me call over there and ask," she said. "I live next door and know the owner, Miss Emily."

She came back a few minutes later with the news I wanted to hear. "Miss Emily says come on over. She's got one room left and says she'll save it for you."

Nineteen

As I'd promised Gladys, I got to The Admiral Hotel pool early.

Excited to talk to her, I'd checked out of Browne Cottage while it was still dark, and the sun was just beginning to light the day when I walked onto the deck at six thirty.

Facing the Atlantic Ocean, and separated from the hotel by flowering bushes, the huge pool was clearly the place to be during daylight hours. Lounge chairs neatly circled the deck, ready for occupants, and a sign on a bright pink snack bar called the Lazy Crab declared it would open for business at ten that Tuesday morning.

For now, though, I had the place to myself, which boded well because Gladys and I would be able to talk privately. She'd made it clear she had not wanted to discuss Harry O'Toole with me at all, until I mentioned Lily—and that she'd been murdered.

Which had changed everything. Gladys obviously wanted information from me, while I wanted information from her—and I didn't have to wait long for her to show up.

Minutes after I arrived, Gladys came onto the pool deck from the beach and walked over to me perched on one of the lounge chairs. She was dressed in the same uniform as the day before, but there was energy in her step now.

"Thanks for taking the time to meet with me," I said, rising to greet her. "I know you have another busy day ahead of you."

"Sure do," she said. "But I want to know about Lily. She was a good friend once, a long time ago, and I can't believe she was murdered. That's so upsetting."

I asked, "Shall we sit?"

She shook her head. "I'm kind of feeling too fidgety. Let's just walk and talk, okay?"

"Sure. Whatever you want."

"You want to know about Harry," she said as we began circling the pool. She spoke his name with hushed reverence, surprising me. Yesterday, it had been with nervous panic.

"Yes. Harry O'Toole. I'm looking for him. I need to talk to him. Have you seen him around?"

She gave me the kind of look you give someone who has lost their mind. "You're asking about a man who was declared dead years ago," she said. "Why do you think I might have seen him around?"

Oh great, not her, too. "I think you know why I'm asking," I said.

"Know what?"

"That he's not really dead. Or, to put it another way, that he's come back from the dead."

She gawked at me. "I have no idea why you would think that."

"The way you reacted to his name yesterday made me think that."

"I'm sorry, I didn't mean to give you the wrong impression." She didn't sound sorry. She was hiding something.

She stopped and faced me. Holding my gaze, she started fingering something around her neck. Like she wanted me to notice it.

It was a necklace.

Not just any necklace. My heart slammed against my ribs. Peering closer, I saw it wasn't a cheap bauble. It was a quality piece of jewelry. Real gold with large stones that sparkled in the light of the rising sun.

"Wow," I said. "That's gorgeous. Are those diamonds and emeralds?"

The dreamy smile on her face sent chills up and down my arms. "Yes," she said. "Harry gave it to me."

"When?"

She turned her smile upside down, puffing out her lower lip in exaggerated sadness. "He gave this to me a long time ago. Right before he left for the war."

Liar. She was lying. I tried not to let my skepticism show. What kind of game was this woman playing? The necklace matched the description of the one Harry had given Penny. It was the same one— had to be. But if so, how had it ended up around the neck of this hotel maid?

"Why are you wearing such an expensive piece of jewelry now?" I asked. "You're on your way to work. It looks too valuable to wear while cleaning."

"You said you wanted to talk about Harry." She ran her fingers along the diamonds and emeralds. "So, I wanted to show you this. Harry was the love of my life. I miss him, dearly, every day. I wish I could be with him now, but I can't because he's dead. And now I want to know about Lily. Tell me what happened to Lily."

"Someone pushed her off a balcony during a party that she and her husband were giving at their home in Philadelphia."

She pressed a hand to her forehead. "Arty, right? Lily married Arty. Harry's best friend."

"Right," I said. "But Arty didn't push her. I know that for a fact. I also believe Harry was at that party. Disguised as a waiter."

Gladys shook her head. "No, that's not possible. You're talking crazy stuff."

"I also have proof that Harry was in love with Lily."

"No! Not true. He loved me."

"And Penny." I smiled wryly, pointing to the necklace. "I know for a fact that Harry gave Lily's cousin, Penny, a necklace exactly like that. Do you remember Penny? She was engaged to Harry before he left for the war."

Gladys backed away from me. "That's not true. He was going to marry me."

"I think that might be Penny's necklace," I said. "I think Harry gave it to you recently."

"No." She backed further away, edging closer to the pool. "Harry gave it to me years ago."

"I understand you and Harry used to meet on his sailboat, Sweet Sailing."

Her eyes narrowed. "Who told you that?"

"A source who asked not to be named."

"Huh," she said. "What exactly did this source tell you? That I was Harry's girl? Well, I was. I was his only girl."

"To tell you the truth, he said Harry had many girls." I wasn't there to embarrass her or make her angry. That would get me nowhere. I waved a hand. "Anyway, tell me where Harry is now. Is that boat still around? Maybe he's living on it? I need to talk to him."

She huffed a laugh. "He's dead, lady. If you want to talk to him, you might need to find yourself one of those psychic mediums people. You know—the kind that claim to communicate with those who've moved on to the great beyond."

"Hey, I happen to know one of those people," I said, smiling at the idea of hiring Victor Bravo. "Only, I don't think he could put me in touch with Harry. Not if Harry's still alive. Lily, maybe Lily. I watched her die. And I think Harry might know who killed her."

"I don't know why I ever agreed to meet with you." Gladys tucked the necklace back under her uniform. "This was a bad—"

Bam.

Startled, I sprang about five feet into the air and fell backward.

Gladys moaned, pressing her hands to her stomach.

Jumping to my feet, I watched in horror as she pulled her hands away. They were covered with blood.

I gasped. Had somebody shot her?

Confused, my heart pounding, I looked around. I wanted to run. But I couldn't leave her. I ran to grab her arm.

But I couldn't get to her in time. She was too close to the edge of the pool. With a scream, she lost her balance and toppled in.

Blood darkened the water.

I jumped in to save her.

She sank fast in a sea of red. I grabbed for her shoulder, but she slipped away.

I tried again. Got a hand under her armpit. Tried to pull her up. But she was too heavy.

I was out of air. I let go. Swam to the surface. Grabbed the side of the pool and took a deep breath.

Someone ran over and pointed a gun at my face. "Get out," a deep, gruff voice demanded. The voice belonged to a masked, menacing, shadowy figure dressed in black. "Get out now," he growled.

What the hell? Like hell I was getting out.

Heart pounding, I tried to duck back under the water. But he was too fast.

He grabbed me by my hair and yanked me up and out of the pool.

Numb with icy fear, I fell to my knees. Damn. Pain shot through my ankle, which until now had been healing nicely.

He grabbed my wrist and pulled me back up.

I gaped at him and tried to pull away, but he was too strong.

Our eyes met through the holes in his mask. I couldn't see his face, but a shock of black hair fell over his forehead and my heart stopped.

Mystery Waiter? "Harry O'Toole?" I whispered hoarsely, trying again to pull away from him as he held me fast. "Are you Harry?"

He shoved his gun into my side. "Shut up. I'm warning you, play nice or else."

Or else sounded bad, so I keep my mouth shut as he pulled me toward the bushes separating the pool from the hotel. He was gripping my wrist so hard the pain shot up my arm, but I didn't fight back, instead going along with him as I tried to think of a way to escape.

But where was he taking me? And why was he dragging me along with him when it would have been easier to shoot me and leave me for dead, like he had Gladys?

Police sirens wailed in the distance. Good. That was good. Someone must have heard him shoot her and called the police.

"Help!" I screamed, hopeful now that help was on the way. "Someone please, help—"

"Shut up," he growled, shaking me so hard I thought my arm would pull out of the socket. "I said, shut up!"

Far off in the distance, I thought I heard someone calling my name. My heart lurched. Steve? Was it Steve?

No, impossible. It had to be my imagination. Steve had no idea where I was. Stupid me, I hadn't told him where I was going. I hadn't told anyone.

"Please. Let me go help Gladys," I shouted at my assailant. "She's going to drown."

"Let her," he growled in my ear. "You should have stayed out of this, bitch."

His car was parked just beyond the bushes. He opened the passenger side door and shoved me in.

Then, before I could fight back, he hit me over the head with something hard.

And the world went black.

TWENTY

I should have had a gun.

That was the first thought that popped into my aching brain when I came to—flat on my back—in a place that reeked of some horrid combination of odors. Vomit. Sea air. And ... urine?

Gagging, I tried to sit up. But couldn't. My wrists were tied to something, which I couldn't see because I was blindfolded.

I tried to move my legs. But they were bound together at the ankles.

I tried to scream. But that wasn't going to happen, either. Because something was tied around my mouth.

I couldn't move, couldn't see, couldn't yell for help. And my entire head was throbbing with the worse headache I'd ever had, times one hundred.

I told myself not to panic and tried to think through the agony. I had no idea where I was, but at least I was alive.

For now.

Think, think, I told myself. The last thing I remembered was a masked man shooting Gladys Jones. Then abducting me and hitting me over the head with his gun.

I probably had a concussion—the least of my problems right now—and I couldn't stop blaming myself for my predicament. I should never have gone to that pool at dawn to meet that hotel maid without a gun.

Problem was, I'd lost my Smith & Wesson in a shoot-out on my last case. But that was no excuse. I should have bought a new one by now. I had no business being in the private investigation business without protection.

I tugged on my wrists. They were bound tight. How was I going to get out of this? Not without help, I wasn't.

Was my abductor ever coming back? Or had he just left me here to die slowly?

And if he did come back, then what was he going to do to me?

I tried to scream. But no one could hear my pitiful muffled wail. I tried not to cry. I would *not* cry.

I had no business thinking of myself as brave and gutsy. Gal gumshoe who could take on the world. Alone. Not needing anyone's help, thank you very much.

What self-deception. Hadn't I learned that by now? That no one can go it alone, least of all me.

Almost from the get-go, Steve had helped me with my business. Sometimes when I wanted him to and sometimes when I didn't. But what was wrong with that? What was I trying to prove?

That I didn't need a man. That's what I was trying to prove. To myself. That I didn't need a man professionally or personally. That it was better that way.

Because of Dean ...

Shame tormented me, beyond my physical agony.

Dean had been my boyfriend in college, and everyone had expected we would get married, because of course that was what a girl was supposed to do. I might have been going for a B.A. degree in English, but everyone knew I was supposed to be really working on getting an M.R.S. degree in Landing a Husband.

Sadly, when Dean did pop the question, I'd said, yes. But only to stall for time because I didn't love him enough to marry him. He was a good guy and good looking, but my heart didn't do flips when I was with him.

Not the way it does with Steve.

Steve ... why had I not told him where I was going? If I didn't get myself out of this place, I would die. They'd find my body decaying on this stinky mattress, or whatever I was lying on, and Steve would probably cry at my funeral. And then go on with his life.

Behind my blindfold, my eyes filled with tears. Was this what I deserved?

I'd asked Dean to keep our engagement a secret until we could pick out a ring. But when we were driving to the jewelry store, I blurted out the truth. That I couldn't marry him.

And then he went home and put a bullet in his head.

No one ever knew the reason he'd chosen to die young. Until I'd told Steve. Now Steve was the only other person who knew.

Numb with despair, I tried to yank my wrists free. All that got me was more pain.

I tried to pull my ankles apart, but they were bound too tightly.

It was hopeless. I was a prisoner of the man who had brought me here.

Mystery Waiter? Harry O'Toole? Maybe. Probably. But whoever he was, he wasn't going to just let me die in this rathole, was he?

I thought about the letter that Harry had written to Lily and found a sliver of hope in that. Because he had loved the woman who'd rescued him in France and had stayed with her until her death.

Meaning maybe there was some goodness in him. Even if he was a jewel thief.

He'd shot Gladys in the abdomen. But not in the head. Maybe she was still alive. Maybe he hadn't killed her. He could have just shot me too, and killed me, his only witness. But he didn't.

But was he going to come back to me? I hoped so, because if he didn't, I would surely die here. But what if he did return? What would he do to me then?

It was too much. Speculating on the what-if-this and what-if-that sent fear surging through my veins. I rolled my head back and forth to try to loosen the blindfold but all that did was make the pounding in my head worse.

Whimpering, I surrendered. Stopped struggling. Lay still to conserve my strength. If Harry, or whoever he was, did come for me, and tried to do something more to me, I'd fight him to the death.

I couldn't see, but I could hear. So, I sharpened my ears. I had to be in some kind of room because there seemed to be a window to my left. I felt a breeze coming in. And off in the distance, I heard voices and what sounded like the roar of ocean waves.

Then, I heard something else. And my heart stopped. Someone was opening a door.

The door to my room.

———

"Story!"

Steve. Thank God. It was Steve.

A miracle. It didn't seem possible, but it was.

I heard him run across the room. Ripping the blindfold off my eyes, he un-gagged my mouth and planted a quick kiss on my forehead.

"Steve ..." I rasped. "How ...?"

"Shhh," he whispered. "I'll explain later. We need to move fast. I need to get you out of here before he comes back."

Nodding, I lay still as he used a switchblade knife to saw through the ropes binding my wrists and then my ankles.

"Thank you," I whispered, struggling to sit up.

Bad idea. The room started spinning around me like I was on a fast-moving carousel. I fell back, pressing my lips together to keep from crying out from the pain that shot through my skull.

"Oh my God, the blood," Steve whispered, clearly trying not to sound as horrified as the expression on his face.

"Dizzy," I said, "I'm so dizzy." Struggling to sit up again, my eyes followed his gaze. I'd been lying on a horrible, grimy mattress. Now stained with a pool of my blood.

"What did he hit you with?" Steve grabbed hold of my arms to keep me from falling back again.

"I think his gun."

"He might have drugged you, too. To keep you out long enough to tie you up."

"Probably. I feel sick."

Steve lifted me up, cradled me in his arms, then rushed out of the room and down a dingy, dank-smelling stairwell. "I'm taking you to a hospital," he said. "You need stitches. Probably have a concussion."

"Thank you." I squeezed my eyes shut to stop the vertigo. "Where are we?"

"In Atlantic City," he said, breathing hard as he broke into a trot.

I popped my eyes back open. We were outside. In bright sunlight. People were parading by. The beach was to our left. "Atlantic City?" I asked, thinking that was too crazy to be true. "Wait," I said, "Are we on the *boardwalk*?"

"Yep. And it's not far to my car."

"But how'd you find me?" I tried to make my eyes focus and stay focused.

People were staring at us. Like, who was this handsome guy, with a grim expression on his face, racing a bleeding woman past shops and ice cream stands?

I couldn't blame them for staring. If I was one of those happy people on vacation, strolling the boards, heading for the beach, I'd stare, too.

We got to Steve's black Mercedes. He put me down, yanked the passenger side door open, helped me get in, then slammed the door shut and ran to get behind the wheel.

"I'm taking you to the Atlantic City Hospital emergency room," he said as he pulled out onto the street. "Don't worry, it's not far."

The dizziness was easing, but my head still ached. I closed my eyes. Then opened them again. "Steve, wait, the blood. I'm probably getting blood all over your car. Your leather seats."

He shot me a look out of the corner of his eye. "You think I care about *that*?"

I sighed and closed my eyes again. "At least the seats are black."

He grunted. "Story, do you have any idea how close you came to dying back there in that stupid boarding house?"

I moaned. "I have a pretty good idea."

"It's a miracle I found you."

"I *know*. How *did* you find me?"

"I was starting to get the feeling that you weren't telling me everything. That there was something you were holding back. And that the answer was in Cape May."

I glanced back over at him. "You were right, Steve. And after I got myself into a pickle, I realized I should have told you where I was going and why."

His hands gripped the steering wheel as he turned a corner, then braked for a red light. "After we get you fixed up in the E.R., you're going to fill me in on the why. And if you have any ideas about who might have done this to you. Okay?"

"Of course. My abductor had a mask on, so I'm not sure who he was. But how did you find me here, in Atlantic City, miles from Cape May?"

The light turned green. Traffic was slow but steady through the downtown area of the bustling summer resort.

"In Harry's letter to Lily, he told her to meet him at Congress Hall, so I started there." Steve's voice was tight. "A desk clerk remembered you asking about a man named Harry O'Toole but didn't know where you had gone from there. So I went down to the beach, started questioning lifeguards. Met one named Carl, who also remembered you."

"Great detective work," I murmured.

"I can't take all the credit. You're memorable, Story. Gorgeous blonde with lovely, long, tan legs, and a heart-grabbing smile. Those are Carl's words, not mine, although I happen to agree."

"Wait, Carl said that about me?"

"You obviously made an impression."

"Huh," I said. "He sure didn't let it show."

"Anyway, he told me what he'd told you about Gladys Jones, including that she worked at The Admiral Hotel. So, I headed there."

"And let me guess ... you found her ... and she told you about our scheduled meeting by the pool."

"You guessed right. And since it was getting late, I checked myself into a room at The Admiral so I could get myself out to the pool on time to join that meeting."

I pressed a hand to my forehead. My thinking was fuzzy, and I just wanted to pain to stop. "I couldn't afford The Admiral. I stayed at a guest cottage nearby."

"I figured that." Steve's voice was soft. "But I knew you would be on time for that meeting. Problem was, you were early—and so was Gladys."

"You heard the shot?"

"And the screams."

"So ... I really did hear your voice calling my name." I gave a grim smile. "I told myself it was just my imagination."

He nodded. "I saw you being shoved into a car, but I was too far away to do anything about it. Best I could do was follow it. All the way to Atlantic City. But then, I lost sight of it in downtown city traffic and had to drive around awhile until I found it again. Parked in front of a sleazy boarding house."

"Oh my God, Steve ..."

"I figured you were in there somewhere. But the building had five stories, so I had to go door-to-door and floor-to-floor to search for you. I infuriated a lot of people who answered my knock so early in the morning, who had no idea what I was talking about. When no one answered, I would check to see if the door was locked, and if it was, I would just move on."

"So, the room I was in wasn't locked?"

"No, thank God it wasn't. It was on the fourth floor and if I had not found you after searching the entire building, I would have called the police." He pointed to the hospital we were approaching. "Now we can call them from here."

He pulled into the parking lot and then followed signs to the emergency room.

Relief and gratitude flooded through me. And something else. Chagrin. I knew the doctors would be able to fix me up and I was thankful to have Steve in my life.

But I couldn't help feeling embarrassed, and humiliated, for needing his help.

Gutsy girl gumshoe. What a joke. More like silly slow-witted sleuth.

"Oh ... don't be so hard on yourself," Steve said as he opened my door and helped me out.

He was reading my mind. I gave him a weak smile. "How do you know I'm doing that?"

He kissed the top of my bloody head. "Because I know you, Story. And all I can say right now is that we just need to get you another gun."

Twenty-One

The emergency room was crowded but a nurse pushing a wheelchair hurried over to me when she saw Steve carrying me in.

"Is this your wife, sir?" she asked Steve as he lowered me into the wheelchair. "What happened to her?"

"She's not my wife. Her name is Story Smith and she's a friend. Someone hit her over the head with something hard, probably a gun." Steve grabbed my hand and walked next to me as the nurse pushed the wheelchair to one of the emergency room's curtained cubicles. "We'll need to get the police involved," he said, his voice tight. "But first she needs medical attention."

"I see." The nurse whisked the curtain aside and then she and Steve helped me onto a soft cot. Adjusting it so I could sit up, the nurse closed the curtain, then pushed my hair aside and gently touched the top of my head with cool fingers.

I winced and moaned. "I'm dizzy." I cut my eyes to Steve. He reached over and patted my hand. "It's okay, you're going to be okay," he said, his face creased with concern.

"I think I must have a concussion," I said in a voice that didn't sound like mine.

"You'll probably need stitches," the nurse said, then turned to Steve. "I'm going to go get a doctor now. We have a lot of emergencies, so I hope it won't take long. You can stay with her?"

"Of course. However long it takes, I'm not leaving."

Our eyes locked after she left.

"Okay. Now seems like a good time for you to tell me what happened," Steve said, his voice grim. "Why did you come to Cape May, and who do you think did this to you? And don't even think about leaving anything out."

I closed my eyes to stop the room from spinning, and keeping them tightly shut, told him.

Told him everything.

About the mysterious waiter at the party. Who I'd come to suspect was Harry O'Toole, especially when I saw him again at Lily's funeral service in the church and then again at the cemetery.

I also told him that I believed Harry O'Toole was the masked man who'd shot Gladys and abducted me.

When I finished, I waited for Steve to pepper me with questions, but I was met with nothing but silence.

I opened my eyes.

He looked angry. His face was flushed, and he was scowling at me. Steve never scowled at me.

"What?" I asked, tensing up, making my head hurt more. "Why are you looking at me like that?"

"Why didn't you tell me about that mystery waiter, Story?" He deepened his scowl. "You gave me pieces of the puzzle—Harry's letter to Lily, the newspaper articles about Cape May Capers—but deliberately hid other important pieces from me. You kept me in the dark, putting yourself in danger. Why?"

I blew out a sigh. "We're competitors, Steve. We're working the same case from different angles for different clients."

"And you want to prove that you're the better P.I? Incredible."

"No, no. I wanted to prove that I can be *as good* as you."

"We're not in competition, Story. This isn't a game. We both want the same thing. The truth about what happened to Lily. And justice for Lily."

I closed my eyes again. "I agree. I'm sorry."

"I have much more experience than you," Steve said, softening the sharpness of his tone. "It doesn't mean that I'm better than you. It's just that you have a lot to learn. And I can teach you."

I opened my eyes and looked at him. "I know. And you have already taught me so much. It's just that ... it's just that ... for some reason I always think I need to go it alone."

"Because of Dean?"

I couldn't bear the disappointed look on Steve's face. I looked away.

"Dean's death is not your fault, you know."

"I led him on. I led the poor guy on."

"He was obviously troubled. More than you or anyone knew. But a part of you did know. Which is the reason you broke up with him."

I hadn't thought of that. I sniffed. "Maybe."

"Girls break up with their boyfriends all the time. It's as common as the common cold. But do those guys turn around and kill themselves? Hell, no. They nurse their wounds and go on and find another girlfriend. No. Big. Deal."

"Did a girl ever break up with *you*?" I was trying to change the subject, but I could tell he wasn't going to bite. Anyway, the answer was probably no.

"This isn't about me," Steve said.

I squeezed my eyes closed and tried to will away the pain. Steve was right. Maybe when I felt better and could process what he was saying, the truth of it could help heal me. But right now, I just wanted a doctor to stitch up my head and give me some aspirin.

Where the hell was the doctor?

I heard the curtain being pulled aside and opened my eyes.

Halleluiah. A young man wearing round-rimmed glasses and a stethoscope around his neck walked in and introduced himself as Doctor Reedy. In that calm, breezy voice emergency doctors often use, he asked me how I was feeling.

"Crappy." I sighed. "My head hurts."

Steve filled him in on what had happened to me, which was wonderful because I was too, too tired and suddenly just wanted to sleep.

"Incredible," the doctor said when Steve finished telling him about my abduction. "Just lie still now and try to relax while I take a look at you."

"Gladly," I murmured.

He examined and cleaned my head wounds, then told the nurse to give me a shot to numb my scalp. Minutes later, as I kept my eyes firmly closed, I felt him stitch me up.

"Okay," he said, "now open your eyes." He shined a bright light into them. "You do most likely have a concussion," he declared, "although it doesn't look like you have a cracked skull."

I gave a weak smile. Thank the Lord for that.

A nurse came in and gave me some pills.

"Aspirin?" Steve asked.

"A bit stronger than that," Doctor Reedy said. "She needed ten stitches but should heal in good time without further treatment. We'll know for sure tomorrow morning."

"Tomorrow morning?" I squeaked.

"We'll need to keep an eye on you all night to be sure you don't have any bleeding on the brain." His voice was firm. "We're admitting you to the main hospital." He turned to Steve. "You can stay with her in her room until eight p.m., when visitors have to leave."

Steve frowned. "I'm not going to leave her. I'll sleep in the lobby all night if I have to because I have no idea who did this to her—or if the monster will come looking for her once he discovers she escaped him."

The doctor pursed his lips, then nodded. "Good idea. You'll be glad to know that we've called the police and they're on their way here to interview Miss Smith. We'll request that they guard her room tonight as well."

———

I was comfortably settled all snug in my bed in my private, third floor, medical surgical hospital room by the time two police officers came to see me.

The pills, whatever I'd been given, were doing the trick because my head felt much better, and the dizziness was subsiding. I was also feeling so floaty and calm—serene, even—that I didn't mind being interviewed by two men while wearing nothing but a flimsy hospital gown, with Steve in the chair beside me.

The policemen introduced themselves as Detectives Bob Marr and John Crisper, from the Atlantic City Police Department. And they didn't waste any time getting straight to the point.

"We understand you were involved in the shooting at The Admiral Hotel this morning," Detective Crisper said, stepping up to my bed. Like his partner, he was dressed in plainclothes, in dress slacks, dress shirt, and tie, and appeared to be around forty, with slicked back dark brown hair and a no-nonsense demeanor.

"I was meeting one of the hotel maids, Gladys Jones, by the pool," I said, aware of how weak my voice sounded. It also sounded like my words were coming from someone else's mouth from somewhere across the room. Kind of funny. Had to be the pills. At least, I sure hoped it was the pills.

"Gladys and I were talking," I said, slurring my words as a feeling of sleepiness returned. "And then somebody shot her. Shot Gladys. And she fell in the pool. And I jumped in. And I tried to save her. But I couldn't. And then he grabbed me."

"Who grabbed you?" Detective Marr asked. He was younger and shorter than his partner and his red hair was cut short, in a buzz cut. He was kind of cute. Except for the buzz cut.

Trying to picture him with more hair, I yawned. "He wore a mask. I'm not sure who he was."

That perked the cute detective's interest. "Not sure? Do you have any ideas?"

I struggled to sit up straighter, and Steve reached over and arranged the blanket on my bed to cover more of my hospital gown, which seemed to keep slipping off one shoulder. Stupid hospital gown.

"How is Gladys?" I asked. "Is she alive? I hope she's still alive."

Detective Marr shook his head. "We would like you to answer our questions before we answer yours."

I sighed. "I think maybe Harry O'Toole grabbed me." I let my eyes close because it was too hard to keep them open. "Harry O'Toole," I repeated. "You need to go find Harry O'Toole. Steve, please tell them about Harry. I'm too tired."

Steve patted my hand. "Sure, Super Sleuth. You just rest."

Super Sleuth. I liked the sound of that.

"The problem is, Harry O'Toole was declared missing and dead in the war," Steve told the officers. Which I was sure they wouldn't like. Which wasn't my problem. Because Steve told me to just rest.

I dozed off as he started to explain Harry O'Toole to them and then drifted in and out of sleep, catching bits and pieces of what he was saying. About Mystery Waiter. And Lily and how she died. And the Prince of Pearls and the missing jewelry.

It was all so complicated and I was so happy Steve could tell them. Until I remembered the necklace.

"The necklace. Where's the necklace that Gladys Jones was wearing?" I mumbled. Prying my eyes open, I tried to sit up. Frantically, I peered at Detective Marr and then at Detective Crisper. "It's not on the bottom of the pool, is it?"

Steve reached for my hand again. "Calm down, Story. I'm sure the police have it, along with her clothes. It's probably locked away in an evidence locker."

"It is," Detective Marr said. "Mighty pricey piece of jewelry for a hotel maid to be wearing. But don't worry, it's in safe keeping."

I swallowed hard. "And Gladys? Where is she now? She's not dead, is she? Please tell me she's not dead."

"Okay, we can tell you that she is alive," Detective Crisper said. "She's recovering in a hospital north of Cape May. Burdette Tomlin Memorial. Unfortunately, she can't tell us any more than you can about who shot her because she's in a coma."

A profound sense of relief calmed me. I whispered, "Thank God, she survived."

Detective Marr gave a curt nod. "That's still touch and go."

My eyes met Steve's. "We need to go see her. As soon as I get out of here, we need to go see her."

Detective Crisper cleared his throat. "That will be up to her family. She is currently under police guard, like you will be as long as you're here, Miss Smith."

"I have so many questions for her," I said. "So many ...."

"As do I," Steve smiled at me. "So, we'll be going together, Story. You and I. Agreed?"

"Agreed." I smiled back. "Together."

Twenty-Two

Doc Reedy came to see me early the next morning, and after examining my stitches, and shining that bright light into my eyes again, pronounced me well enough to be discharged.

"That is, depending on how you feel," he said. "How is the dizziness?"

I glanced around the room—at the sunlight pouring in the window, at Steve in the chair beside me, watching me with slightly bloodshot eyes. I suspected he hadn't gotten much sleep.

"Amazing. It's gone—the dizziness is gone." I blew out a sigh of relief. "I feel so much better today."

"And the pain?" The doctor's clinical tone told me he asked patients that question multiple times a day.

I blinked at him. "Gone." I grinned. "It's gone. Am I a fast healer, or what?"

The doctor let a smile escape his lips. "You're young and despite your injuries, in good health. Although I notice you also seem to be recovering from an old injury to your ankle. It's slightly swollen."

"I did sprain it, yes. But it's almost better."

"Then, good. You're free to go." He let his smile fade. "You will need to have those stiches removed in about a week, but that can be done by any doctor. If the pain in your head returns, or the dizziness, you'll need to get yourself back to a hospital."

"Wait." Steve stood up. "Are you sure about this, doc? Maybe she should stay here another day, just to be sure."

"No." I clutched my flimsy hospital gown and yanked it higher toward my neck, suddenly feeling vulnerably underdressed. "I don't need to stay here another day. I'll be fine."

"I'm also worried about your safety." Steve frowned at me, then at the doctor. "If Story can stay here another day, that will give police more time to find the man who did this to her."

"No," I said, annoyed. "My safety is not the hospital's problem, Steve. And you and I need to go find that man. The man who shot Gladys—and for all we know, who might have killed Lily."

"Right." Steve pressed his lips together and nodded. "You're right." He walked over to a small closet next to the window, opened the door, and pulled out a large brown bag with handles.

A department store bag?

I sat up straighter in bed. "What's that?"

"Clothes." Steve sauntered over to me, swinging the bag, wearing his too-cute, heart-grabbing grin. "Last night, after you fell asleep, I went out and bought you new clothes, so you'd have something to wear out of here. The ones you came in with are dirty and bloody."

"Oh ..." Tears welled in my eyes as I reached for the bag and pulled out adorable denim shorts, a matching flowered top, and socks and sneakers. New navy-blue sneakers that appeared to be just my size.

"Thank you, Steve," I whispered. "But how did you know my size?"

His face flushed. "Come on, Story. Don't we know each other well enough by now? I cherish you and everything about you. You're with me even when you're not with me. Of course, I know your size."

"Wow." A tear escaped and slid down my cheek.

Steve leaned close to my ear and whispered, "There's also new underwear in the bag for you, under the tissue paper, but you don't need to pull it out right now in front of ... you know ..."

He glanced at the doctor, then turned back to me with a wink. "I'm sure it will fit." He was blushing. Steve was blushing. Adorable.

Doc Reedy cleared his throat. "Well, it seems you have what you need to get dressed now, Miss Smith. I'll send a nurse in to help you get a shower first. Just make sure you don't get your stitches wet." Shooting Steve a raised eyebrow look that said, "follow me," he headed for the door.

Hesitating, Steve's eyes met mine. "I'll be waiting right out there with the police guard. Take your time and don't slip in the shower. I need you healthy, partner."

"Will do, partner." I liked the sound of partner and gave him a thumbs-up. Moments later, when the nurse came in, I was still smiling.

Probably since she'd had experience with it before, she turned out to be a whiz at helping me wash my hair without wetting the stitches. And since I had not had access to a mirror to see the horror of my appearance before my shower, I had no idea how much of my hair had been cut off. Until now, the least of my concerns.

I slipped into my new clothes, then faced the bathroom mirror, and holding my breath, took a comb from the nurse and gingerly ran it through my hair.

"I look okay," I told her, surprised. "How much had to be cut away?"

"Only as much as needed." Her eyes met mine in the mirror and lit up in a smile. "We're pretty good at that."

Touching my fingers lightly to the top of my head, I felt the raised, rough stiches and carefully combed the rest of my hair around them.

"Your hair should dry by the time you've finished your breakfast," the nurse said. "A tray will be delivered shortly. Do you want me to go fetch your boyfriend now?"

Boyfriend. Steve was not my boyfriend, but I liked the sound of it, and pretending that he was, so I didn't correct her.

"Yes, please let him know that I'm ready," I said. Sitting back down on my bed, I let my feet dangle over the edge and gave her a dreamy smile. Probably too dreamy, but I couldn't help it. My face couldn't help it. "Yes," I said. "Please tell Steve it's okay to come back in."

———

Burdette Tomlin Memorial was in Cape May Courthouse, a town about forty miles south of Atlantic City.

Steve and I headed straight there after I finished my breakfast and he paid my hospital bill, which he insisted on doing because he knew I couldn't afford it.

I knew I couldn't afford it, so I didn't try to argue, but I told him I'd pay him back as soon as I could.

"Don't worry about it, Story," he said, gripping the wheel of his Mercedes as we headed south along the coast. "I'm just glad you're going to be okay." He reached over and patted my knee. "Let's just hope Gladys Jones gets as lucky as you."

Unfortunately, Gladys was still in a coma.

Fortunately, she still had a police guard outside the door of her private room. And fortunately, her parents gave us permission to enter.

"Hi, I'm Joe Jones and this is my wife, Bertha." Gladys's father shook Steve's hand and gave me a weak smile. Appearing older than I'd expected, he was stooped and wiry, looking vulnerably weak and pale, as if he might suffer from a bad heart.

Or maybe his daughter's dire condition was taking a toll on him.

Lying eerily still, face up, there were tubes up her nose, another tube was dripping something into her arm, and wires were taped to her chest to monitor her heartbeat.

From the other side of the bed, Bertha Jones—her gray hair frizzy and uncombed—looked over at me with grief-stricken eyes. "The police told us what happened, Miss Smith." She reached over and put a hand on her daughter's hand. "About how you jumped in the pool and tried to save Gladys. Thank you. Thank you for that ..."

I sighed. "I wish I could have done more. I didn't understand what was happening when Gladys got shot. I was meeting with her to ask her some questions, but someone clearly didn't want her to talk to me."

"Yeah. And we're betting it was Harry O'Toole." Bertha spit out his name with bitter authority, as if she had no doubt at all that he was the shooter.

Bingo. Gladys might be in a coma, but her mother wasn't, and she seemed eager to talk.

Her father, too. "That Harry O'Toole caused our Gladys nothing but trouble for years," he said. "Started when she was in high school. She couldn't resist him. Believed he was in love with her, and only her, even though it was obvious to the rest of the town that he had lots of girls."

Steve and I looked at each other. He gave me a silent nod, which I took to mean that I should be the one to keep questioning. I decided to hold back most of what I knew about Harry O'Toole and let the parents tell me what they knew.

Steve dragged two chairs that were against the wall over to the bed, and waving me into one, took the other as Joe Jones sat back down.

"I've been told Harry O'Toole died in the war," I said, staring at Gladys's face, hoping she could hear me, willing her to wake up. "But while investigating the death of a woman in Philadelphia, I came to believe that maybe he hadn't, that he was very much alive."

"Oh, that devil's alive alright," Bertha Jones said. "You can take that to the bank."

"How do you know?" I pressed. "Have you seen him around?"

"No." Joe Jones shook his head. "Nothing like that."

"Did Gladys tell you she'd seen him around?" I held my breath as both parents stared at each other, as if trying to decide how to answer.

"Gladys didn't tell us she'd seen him, but she'd started acting weird lately. Real nervous," Joe Jones said finally, lowering his voice. "We just know from experience that when trouble is happening, Harry O'Toole is behind it."

I needed more specific information, but they suddenly seemed cagey. "What about the expensive necklace Gladys was wearing when she got shot?" I asked. "Diamonds and emeralds aren't something one normally wears to work as a hotel maid."

Again, silence. Color bloomed on Bertha Jones's cheeks as she narrowed her gaze on something beyond my shoulder—as if peering into the past. She took a deep breath, swallowed hard, glanced at her husband, then at me. "Gladys might have got herself involved in a crime years ago." She squeezed her daughter's hand, then released it and sat back. "You heard of the Prince of Pearls?"

I sucked in a breath, managed not to gasp. "Uh, yes ... the Cape May Capers is what they called his crimes. An unknown jewel thief or thieves. I learned about those robberies while investigating the death of the woman in Philly."

"Well, we think Harry O'Toole was the Prince of Pearls," Joe Jones said. "Because he might have given some of his loot to Gladys when he went off to war."

"*What*?" Steve had let me do the talking until now, but he was clearly so shocked that he could no longer keep quiet. "Are you saying that he gave Gladys some of the stolen jewelry?"

Bertha clapped a hand to her mouth and closed her eyes. Suddenly appearing years older, I felt sorry for the woman. If she and her husband had known about evidence of a long-ago crime and kept quiet about it, they could be arrested.

I didn't want her to worry about that. "Anything you reveal to Steve and me right now will stay confidential," I assured her. "We just want to catch the man who shot Gladys."

"That cad, Harry, gave Gladys a package before he shipped off to the Army," Joe Jones said, meeting my gaze with determination in his eyes. As if he was no longer afraid to tell what he knew and was prepared to deal with whatever happened after that.

"What kind of package?" I asked. "What did it look like?"

"A brown paper package, about the size of a loaf of bread," Bertha Jones said. "Gladys showed it to us and said she had to hide it, and that we were better off not knowing what was in it."

"So ... you don't know if it contained stolen jewelry?" Steve frowned.

"We never saw what was in it," Bertha said. "But we could tell by the way Gladys was acting, all nervous and excited, that it could be something illegal. And since rumors were going around about Harry O'Toole and his friend, Arty Duncan, being the jewel thieves, we put two and two together, and ..."

"And you kept quiet," I remarked, unable to keep the judgmental surprise out of my voice. It was just that the Joneses seemed like honest, upstanding folks. Hard working, loving parents, salt of the earth-people. "Your daughter put you in a difficult position," I said, softening my tone.

"We never saw the package again," Joe Jones said stiffly, defensive. "Gladys told us that Harry told her to hide it, so she did. Told us that she promised to give it to him when he returned from the war and that we were never to speak of it again. So, for our daughter's sake, we haven't."

"She's our only child." Bertha Jones pursed her lips, like that justified their decision. "And anyway, we didn't know for sure what was in that package, so we didn't ask. We just tried to forget about it."

"But Harry never returned from the war." I was half-whispering now, worried about being overheard by someone out in the hallway. "So ... what did Gladys do with the package?"

"We don't know," Joe Jones blurted, exchanging a knowing look with his wife, who with a quick nod, told him she understood.

They knew more than they were willing to tell. But I had gotten enough information from them that I decided to leave off pressing for more until later.

Steve wasn't as patient. "I think you do know." He narrowed his eyes at Joe Jones. "And it might have something to do with Gladys getting shot."

"Gladys never told us what she did with the package." Bertha Jones reached for her daughter's hand again. "We never asked her—and she never told."

I stared at Bertha's quivering hand on Gladys's lifeless one. Interesting family. Interesting family dynamics. They clearly believed that if a secret stayed a secret, it couldn't hurt you. But secrets have a way of blowing up. And Gladys was fighting for her life.

My head was starting to hurt again, and it had nothing to do with my injury. I needed to rest. I needed to think. I needed to figure out what to do next. Because I was no closer to solving Lily's murder than I'd ever been, let alone finding the man who had tried to kill Gladys and abducted me.

"You look tired, Story," Steve said, standing and reaching for my hand. "I think we have learned enough for now. Hopefully Gladys will wake up soon and be able to tell us more. Ready to go?"

I nodded and let him pull me to my feet. I thanked the Joneses. "You have been a big help. We'll keep in touch with the hospital to see how Gladys is doing and, with your permission, come back to talk to her when she's able."

Bertha Jones gave a nod. "God willing, she'll be able to talk soon."

Steve and I left the room hand in hand. He pulled me to a stop when we reached the nursing station. "I need to call Arty," he said, pointing to the phone on the counter. "I want to let him know where

I am and what I've been up to." He lowered his voice. "I also want to ask him about the rumors going around about him and Harry and the Cape May Capers."

I winced. "He's not going to like that. He'll just deny it."

Steve shrugged. "Even so, I want to hear what he has to say."

The young nurse behind the counter gave Steve permission to make a quick call even though it meant calling long distance to Philadelphia. Probably because he told her he'd pay the bill. And probably because she thought he was cute.

Flashing her a thank-you-honey-smile that no doubt made her day, Steve dialed Arty's number. Then almost dropped the phone when Arty answered by shouting into his ear.

"Janey and Jeannie have been kidnapped," Arty screamed, loud enough for me and most of the hospital to hear. "Somebody took my little girls and they're holding them for ransom!"

TWENTY-THREE

"Calm down, Arty," Steve said, his voice tight. "This is terrible news. And I want to help you. Are the police there?"

Steve motioned for me to come over and put my ear next to his so I could hear what was being said, too. I couldn't believe this was happening.

"Yeah, the police are here," Arty said.

"Then, good. Let me speak to one of them."

"Okay, okay."

"Hello," a deep voice said. "This is Officer Powell. Who's this?"

"My name's Steve Evans. I'm a private eye hired by Mr. Duncan to investigate the death of his wife. And this might be related. Mr. Duncan says his children have been kidnapped?"

"Looks like it. They're gone and there's a note."

"I'm in Cape May, working on a lead," Steve said, lowering his voice. "Maybe I can help. Can you tell me what the note says?"

Silence for a moment. Followed by mumbling in the background. Then, "I have it in my hand. Mr. Duncan says it's okay for me to read it to you."

Steve gripped the phone tighter. "Okay, go ahead."

I pressed my ear harder against the receiver.

Officer Powell cleared his throat. "It says, 'Arty Duncan, I have your girls. If you want to see them again, bring fifty thousand dollars in cash to Batsto Village, the historic park in Hammonton, New Jersey. Listen up! In the village is a mansion with a wide front porch. On the porch is a wooden bench and a rain barrel is next to the bench. Wrap the money securely and put it in the rain barrel. Come alone. No cops. After I get the money, you will get your kids back. Don't worry, they're safe and won't be harmed as long as you follow instructions.'"

"That's it?" Steve said.

"That's it."

"When were they taken?" Steve asked. "And how? Was nobody watching them?"

"We're not sure how long they've been gone." Officer Powell cleared his throat again. "They were in the playroom and apparently Mr. Duncan and the nanny, Stella Murphy, were in another room."

"Together?" I blurted into the phone.

"Who's that?" the officer asked.

"This is Story Smith. I'm a private investigator working with Mr. Evans," I said.

"Your name is Story Smith?"

Arty began shouting in the background but was interrupted by a woman. "Is that Miss Smith?" she shouted over Arty. "Let me speak to her!"

It was Anna Ash.

"Hello, Story?" she said, her voice shaky.

"Yes, it's me," I assured her. "I'm here."

"I'm so upset," she cried. "It's Arty's fault that my granddaughters were kidnapped. The idiot. The fool." Her voice was laced with contempt.

Heavens. I turned to Steve and gave him a wide-eyed look.

"What are you talking about, Anna?" I asked her.

"Arty and Stella were fooling around when Jeannie and Janey were taken," she said. "Arty insisted that the girls and Stella come back to live with him. And then he and his 'so-called nanny' resumed their affair. This time without worrying about my Lily catching them. Because she's *conveniently dead.*"

Yowie. The poor woman. She was not holding back. And good for her. Then again, she had nothing left to lose.

"Where is Stella?" Steve asked her, sounding disgusted and concerned at the same time.

With our heads pressed together so we could share the phone, I could feel the tight tension in his body.

"Upstairs in her room, where I sent her, because I can't bear the sight of her right now," Anna said. "When Officer Powell and the other officers got here, she didn't even try to lie."

I swallowed hard. "Wow."

"She blurted it all out, the little twit," Anna snapped. "Admitted that she and Arty were in his bedroom while the girls were in their playroom. Claimed she was keeping an ear on them. Do you believe that? She was keeping an ear on my granddaughters while engaging in unspeakable acts with their father?"

Sadly, I could believe it. Stella and Arty were quite a pair. She was clearly none too bright. And he apparently liked his women young and stupid.

"Anna," Steve said, "could you please put Arty back on the phone?"

"Gladly, just a minute."

We heard moaning and rustling and then Arty came on. "Evans ..." he wailed. "Help me, help me."

"I'm trying," Steve said. "The important thing is that we find your girls and quickly."

"Where are you, Evans?"

"In Cape May, New Jersey, following up on a lead about Lily's death."

"Cape May?" Arty shouted. "What the hell are you doing there? And with Story Smith? I'm not paying you good money to hang out at the Shore with your private detective lady friend."

I gritted my teeth. *Lady friend*. What a jerk. Even during a crisis, Arty showed no respect for me.

"Story's a hell of a private eye, Arty—and leave her out of this," Steve said. "Calm down and tell me what you're going to do about the ransom. That note is rather vague about when you're supposed to deliver the money and how you're supposed to get your kids back."

"That's why I called the cops." Arty was wailing again. "I didn't know what else to do."

"Batsto Village is between Philly and the Shore," Steve said. "It's in the middle of deep woods, which makes it a challenging location. And the kidnapper's demand is a lot of cash for you to come up with on short notice."

"Anna has ordered her banker to bring the cash here," Arty said stiffly. "We're going to do what the kidnapper said."

"Okay."

"So tell me, what are *you* going to do now, Evans?" Arty's tone had changed again. Now it was snide. "The police are going to deal with taking the money to Batsto. But what are *you* going to do?"

Steve glanced at me. Our eyes met, and bless him, he was reading my mind.

He gave a grim smile. "Story and I are going to work the lead we have in Cape May," he said. "The person we suspect might have murdered Lily might also have kidnapped your girls."

"Who?!" Arty shouted. "Who is it?"

I took a deep breath. Was Steve going to tell him, or was I? I decided to go for broke. Time was of the essence—and we needed to get cracking. "You're not going to like this Arty," I said. "But your friend Harry O'Toole might still be alive."

"What!?" he screamed.

"There's a good chance—or maybe a longshot chance," I said calmly, "that if we find him, we'll find Jeannie and Janey."

"What?!" he screamed again. "Are you *crazy*? My wife's dead and my kids have been kidnapped—and you guys are wasting time looking for a dead man? Evans, I should fire you."

"I wouldn't," Steve said. "This is why I called you. To ask you about Harry."

Arty grunted. "Why? This is idiotic."

"Did you know that shortly before she died, Lily traveled to Cape May to meet a former lover?" Steve asked.

Arty didn't answer at first. When he finally did, he sounded wary. "No. I knew of no such thing. That's preposterous."

"She did," Steve said. "And we believe it was Harry O'Toole."

Arty growled, "Impossible. Harry is dead, I tell you. He died in the war."

"I understand that Harry was your friend through high school," I said calmly, ignoring his anger.

"Yeah, so what?"

"So just humor us and answer a few questions," Steve said. "Harry had a lot of girlfriends, right?"

"Yeah ..."

"Was Lily one of them?" Steve asked.

"No ..."

"When you were high school buddies, did you own a sailboat together?" I asked.

Arty grunted, like he was surprised at the question. "Yeah. So ...?"

"Was it named Sweet Sailing?"

"Yeah. Who told you?"

"A lifeguard friend of yours named Carl," I said. "And now you own a motor yacht named Sweet Sailing Two."

"That's right." There was a smidgen of reluctant respect in his voice that I knew that.

"I spotted it in a marina near The Lobster House and figured it must be yours," I said.

"Clever name, if I do say so myself," he said with what sounded like a smirk.

"Whatever happened to your sailboat named Sweet Sailing?" Steve asked.

"Why?" Arty shouted. "Why are you wasting my time with these questions? Go find my kids."

"We'll have a better chance of finding them if you do answer our questions," Steve said. "Trust me, this is important."

Arty groaned. "I sold the sailboat, okay? A long time ago. To another lifeguard. Jeff something. Can't remember his last name."

"Do you know if Jeff still owns it?" I asked.

"No, but somebody does. I've seen it around."

I blew out a breath, relieved. Sweet Sailing still sailed. Meaning Harry O'Toole could be living on it. Meaning he might be keeping Jeannie and Janey captive on it.

It was a longshot in a complicated case full of them, but it was possible.

Steve obviously thought so, too. "You've given us a lot to go on," he told Arty. "Rest assured that I'm on the job. And I'll be back in touch."

TWENTY-FOUR

Steve hung up the phone.

"I'll send the hospital a check for that call," he promised the young nurse still behind the counter. "Sorry it went longer than expected."

She gaped at him. "You were talking about kidnapping and murder. Oh my."

"We're private eyes," I said, as if that explained everything. "Thanks for your help."

"Sure ..." she squeaked as we took off running to the hospital parking lot.

We jumped in Steve's Mercedes, then he started the engine and looked over at me. "Where to now, partner?"

"We need to find that sailboat. Find out if Jeff still owns it. Or if he doesn't, who does." I chewed my lip. "I say we head to the lifeguard station."

Unfortunately, Jeff was no longer a lifeguard. And unfortunately, Carl couldn't remember Jeff's last name.

"But whoever owns that old sloop now, I've heard rumors they're renting it out," Carl said. "Probably by the hour to teenage punks, like back in the day, though I've seen it sailing around the bay. Still has the original name of Sweet Sailing, so you should be able to track it down. There are a bunch of marinas around and the owner is probably keeping it in one of them."

"Maybe it is being rented to Harry O'Toole," I told Steve as we walked back to his car. "Don't have any idea where we should start looking for it, but let's head to Arty's motor yacht and nose around, see if anyone knows anything."

We drove to The Lobster House, parked, then walked to the marina where I'd first spotted Sweet Sailing Two. I was relieved to see the motor yacht was still in its slip.

"Nice boat," Steve said. "Should we see if anyone is aboard?"

"Might as well," I said. "Although it doesn't appear so. It's highly unlikely Harry has the girls here."

Steve stepped aboard and shouted, "Hello ... hello?"

"Nobody's answering," he yelled over to me. "I can see partly in the windows and there's no evidence that Harry or anyone else is living here."

"Try the door." I pointed to it.

Steve knocked, then jumped back in surprise when it squeaked open a few inches. "You believe this?" He turned and looked at me. "Arty just leaves it unlocked?"

"Trusting soul," I said, hopping aboard to join him. "Guess he relies on his neighbors at nearby slips to keep an eye on things. Do you think it's okay if we go—"

"Hey, what are you doing?" A burly guy wearing a cap with the word "Captain" in big letters across the front yelled at us from the dock.

"Looking for Arty," Steve shouted back.

Captain shook his head. "He's not here—so get off his boat."

Steve raised his hands in the air, like he was surrendering. "Sure, sure, no problem."

We jumped back onto the dock. I could tell Steve had a plan, so I gave Captain a sheepishly friendly smile and let Steve run with it.

"We're looking for Arty's friend, Harry O'Toole," Steve said. "Thought he might be staying here. Have you seen him?"

"Never heard of the guy." Captain's eyes narrowed in a puzzled, suspicious frown.

Good. At least we didn't have to hear about Harry being long dead. I widened my friendly smile to put Captain at ease.

"Oh well." Steve rubbed his chin. "Maybe we heard wrong. We heard that Harry was staying on Sweet Sailing, and we thought this was the boat."

Clever. I liked Steve's plan.

And it worked.

Captain waved a hand. "Oh, no. This is Sweet Sailing *Two*. You must be looking for that ratty old sloop by the name of Sweet Sailing. Arty's first boat. Which is not here. No ragtag vessels allowed in this marina."

"Oh ..." Steve grinned. "That could be it. You happen to know where that old sloop might be docked?"

Captain grimaced, like he was annoyed by the question, or maybe insulted that he looked like the kind of guy who would step foot in the kind of place that housed ratty old sloops. He scoffed. "Not a clue, son."

"Have you by any chance seen it sailing around?" Steve asked.

Captain cupped a hand over his eyes and peered out at the water. "Maybe. I think I might have seen it go by about a week ago."

"Which direction?" Steve pressed.

Captain jerked a finger east, toward the coast. "That way—and I just thought of something. There are some small marinas along an old road that runs through marshland to the Diamond Beach area, near Wildwood. Where are you parked?"

"The Lobster House," Steve said.

"When you leave there, head north, go over the canal and turn right on Ocean Drive. You'll cross three bridges. In about another mile or so, turn left on Fish Dock Road. Good luck."

He sounded eager to get rid of us.

And I was eager to oblige.

"Thanks," I said, restraining myself from running down the dock toward my car. Because an idea had just come to me that I was eager to explore before leaving Cape May.

Harry's abandoned childhood house was not far away.

What if?

I turned and waited for Steve to catch up to me. "There's a place we need to check out right now," I said. "What if Harry took Janey and Jeannie to his father's house? No one has lived there for years."

Steve's eyes went big. "Oh, yeah, good thinking. You never know."

"Yep," I said. "It's worth a shot."

———

"If Harry does have the twins at his father's house on Jackson Street, we can't give him any warning that we're coming to the rescue," I warned Steve as he pulled into the neighborhood.

He flicked me a knowing smile as he turned into the parking lot of the hardware store a few doors down. "Trust me, sweetie, I've been at this game far longer than you and I know what I'm doing. He's not going to see us coming."

He cut the engine and turned to face me. "Ready?"

"What's the plan?" I asked, suddenly not so sure this was a good idea after all. "It's broad daylight. In July. At the peak of the summer season. How is Harry, or anyone else—neighbors, tourists—not going to notice us going into a clearly abandoned building?"

"Easy." A corner of Steve's lips quirked upward. "We're going in fast."

"Fast?" I narrowed my eyes at him. "What do you mean, fast? You mean we're just going to run in? The place is dilapidated, the steps leading up to the porch are crumbling, the porch is missing a bunch of boards, and I'm not in the mood for another sprained ankle. Or being arrested for breaking and entering while in the ambulance on the way to the hospital. Again."

Steve grinned. "Just be careful. Watch where you step."

"But there are spiders," I hissed.

Steve's lips quirked upward. "So what, Little Miss Arachnophobe? Like I said, just watch where—"

"No, wait."

Steve gave me an eyeroll. "What?"

"What about the door? We're going in the front door, right?"

"Yeah. What about it?"

"It's probably locked."

"If it is, we kick it in," Steve said. "No more talking. Time for action. Let's go."

He got out of the car and came around to get me. "Here's the plan, Story. We head toward the house, strolling along the sidewalk like regular old tourists. Then, when we get to the house, we make a quick turn onto the front walk and run up to the porch. What happens next depends on the door."

"Let's hope it's unlocked," I whispered as Steve reached for my hand.

"Buck up, dear one." He said as we started our stroll up Jackson Street. "Just stay with me."

When we got to the sad-looking wooden bungalow, it looked even more unkempt than it had the last time I saw it. The front door grimier, the windows dirtier, and the front porch pillars in even more danger of collapsing.

Was Harry crazy enough to bring his captives here?

Were we crazy enough to go in and see?

"Got my gun and we're going in," Steve said, his voice low in my ear. "Unless you want to wait out here and let me go alone."

No way was I going to agree to that, as tempting as it was. I had to do this. "No." I shook my head. "I'm going with you."

"Okay, then," he said, tightening his grip on my hand. "Let's move."

We moved. Fast. Up the walk, up the front steps, and onto the porch.

Skirting loose boards, we made our way to the door—which, up close, didn't look so formidable because it was wooden and weather-beaten.

Steve tried the knob.

Of course, the door was locked.

With a grunt, he threw the weight of his body against it.

Crack. It creaked open.

It was dark inside. And the place stunk. Of dankness, dust, and mildew. And something else. Horrible and disgusting. Rat droppings ...? Oh my God. I clapped a hand over my mouth and nose, forcing back the shriek building in my throat. Were there rats *and* spiders in here? Oh, my God, and what about snakes?

Steve closed the door, put a finger to his lips to signal silence, and tip-toed ahead of me into the gloom.

Quivering with fear, afraid to take a step, I looked around the living room. No rats. No spiders. But then again, I couldn't see much of anything.

Just dust-covered, decaying furniture. A couch with holes in the cushions. Two wooden chairs, one, broken, on its side. A dirt-streaked mirror on the wall across from me. And seascape paintings on another wall, tilting precariously like they were about to fall and crash onto the floor, which was covered with area rugs dotted with some kind of animal feces.

Steve tiptoed ahead of me into an equally depressing dining room. Long, oval mahogany table, covered with inch-thick dust. Straight back chairs strewn about. Creepy cobwebs, covering a once elegant crystal chandelier, sent chills up my spine.

Hugging myself, averting my eyes from the cobwebs lest they were crawling with creatures I didn't want to see, I followed Steve into the kitchen, where unwashed dishes, now covered with some kind of green goo, sat piled in the sink.

My fear of running into creepy critters, not to mention a potentially armed and dangerous kidnapper, gave way to sorrow for the sadness this home had seen. Because it was clear even before Steve and I headed to the bedrooms that no one was here.

And that no one had been here for years.

No Janey, no Jeannie, no Harry.

Steve and I stared at each other.

"It was worth a try," he said, his voice hollow.

Frustrated, anxious, my heart heavy, I nodded. "Now we have to go find that sailboat," I said. "Let's hope we *can* find it. And let's hope the girls are on it."

TWENTY-FIVE

It didn't take us long to find the two-lane road that led to Diamond Beach.

We followed Captain's directions and within minutes found ourselves motoring past marshes and saltwater ponds in the middle of what felt like nowhere.

Fearing that maybe Captain had sent us on a wild goose chase, I kept my eyes peeled for signs of a marina.

Finally, after about ten minutes, we finally spotted one off to our right. It was modest, just several docks lined with sailboats and motorboats that jutted into a saltwater bay. There was no sign indicating a name, but a sandy road served as an entrance, so Steve turned onto it and parked in front of a shack that appeared to serve as an office.

A pretty young woman wearing a cowboy hat and overalls stepped out and came over to us. "Can I help you folks?" she asked, eyeing Steve's Mercedes. She grinned. "Nice car."

I swatted a greenhead fly away from my face. "We're looking for a sailboat named Sweet Sailing," I said. "Any chance it's docked here?"

"Don't know of any boat by that name." She looked Steve over with the same kind of admiration she'd just given his car. "Sorry."

"Mind if we go take a looksee anyway?" Steve asked, flashing her a grin a shade short of flirtatious. "Maybe it pulled in here when you weren't looking."

"Unlikely." Giving him a clearly flirtatious grin back, she waved a hand in the direction of the boats. "But go over and see for yourself. You never know. Belong to a friend of yours?"

"Not exactly," Steve said. "More of an acquaintance."

"His name is Harry, and he walks with a limp," I said, hoping that would trigger a look of recognition in her eyes.

Nope.

My description triggered a look of suspicion instead. "I don't know of anybody named Harry and I haven't seen a guy around who walks with a limp," she said. "Why? You guys aren't cops, are you?"

"No," Steve said. "Nothing like that. We'll just take a quick peek at the boats and then we'll be on our way."

Unfortunately, Cowboy Hat was right. No Sweet Sailing, although based on the boat's description, it would have fit in among the other modest vessels being kept there. It was clearly a lower rent marina. Too buggy out in the marsh to attract the moneyed crowd.

We stopped to ask a few boaters milling about if they'd ever seen Sweet Sailing, but no one had. No one had seen a man fitting Harry's description either, so we headed back to the car and hit the road again.

Captain turned out to be right. We came upon several more marinas and stopped at them all. Again, with no luck.

I was beginning to panic. What if we got to Diamond Beach with nothing to show for our efforts? "How many marinas could there be out here?" I cried.

"We can't give up," Steve said, peering ahead. "There must be more."

"Oh, wait, I see a large body of water ahead, like a big bay or a sound." I grinned, feeling suddenly hopeful. "And I see a place coming up that looks larger than the other marinas. With a name—Star Light Marina." I pointed to a big wooden sign at the entrance. "Maybe our boat's here. I have a good feeling about this."

Steve pulled into the parking lot and my heart started racing.

It was obviously not a fancy marina, or pretentious. It was the perfect place to keep an old sloop like the one we were trying to find.

Three wooden piers jutted out into a wide bay. Maybe thirty boats, most of them old wooden sailboats.

"Improv time," Steve announced as we got out of the car and headed to the nearest pier. "We're tourists, remember, and if anyone asks, we're just looking for our friend, Harry."

I nodded and fixed a smile to my face. But as we passed boat after boat, it was hard to keep smiling because every boat had a name and none of them was the right one.

We headed to the second pier. Still, no dice.

And then, finally, there it was, at the end of the third pier. A sailboat with the name of Sweet Sailing. The old wooden craft, which needed a paint job, looked like a dinghy compared to Sweet Sailing Two.

My heart stopped. Because unlike Sweet Sailing Two, it appeared that someone might be living here. A beach chair sat by the closed cabin door.

"Steve, come on, let's go aboard," I whispered.

He shook his head. "That would be rude—we have no idea who's living here. Might not be Harry. And if it is Harry, he's probably not going to want visitors. And he's probably armed."

"Well, we can't just shout out yoo-hoo, Harry, you home?" I blew out a breath. "What's the plan? Did you bring your gun?"

He gave a quiet grunt. "Of course, I did. Did you bring yours? Oh, wait ..."

"Seriously," I said, "I think we need to go aboard and surprise him if he's there."

Steve gave a nod. "I agree. Let's hop on together at the count of three."

Clunk. The boat rocked back and forth with our combined weight at "three." But no one came out of the cabin to see who'd come to call. Maybe nobody was home. Or ...

Steve pulled his gun from his waistband as I tried the cabin door.

It was locked. Darn.

Then we heard muffled sounds inside. Crying. Whimpering.

"Steve ..." I whispered.

"Stand back," he muttered. He kicked the door open. We rushed into the cabin.

It was dark and stuffy in there.

And then, in the dim light, we saw them. Bound. Gagged. Blindfolded.

Two terrified little girls. Thankfully, alive.

And alone.

———

Steve ran to one of the girls and I ran over to the other.

"Shhh ..." I whispered as we ripped away the blindfolds and then the gags around their mouths. "We're here to help you but you need to be quiet because we don't know when the bad man is coming back."

"He said he would kill us if we tried to get away," the child I was helping whimpered. "I'm so scared."

"You're okay, now," I said as I worked to untie the rope around her ankles. "What's your name, honey?"

"Janey."

"Okay, Janey, everything's going to be okay."

"What did the bad man look like?" Steve whispered as he untied the ropes around Jeannie's ankles.

"Big and scary," she said, then started to sob.

"Where did he go?" I asked Janey as I quickly undid the rope binding her wrists in front of her. "Did he tell you?"

"No." A tear ran down her cheek. "He just said he'd be right back. And that he'd kill us if we tried to leave."

"Well, you're safe—"

"Jeannie!" Her feet and hands free, Janey threw herself at her sister. Shaking, they clung to each other and sobbed.

"We need to get out of here, now," Steve said, clearly unnerved by their tears. "We have no idea when the bad man will come back. Let's go."

Without another word, I peeled Janey away from her sister and rushed out of the cabin with her in my arms. Carrying Jeannie behind me, Steve and I raced down the pier to his car, keeping our eyes peeled for Harry, who we knew had a gun.

Steve opened the door to his back seat and quickly slid Jeannie in.

I put Janey next to her and closed the door.

Steve gunned the engine and took off for the nearest police station in Cape May. When we pulled up, Steve ran in to get help.

Minutes later, two officers wearing grim expressions came out and carried the twins inside as I followed them into the lobby, where Steve was waiting.

Seeing a sofa against a wall, I took the twins over to it and reassured them that everything would be okay.

I could only imagine the terror the poor things had experienced. Actually—I didn't have to imagine it because I'd lived it myself. I had no doubt that the man who'd kidnapped Arty's twins was the same man who'd abducted me. Insane. And pure evil.

I turned to face Steve and the police officers, who'd been joined by an officer who appeared to be their chief.

Tall, with neatly cropped gray hair and keen blue intelligent eyes, he had an unmistakable air of authority, which under the circumstances I found comforting.

"Chief Dallas Marino," he said, coming over to shake my hand. "I understand these children have been kidnapped?"

"I was able to fill them in a little bit," Steve told me. "But not much."

I glanced over at the girls, who were clinging together, shaking so hard their teeth were clattering. Now, in the bright light of the station, I could see they were dressed alike in blue shorts and pink T-shirts, and that they were barefoot. Their pigtails were coming undone and the only way I could tell them apart was by the color of their hair ribbons—Jeannie's, blue and Janey's, purple. One of Janey's was missing.

I introduced them to the captain, told him how we had rescued them, then filled him in about what we knew about the abduction in Philadelphia.

"But there's more," I whispered, taking him aside so the girls couldn't overhear me. I told him about Lily's death, that Steve and I were private eyes hired to investigate the probable murder, and that it was possible that the murderer and kidnapper were the same person. "Information that we uncovered during our murder investigation led us to the sailboat where we found the girls," I said. "Luckily we found them unharmed and unguarded."

"Good work," Captain Marino said. "Do you happen to know the suspected kidnapper's name?"

"Not yet." I swallowed hard. It was true that I wasn't sure about his name. And I didn't want to say any more until we knew for sure.

"Kidnapped from Philly, you say?" Chief Marino squinted at me, looking confused. "So why were they brought to Cape May?"

"Could we go somewhere private to talk ...?" I asked. "And perhaps get these children something to eat and drink?"

"Good idea," Steve agreed, "it's been a long, traumatizing day."

Nodding, the chief directed us into a meeting room at the back of the station, waited for the twins to settle themselves on another sofa back there, then told Steve and I to take seats at a table on the other side of the room.

A woman came in bearing glasses of water and cookies for the girls. After watching them guzzle the water and gobble down the cookies, Chief Marino dragged a chair over to them.

"Feeling better?" He asked, his voice soft and patient.

They nodded.

I couldn't help but smile. Now holding hands, the twins were clearly devoted to one another. Their togetherness gave them strength.

A strength I envied. When I was abducted, I'd been alone. And the terror of being alone in that horrible boarding house room had not yet left me.

"I'm going to call your father to tell him you're okay," Chief Marino told them. "But first I need to ask you some questions, okay?"

Jeannie sniffed. "Okay."

He leaned forward. "Did a bad person take you out of your house?"

"Yes ..." Janey whimpered.

"Who?" he pressed. "A man or a woman?"

"A bad man," Jeannie said.

"Tell him what the man looked like," I blurted out.

Chief Marino glared at me. "Please let me ask the questions." He turned back to the girls. "Can you remember the color of his hair?"

"Black." Jeannie bit her lip. "Kind of long."

"Like he needed a haircut," Janey said.

"What about his face? Was there anything you remember about his face?" Chief Marino asked.

"It was scary. And ugly." Janey wrinkled her nose. "There were weird marks all over it. I think scars."

Jeannie pointed to her cheeks and nose and chin. "Like bad boo-boos. Bad boo-boo scars."

I sucked in a breath. They were describing Mystery Waiter and almost certainly Harry O'Toole.

"He walked funny, too," Jeannie said. "Like there was something wrong with his feet."

"Like this?" The captain stood up and walked a few steps with an exaggerated limp.

The girls nodded in unison.

"Can you tell me how he took you out of your house?" Captain Marino sat back down. "Did he sneak up on you?"

"We were building a block fort in our playroom," Janey said, "and he ran in, and he grabbed us by our hands."

Jeannie whispered, "He said he would kill us if we screamed."

The captain narrowed his eyes. "Where were the adults in your house? Was anyone watching you?"

"Stella was supposed to." Jeannie nibbled a finger. "But she was with Daddy. In Daddy's room."

The police captain turned to Steve and me with a questioning look in his eyes.

I raised my eyebrows and nodded. "Stella's their nanny and what this child said confirms what we'd been told by their grandmother. And it's exactly what it sounds like."

The captain turned back to the girls. "Did the bad man hurt you?"

They shook their heads.

"Did he touch you in any bad way?"

They shook their heads again. "He tied us up," Janey said. "And then we went for a long ride in his car to his boat. And then he left."

"Did he say why?"

"No," Jeannie said. "But he was gone a long time."

Maybe to get food. Or maybe he was on his way to Batsto Village to collect the ransom money. In any case, I was relieved they hadn't been molested. I shuddered to think what might have happened if Steve and I had not rescued them when we did.

Captain Marino stood up. "I'm going to call your Daddy now." He looked over at Steve and me. "There's a phone in my office and I'd like one of you to come with me."

"Me," I said, jumping up. I could not *wait* to hear what Arty would say when he heard that I—a female detective and his sworn enemy—had played a key role in rescuing his children.

I didn't care that Steve was his private investigator. It was time the man talked to me.

Steve gave me a smile and a thumbs up as I left the room.

I was glad he agreed.

Twenty-Six

Arty thanked me, reluctantly, but it was still gratifying. It was the least he could do given that his twins were safe. Which was all that mattered.

That and finding the kidnapper, which was next on my list.

Arty was surprised to learn that the twins had been found on his old sailboat, but he didn't bring up Harry's name and neither did I. All Arty cared about was that his children were safe. Which suited me just fine since Steve and I planned to look for Harry without getting the police involved.

Captain Marino motioned for me to hand him the phone when I finished talking to Arty. He asked to speak to one of the Philadelphia officers at the house with Arty, then informed him that Cape May police would transport the twins back to Philadelphia under guard, and that his department would work with Philadelphia police to find the kidnapper.

"The Philly police have Batsto staked out," Marino told me after he hung up the phone. "With the ransom money stashed in the barrel as directed."

"Good," I said, relieved. Maybe the cops would get lucky. Maybe they would catch the kidnapper with no problem. And maybe he'd confess. But I wasn't counting on it.

The Harry O'Toole I knew was too clever to be caught.

"So where does this leave us now?" I asked Steve as we left the station, feeling proud of what we'd accomplished. "What's our next move?"

He chuckled and reached for my hand. "Aren't you exhausted, super sleuth?"

I squeezed his hand and met his eyes. "Well, now that you mention it, yes."

He smiled. "You're an incredible woman, Story, do you know that?"

Uh-oh. He was giving me *that* smile.

"You started today by getting discharged from the hospital after being treated for a head injury from a brutal abduction," he said. "Then you ended today by rescuing two little girls who'd also been abducted, most likely by the same man."

"Well, yeah. Now that you mention it, it is kind of crazy." Suddenly wary, I dropped his hand. "But where are you going with this, Steve?"

He kept that smile on his face but didn't say anything until we reached his car.

Then he helped me into the passenger seat, went around to the trunk, opened it, and removed something.

Hopping into the driver's seat, he handed me a bag—another brown department store bag.

Widening my eyes, I peeked inside. "More clothes?" I was still wearing the outfit he'd given me at the hospital.

He chuckled. "No. It's a nightgown."

"A nightgown?"

"It's getting late and we're not going to drive back to Philly. Your car is still parked at The Admiral Hotel, remember? Plus, you're in no condition to drive."

He was right. I looked back in the bag, pulled out a frilly, pale pink nightie, and rubbed it against my cheek. "It's beautiful, so soft," I said, overcome with gratitude and a growing apprehension about where this was leading. "But—"

"No buts. We're going to leave your car at The Admiral for the night, where I'll get us rooms." He gave me lopsided grin. "I know what you're thinking, and don't worry. Two separate rooms. Since it's Wednesday, I don't expect the hotel to be full."

———

Steve did manage to get us two oceanfront rooms at The Admiral. And since we hadn't eaten all day, he treated me to dinner in the hotel dining room after checking in.

I was too hungry and too broke to protest. And I was thrilled to be in one of Cape May's finest restaurants in his company.

But I was still so wound up from the day's events that I was finding it hard to relax. "We need to find Harry O'Toole," I said for probably the millionth time as I looked around the grand room, every table filled with chatty vacationers. "And I have so many more questions for Arty. This case is getting more and more complicated by the day."

Steve grinned at me from across the table, the flickering golden light of the candle between us sculping the amazing angles of his handsome face. "Relax. We'll figure it out. We've made great progress so far—for now can we just eat and enjoy each other's company?"

He was right. "Sure, Steve, you're right," I said, flicking him a guilty smile as I took another bite of lobster.

I was trying to enjoy his company, but my jumble of jittery emotions was making it hard for me to eat the lobster entrée I'd ordered. In addition to my case, I kept thinking about those two oceanfront rooms he'd booked for us, side by side, on the top floor. They had to cost a fortune, which made me grateful and anxious and excited and scared all at the same time.

If I kept letting Steve pay for everything, that meant I owed him. And I didn't want to owe him anything.

"Don't worry, Story," he said, "I'm not going to sneak into your room in the middle of the night, naked."

I almost choked on my lobster.

His lips formed a suggestive grin as he stabbed a piece of his filet mignon and headed it toward his mouth. "Unless ..." He held the steak in front of his lips, cocked his head, and wiggled his eyebrows. "You want me to."

Oh. My. God. My heart stopped and my mouth dropped open. I blinked at him. My worst fear was colliding with my secret fantasy. A secret fantasy that had to stay secret.

Or it could hurt me.

Because secrets have a way of blowing up.

And if this one did ... I didn't want to think about it. I would not think about it.

Steve laughed. "I'm just kidding, Story. Relax."

"I don't think you're kidding, Steve." My words came out all squeaky. My cheeks were on fire. My lungs didn't seem to be working. I couldn't breathe. *Why* did I just say that?

"I'm not kidding about my feelings for you." Steve put his fork down. His grin faded and he suddenly looked more serious than I'd ever seen him. And we'd been in some serious situations, he and I. "You know how I feel about you." He leaned across the table toward me. "Which means I'm not going to pressure you to do anything that you're not ready for emotionally."

That was one the kindest things anyone had ever said to me. Steve was so good. Better than I deserved. "Thank you," I said, my voice breaking. "But I don't know if I will ever be ready."

"Oh, Story ..." Flickers of candlelight danced in his eyes as he reached for my hand. "I know one day you will. And I'm a patient man."

———

Steve did not sneak into my room during the night, naked or otherwise.

Whew. And darn.

I didn't sneak into his, either, although fantasizing about what could happen if I did cost me several hours of sleep.

As did thinking about my case. While tossing and turning and wrestling with my pillow, it kept coming back to me that my next move was obvious. I had to talk to Arty. Again. I had so many questions I needed to ask him regarding his friendship with Harry O'Toole, and without those answers, I felt stuck.

Not that I expected Arty to blurt out a confession that he and

Harry were the jewel thieves who never got caught. But I did want to see the expression on his face when I brought up the subjects of the Cape May Capers and Gladys Jones, who had to be a key piece to the puzzle.

"It's no use, Story, he's still not going to agree to talk to you about those things or anything else," Steve told me over breakfast the next morning in The Admiral dining room.

Steve looked great. Refreshed. Like he'd gotten a good night sleep. Unlike me.

Envious, I took a sip of orange juice. "I was hoping you could plead my case," I said, trying not to whine, although it was hard not to. "I was hoping you could convince him that it would be in his best interest to talk to me. We all want to find Lily's killer. We're all on the same side here. And I did rescue his twins."

Steve shrugged. "Sure, I'll try."

Goody. I smiled. "Thanks."

"Don't get your hopes up, though. I don't expect to succeed." Steve pushed his scrambled eggs around on his plate, then looked back at me. "I'm pretty sure Arty still heartedly dislikes you."

"Gee, thanks." I let out a deep sigh.

Steve finished his eggs, drank his coffee, then waved for the waiter to bring the check. "Aren't you hungry?" he asked, pointing his fork at my barely touched plate of pancakes smothered in butter and syrup. He cocked his head. "Did you sleep okay?"

"Not really." I dumped two spoons of sugar into my coffee and brought the cup to my lips. Maybe all I needed was sugar and caffeine.

He grinned. "Was it me?"

I almost choked on my coffee. "You?" Swallowing hard, I stared at him. "What do you mean?" My hands shaking, I set my cup down.

He laughed. "Never mind, I'm just teasing you. I wish you didn't need to drive your car back to Philly, but I don't think you want to leave it here."

"I'll be fine."

"You sure?"

"I'm sure."

But that was a lie. I wasn't sure about anything anymore. I wasn't sure how I was going to get Arty to talk to me. I wasn't sure how I was going to find out who killed Lily. I wasn't sure how I was going to find out who tried to kill Gladys and left me for dead. And, if this monster was indeed Harry O'Toole or someone else. An imposter?

How could a missing necklace case have turned so complicated?

Steve seemed to be reading my mind. Something I was learning he was eerily good at. "One step at a time, Story," he said, "that's how this business works. Don't doubt yourself, you're doing great."

He came over to me and reached for my hand and I stood and faced him. Draping his arm around my shoulder, he pulled me close. "Don't worry, together we're going to find the bad guy or guys. And Penny's necklace, while we're at it."

I leaned my head on his shoulder. "I already found the necklace—remember? It's in police custody."

"See ..." Steve murmured. "That's progress. We'll just keep going. During investigations, one thing always leads to another. You just need to follow the trail, be doggedly persistent, keep your eyes and ears open. Be open to what unfolds."

"Great advice—just what I needed to hear," I told him as we headed out to the parking lot. "Thanks."

We walked over to my T-Bird. Then it hit me that I had pocketed my car keys in the shorts I was wearing when I went to meet Gladys, which felt like a thousand years ago. Where ...?

Grinning, Steve pulled the keys out of his pocket and dangled them in front of me. "Thought you might need these. I found them in your shorts at the hospital. Good thing they didn't end up on the bottom of the pool."

Returning his grin, I reached for them and gave him a hug. "Thanks. Damn if you don't seem to think of everything."

"I try." He watched me get in my car and start the engine. "You look dog tired, and I'm concerned about you, so I'll follow you to Arty's house. When we get there, just wait in the car and I'll go in and talk to him. Hopefully he'll listen to reason."

It didn't turn out that way.

I managed the drive back to Philly okay. And luckily, Arty was home.

But Steve was unable to convince him to let me come in. Twenty minutes after entering the Duncan residence, Steve came out and gave me the bad news. "Arty's spending time with his girls and he wants you off his property. *Now.*" Steve winced. "I'm sorry."

I wasn't surprised. Disappointed, but not surprised. Anyway, I was ready for my next move, which I'd been mulling over while waiting for Steve to return.

As silly—and as desperate—as it sounded, I couldn't think of anything else. I was going home to change my clothes, and then ...

"Okay." I flashed Steve my best super-sleuth smile. "I'm going to go see Victor Bravo and see if our psychic medium friend can get in touch with Lily on the other side."

TWENTY-SEVEN

"Well, look who it is, my favorite gal detective." Victor Bravo greeted me with an elaborate bow when he opened his door to find me on his doorstep. Then, stepping aside to peek over my shoulder, he frowned. "But where's that handsome future husband of yours?"

Blushing, I said, "Just me today, I'm afraid." No use arguing with Victor that Steve was not my future husband. It would have come across as an insult—because predicting the future, in addition to contacting dead people, was how the psychic medium made his living.

Anyway, it didn't take a psychic to see there was something between Steve and me. That didn't mean we'd ever get married.

Victor had not directly helped me solve my last case, but he had seemed to know things he shouldn't have. Which I found uncanny. And he was fun to be around. Maybe because he was one of the most honest people I'd ever met when it came to being totally himself.

He usually wore a turban, and the one now covering his bald

head was bright purple, a perfect match for his billowy lavender and white striped pants and knee-length, cotton-candy-pink tunic. As usual, he was also barefoot, and today his toenails were painted bright-sky blue.

"Come in, come in," he said, waving me into his modest bungalow. "How can I help you, dear one? Have you come about another murder? I certainly hope not ... but then again, you are in that type of business."

I walked over to his sofa and sat down. I'd met Victor on my previous case, which had ended up involving two murders, and while the jury was out on whether I believed his powers were real, I was leaning toward becoming a believer. Or at least becoming more and more intrigued. And in this situation, hopeful.

"I would like you to try to contact two departed souls for me," I said. "The first is a woman named Lily, who died recently from a fall off her second-floor balcony. She may have jumped, but more likely she was pushed."

"Ah ... I see." Victor's eyes bore into mine as he sat down in a soft-cushioned chair across from me. "And the other?"

"A man who was reported missing and dead during World War II. His name was Harry O'Toole. While investigating Lily's death, I've uncovered evidence that Harry might still be alive, or it could be that someone is impersonating him."

"Interesting," Victor said, dropping his voice to a deep croon. "I shall try Lily first. Her last name?"

"Duncan."

"Lily Duncan ..." Victor closed his eyes, deepening his tone even more. "Lily, are you here?"

I sat forward, elbows on my knees, and watched Victor breathe.

Mouth slightly open, abdomen moving in and out, the rest of him motionless. For a long time. For what seemed like forever.

Finally, just as I was beginning to fear he'd fallen asleep, he opened his eyes and blinked at me. "Lily has come through. Pretty woman. Petite blonde."

I beamed. "Yes. That's her."

He lifted his eyes to the ceiling and after a minute announced, "She did not jump."

I pressed a hand to my chest. "Okay, okay. That's good. I didn't think she did."

Keeping his gaze on the ceiling, he added, "Seems she was murdered. Pushed?"

I sucked in a breath. "Who pushed her?"

Victor lowered his head and closed his eyes again. He waited. "She keeps saying, 'I loved him, I loved him.'" He shook his head back and forth, back and forth, squeezing his eyes tighter, looking confused. "She says not pushed. I'm hearing the word *tossed*."

"Tossed?"

He pushed his bushy eyebrows together. "I'm seeing strong arms lift her up. Picking her up, tossing her over the balcony. Like a rag doll."

"Who?" I hissed. "Who's tossing her?"

Victor opened his eyes and stared at me. "I don't know. She keeps saying, 'I was betrayed by love. Betrayed by love.'"

I leaned forward. "Betrayed by *whom*?"

"Tricked ... she keeps saying she was tricked ..."

"Tricked by *whom*?"

Victor looked up at the ceiling again.

"Man? Woman?" I shouted. "Was it a man or a woman who tricked her?"

"Shhh." Victor lowered his head and fixed his gaze on me. "She's fading away."

"No!" I cried. "No, Lily, don't go. Tell me more. I need to find your killer."

Victor whispered, "She's left."

"*No* ... why?"

"It takes a lot of energy for souls to come through." He raised his hands high and held them there, palms up. "I sensed this was causing her pain." He lowered his hands and folded them into a prayer position. "I'm sorry I could not get her to say more."

I sighed. What had I learned? If Victor was right, only that Lily had been killed by someone she'd loved. And that she'd been tossed over the balcony, not pushed. Not super helpful.

Frustrated, I was beginning to feel like a fool. "Okay, then," I said, "what about Harry? Can you try to reach Harry?"

Nodding, Victor shut his eyes and whispered, "I'll try."

Again, I watched him breathe. Still and silent.

Again, I waited. Only longer this time.

Finally, he opened his eyes. "He's not coming through. Nothing."

I wasn't surprised. In truth, I would have been surprised, and disappointed, if Victor had been able to summon the spirit of Harry O'Toole. "What does that mean?" I asked, excited. "Does this mean he's still alive?"

"I can't guarantee that." Victor gave me a wry smile. "I can only tell you that I can't reach him in the realm of the dead. It's possible he's in the place called hell. But I cannot communicate with souls in hell. Which is just as ..."

"Which is just as well," I said. "It wouldn't be pretty. I understand."

He nodded. "Good, anything else I can help you with?"

"No," I said, "you've given me some good information. About Harry, at least. I just wish Lily could have given me more." Lifting my purse off the floor, I dug for my wallet. "How much do I owe you?"

"Wait, there's more," Victor said, his tone ominous. Stroking his chin, he stared at me, eyes wide and unblinking. "I must tell you that when I was trying to summon Harry, I kept getting a vision about you."

"Me?" I braced myself. "About *me*?"

"I saw you in great danger."

"Oh. Well. That's nothing new." I waved a hand. "In this business, I'm often finding myself in some kind of pickle."

"*Great danger*," Victor said, his voice sharp. "You need to take this seriously."

I swallowed the lump in my throat. "Okay. What did you see in your vision?"

He closed his eyes again and waited, then, frowning, said, "You're in water."

"Okay ... good thing I can swim ...oh, wait." I chuckled. "Wait a minute, wait a minute—maybe you're seeing the past. Something that recently happened to me, when I jumped into a pool to try to save someone. I was in danger then, for sure."

"Not the past." He sounded annoyed. "I don't see things that have already occurred. This is something that has yet to come. You are going down, down, down, deeper and deeper in water."

I sucked in a breath. "Oh ..."

"Deeper and deeper and deeper and deeper.""

My heart clutched. He was scaring me. I whispered, "What else do you see?"

He circled his hands over his eyes. "You are wearing some kind of mask. A swim mask."

"What? I don't own a swim mask."

Victor opened his eyes. He regarded me with a grave expression. "Take this as a warning, Story Smith. Consider yourself fortunate."

"Fortunate?" I said, aghast. "This sounds awful."

"Fortunate because now you know. When you see a swim mask, *put it on.*"

Rattled, I was shaking. There was something about this warning that sounded too real to dismiss. "Okay. I will keep my eyes open. And when I see a swim mask, I will put it on."

"Good girl." Victor clapped in delight. "Good girl. That might just save your life."

———

Victor didn't come cheap, and as I made the half hour drive from his house in West Chester to my office in Philly, I wondered again and again if I had received my money's worth from him.

Time would tell, I assured myself.

Ideally, I'd be able to get Penny and Jonathan to reimburse my visit to Victor. If I solved the case that is and could prove the psychic medium's pronouncements had helped.

It had been a long day and was getting close to dinner time, but I told my hungry stomach it would have to wait. First, I had to type up daily reports—today's, and the days I'd spent in Cape May and Atlantic City because it was already Thursday, and I was behind.

Wendy greeted me with her customary cheerful smile when I got to the office, because as usual, she was still hard at work.

"Jonathan's lucky to have you," I said, fishing in my purse for the key to my office. "Is he here by any chance?"

"No, he left for the day."

"Oh." I sighed. "I was hoping to bring him up to date on my investigation into Lily's death. I'll just put it all in writing and talk to him later."

"I'll call him and tell him you're here." Wendy picked up the phone and dialed his home number. "I don't think he'll mind coming back to see you and maybe Penny will come with him. They've both been quite concerned about your case."

"Hello, Jonathan," she said when he answered. It was a quick call because as she'd predicted, Jonathan said he did want to see me and so did Penny.

"They'll be here soon," Wendy said, hanging up the phone. "But, boy, do you look exhausted, Story. You must be working hard. Haven't seen you in days."

I twirled my key ring on my finger. "Yep. I'm tired, but I still have work to do. Penny's missing- necklace-turned-murder case has turned extremely complicated."

Wendy gave me an admiring grin. "But that's good, right? Because boring doesn't seem to be in your vocabulary. I'm also betting that, by complicated, you mean your hunky sidekick, Steve, has gotten involved."

I had to smile at that. "You know me too well, Wendy. And yes, he has."

I backed away from her desk. "I've got to go get to work. I'll let

Jonathan fill you in once I fill him in." I gave her a flutter finger wave. "Let me know when he gets here."

Letting myself into my office, I found it hot and stuffy, so I opened my window, left the door to the hall open, and got to work.

A half hour later, the Millers arrived.

"Have you found Lily's killer?" Penny asked, rushing into my office with breathless with expectation, Jonathan right behind her.

"Not yet but I'm working on it and expect to have good news soon." That was rather optimistic but hey, I'm an optimist.

I waved for Penny to sit in the chair in front of my desk, pulled another one out of the corner for Jonathan, then brought them up to date on everything so far. Everything—Harry O'Toole's letter to Lily, the shooting of Gladys Jones, my abduction, the abduction of Arty's twins, how Steve and I had rescued the twins, and my visit to Victor Bravo.

"I'm putting it all in writing now," I said.

"Incredible," Jonathan said. "Good work. You certainly leave no stone unturned." He pushed his brows together. "But a psychic medium?"

"I'm currently at a standstill," I admitted. "Not sure Victor told me anything helpful, but one never knows."

"I'm sorry to hear about your abduction and injuries, how awful," Penny said. "And the twins being kidnapped? I can only imagine Arty's fear. I bet he was hysterical."

"He was. But it ended well. The problem is that the kidnapper is still out there."

"And you and Steve Evans believe it might be Harry O'Toole." Penny shook her head. "I can't believe that—but I guess I must."

"How well did you know Gladys Jones?" I asked Penny. "Sadly,

Gladys is still in a coma, and I suspect she holds the answers to many of my questions."

Penny sighed. "I'm afraid I didn't know her well at all. I hate to sound like a snob, but she wasn't in my social circle. She had a reputation for being fast."

"Yes, I've heard that." I picked up a pencil and tapped it on my desk. "But what about her and Harry? Was she fast with him?"

Penny pressed a hand to her chest. "Oh, no. Not Harry. He was going to marry me. He loved me."

I bit down on my lip and nodded sympathetically, biting back what I wanted to say about good old Harry. He'd sure had the girls fooled. And he was still up to being a bad boy. Only now, instead of womanizing and robbing homes he was committing murder, abducting women, and kidnapping children.

If my theory was about him was correct, that is. If he truly was a war hero returned from the dead. But if I was right, what would he try next? The man was batty, dangerous, and desperate.

"I'm afraid Gladys is the only lead I have to my suspect right now so if you recall anything about her that might be helpful, let me know," I told Penny.

"And so, what will you do in the meantime?" Jonathan asked.

"I have a plan," I assured him. "I always have a plan."

"Good," He smiled. "Just don't get hurt again."

I couldn't promise him that, but after he and Penny left, I picked up the phone and dialed Steve's office.

He answered. Of course. It was late but he was doing what I was doing—writing his daily reports.

"Story," he said with a smile in his voice. "I'm surprised to hear from you. You didn't get much sleep last night and I thought you'd be in bed by now."

"I will be soon," I said. "But I need a plan in order to be able to sleep and I want to know if you want to join me."

"Join you in doing what? Where?"

"We need to go back to Burdette Tomlin Hospital to see Gladys. She's got to wake up soon and if not, I have more questions for her parents. They haven't told us everything."

"I agree."

"You agree?"

"Yes, I agree that they know more than they've told us. And I agree that we need to go back to that hospital tomorrow. We've got nothing else. So, see you tomorrow."

Twenty-Eight

Steve met me at my office early the next morning, and this time we took my T-Bird.

Fortunately, Gladys was still among the living. Still in the hospital. Still the same room. Still under police guard. But unfortunately, still comatose.

Only now, she was alone in her room.

"Her parents left about an hour ago," a nurse told me when I questioned their whereabouts. "They've become rather discouraged about her condition. Her mother looked weary, so I encouraged them to go home and get some rest."

"Any change at all?" I tried not to sound as discouraged as I felt.

"Not yet." The nurse lay a hand on Gladys's forehead. "No fever, which is good. Indicates she's not developed any infections. She has not stirred, though, or opened her eyes."

Steve's gaze met mine. "I have an idea."

I sighed. "Good, partner, because I'm out of them."

"Let's go see her parents. Weary or not, they can at least answer some questions."

"Can't hurt," I agreed. I asked the nurse if she could get us their address.

Minutes later, she came back with it scrawled on a slip of paper.

I showed it to Steve. "They don't live far from Harry O'Toole's childhood home," I said. "Let's head there now."

———

Joe and Bertha Jones lived in a modest bungalow. Single story, small, well-kept front yard.

Painted a light shade of sea green, its windows framed by white shutters, the house had a cool beachy feel. Nice, since it sat only a few blocks from the ocean.

Steve parked out front, and we walked up the three steps to the front door and knocked.

Joe Jones opened the door and seemed surprised to see us, then alarmed. "Is it Gladys? Have you been to the hospital?" he asked, anxiously waving us inside.

"Relax Mr. Jones." Steve put a reassuring hand on the elderly man's shoulder. "Yes, we've just come from the hospital, but we're not here to discuss your daughter's condition. That hasn't changed."

"Oh, then ..." Blinking at us like a man trying to wake up from a nightmare, he pointed a shaky hand at his couch. "Please, have a seat. And tell me why you've come. I don't understand."

I asked, "Is your wife here? We were hoping to speak to both of you. We have more questions about Harry O'Toole."

He ran a hand over his weary face. "My wife is asleep, and I'd rather not wake her. This whole ordeal with Gladys has been hell."

"I'm awake, Joe."

Bertha, tying the belt of a terrycloth robe around her middle, came into the living room. "I can't sleep," she said, eyeing me and Steve in confusion. "My nerves are too bad. Then I heard somebody knocking. Was afraid it was the police come to tell us bad news about Gladys."

"You remember these detectives? They want to ask us questions about Harry." Her husband took her arm, guided her to an armchair across from the couch, then went into an adjacent dining room and grabbed a chair for himself.

"I don't know what else we can tell you." Bertha rubbed her eyes. "We told you all we knew when we saw you in the hospital."

Steve leaned toward her. "About that package that Harry O'Toole gave Gladys before he shipped off for the war—tell us what you suspect was in it."

"We told you before, we never saw what was in it," Bertha said. "But …

"But what?" I pressed.

She wouldn't meet my eye. "It was probably stolen jewelry. But that's all I'm going to say."

"Because Harry O'Toole was the Prince of Pearls," Steve said.

"That was the rumor," Joe said. "Never proven, so if he was, the guy got away with his crimes."

"And his friend, Arty Duncan?" I asked. "Do you think he and Harry were partners? Because if they were, he got away with it, too. And now he's living a life of luxury."

Bertha shrugged.

Really? Confused, I leaned forward and met her gaze. "Doesn't that make you angry?"

"All I care about right now is my daughter," she said, then folded her hands and closed her eyes, and sat stone still, making it clear she was done answering questions.

"Harry O'Toole is an extremely dangerous man." I cut my eyes to her husband. "We believe, like you, that he is still alive. We suspect he murdered Arty's wife, Lily. And that he recently kidnapped Arty's children—who, you'll be glad to know, have been rescued. Harry was holding them for ransom, which shows he is desperate for money. We believe he's after the package he gave to Gladys for safekeeping."

Bertha didn't open her eyes, not even at the mention of children being kidnapped. She didn't move.

Joe shook his head. "We don't know where that package could—"

Rap, rap, rap.

Somebody was at the door. Joe seemed surprised but didn't get up to answer the knock.

Bertha's eyes popped open. She looked at her husband. "Who could that be?"

He shook his head. "I don't know."

Steve stood. "I'll get it."

He opened the door.

A man dressed all in black shoved him forcefully.

Steve flew backward, then stumbled back onto to his feet.

The man pointed a gun at Steve, then waved it at the rest of us. "Nobody moves."

Swallowing hard, fear flooded through me. And shock. Mystery Waiter, a.k.a., Harry O'Toole. The very guy we were looking for.

Steve pulled his pistol from the waistband of his shorts.

Mystery Waiter aimed his gun at him. "Drop it. Now."

Steve dropped it.

"Now go sit down," he snapped.

Steve rejoined me on the couch.

"Harry O'Toole," Joe hissed. "So, it's true. You really are still alive, you *bastard*."

I sucked in a gasp. Here was the proof I needed. Mystery Waiter was indeed Harry O'Toole.

"Where's the package, Joe?" Harry advanced on him with his gun. "That package I gave Gladys before the war," he growled. "Where is it?"

Joe shook his head. "What package?"

Harry pointed the gun at Joe's forehead. "Stop pretending you don't know."

"We don't know about any package," Bertha cried. "What are you talking about?"

Harry turned his gun on Bertha. "Where did your daughter hide my package?" His eyes flashed fury. "Tell me now or I'll kill you."

"She doesn't know, Harry." Joe was pleading. "Don't hurt her."

"What happened to you, Harry?" Bertha's voice quivered. "What did the war do to your face?"

Uh-oh. If she was trying to change the subject, that was the worst thing she could have said. His scarred face turned a deep shade of red. "Your daughter lied to me about where she was keeping my package," he snarled. "Claimed it was in a safety deposit box in a bank. But the bank never heard of her or any such box. Now you have three seconds to tell me where that package is—or you're dead, lady."

I jumped up. "Don't shoot her. I know where it is," I lied.

He turned his gun on me. "Where?"

I had to think fast. "Uhm ... it's on a boat."

He narrowed his eyes. "What boat?"

"I need to take you to it."

He glared at me. "You're lying."

"No ... I'm not."

He pointed his gun at my face. "How do you know where the package is, blondie?"

"Gladys told me," I said, making it up as I went along. "Right before you shot her at the pool. Remember me? I was with her. You knocked me out with your gun. Gave me a concussion. Dragged me off and left me for dead in that horrid Atlantic City rathole."

"Of course I remember you." He snickered.

"Thanks for not outright killing me," I said, laying on the sarcasm. "Good thing you didn't because I know where your package is, and I can lead you to it."

I was laying it on thick, but something changed in his eyes. They went a little soft. "I was nice to you because you reminded me of someone I once loved. Her name was Sophie. Your hair, your eyes, that sweet, sweet body of yours. So much like her."

His smile chilled me to the bone.

I felt Steve stiffen next to me, but he kept quiet. Smart thinking.

"I was disappointed to find that you'd escaped, dolly, because I was never going to leave you tied up like that." Harry's smile went creepier. "After you came to, I was looking forward to you and I having some fun."

The look in his eyes left no doubt as to what he meant by fun. "Should have just killed you when I had the chance, though." He moved closer and pressed his gun to my forehead. "You're no fun at all."

"Oh, but I can be," I blurted out, shaking inside while striving to appear cool and confident. "Because I know where your package is. Because Gladys told me. It wasn't nice of you to shoot her. Don't know why you did that."

Harry scoffed. "Bitch lied to me. Made me give her the necklace she knew I'd given Penny Ash all those years ago. Said she'd tell me where my package was if I gave it to her—since it should have been hers to begin with. Because we were engaged." He hacked a dry laugh. "I was never going to marry that floozy."

"But why did you have to shoot Gladys? Were you planning to kill her?"

"Revenge. I wanted to hurt her like she hurt me. I went to a lot of trouble to get that necklace from Penny. And thanks to Penny's cousin, Lily, I succeeded." He sighed. "Poor Lily ..."

He pressed the gun harder to my head. "Imagine my disappointment when I found out the package wasn't at that bank after all. So, tell me where it is. Now. Or ..."

"I need to take you there," I said, holding my ground, stalling for time. I grabbed hold of Steve's hand. "Steve and I will take you to it. But only if you leave Mr. and Mrs. Jones alone."

"Alone?" He laughed. "You must take me for an idiot. As soon as we leave, they'll call the police."

"Tie them up, then," Steve said. "I'll help you. Just don't hurt them."

Harry hesitated. He obviously didn't like it, but what was he going to do? He wanted that package, and I could tell by the look on his face that he wanted to believe I knew where it was.

Keeping the cold barrel of his gun pressed to my head, he barked at Joe to go get some clothing that he could rip up to use as makeshift ropes. "If you don't come *right* back, everybody here dies," he barked, "including your wife."

Joe did as he was told.

Twenty minutes later, with Harry continuing to point his gun at me, Steve had Joe and Bertha tightly bound to kitchen chairs, gags stuffed in their mouths.

Harry nodded, satisfied.

Then, keeping his gun aimed at our backs, he ordered Steve and me out the door and to my car.

Steve glanced at me and silently mouthed, "Where are we going?"

I mouthed back, "Sweet Sailing Two."

Twenty-Nine

hy did I lie that Gladys had hidden that package aboard Sweet Sailing Two?

Because I couldn't think of anything else. Steve and I had been there, so I knew the cabin was kept unlocked. And that it was a good place to stall for more time.

My only hope was that Steve would find a way to overpower Harry while I pretended to search for the package.

I didn't know if Harry even knew that Sweet Sailing Two existed. That his childhood chum, Arty, now owned a million-dollar motor yacht named after their old sailboat.

It really didn't matter. If he knew about it, fine. It would hopefully strike him as a plausible place for Gladys to hide stolen jewels. Gladys had known all the lifeguards back in her day, and I was ready with the lie that she and Arty had become lovers after the war. Given her reputation, it was a believable one, and for all I knew, might even be true.

Given the rumors about Harry and Arty, I was almost certain the jewels in the package had been stolen by them as a team.

On the other hand, if Harry had no idea that Sweet Sailing Two existed, I was hoping the shock of seeing the luxury yacht with that name would distract him long enough for Steve to grab Harry's gun away from him.

Harry demanded that Steve drive my car and held me on his lap in the passenger seat, keeping his gun pressed to my side.

Then, when the three of us got to the marina, Harry took my arm and kept the gun aimed at me as he forced Steve to walk ahead of us down the pier.

"Where we going, blondie?" Harry asked me.

"To a boat," I said, flippantly. "I'll tell you when we get there."

Steve stopped at Sweet Sailing Two.

"This it?" Harry pressed the gun into my side.

I nodded. "Recognize it?" I taunted.

He grunted. "Maybe I do and maybe I don't. Who cares? If this is where Gladys hid the package let's go ahead and board. Your boyfriend first."

Steve hopped on.

Harry and I followed.

Steve pushed the cabin door open, and Harry and I followed him in.

Harry closed the door behind us. It was dark in the cabin, so he ordered Steve to open the curtains.

I looked around, trying to figure out what I was going to do next.

The interior of the yacht was laid out like a small house. My eyes landed on many places where a package could conceivably be hidden, including teak cabinets in the kitchen area, and glass-enclosed shelves filled with books in what looked like a living room.

Past the living room I spotted several closed doors that likely led to bedrooms.

I wondered how long could I keep up a fake search? I met Steve's eyes and gave him a just-play-along-with-me look.

He pressed his lips together and nodded.

"Get over here, boyfriend, hands up," Harry shouted at him. "What's your name so I don't have to keep calling you that."

"Steve Evans and that's Story Smith." Steve nodded at me. "Female private eye extraordinaire. Who's been on to you from the get-go."

"Yeah, yeah. She's been a thorn in my side for way too long." He shoved his gun into my ribs.

I gasped but didn't move.

"So, where's the package, blondie?" he growled at me. "Where'd Gladys tell you she put it?"

I took a deep breath and willed myself to stay calm. "She didn't tell me exactly." I sniffed. "I need to look for it."

"She didn't tell you *exactly*?" Harry shot daggers at me with his eyes. "What *did* she tell you?"

"Just that she hid it on Arty's yacht, Sweet Sailing Two. She said it was named after the sailboat you and Arty once owned. And then she told me the name of the marina."

"So ... why here? You better not be lying. Why did she hide it here?"

Okay, it was time for my preplanned lie. "Don't you know, Harry?" I shot him a look of profound pity. "You and Gladys were lovers once but when you didn't come back from the war, she and Arty became lovers."

Harry blinked at me in disbelief. "You're lying."

"No, I'm not."

"Arty married Lily," he snapped. "Gladys lied to you—or you're making this up."

"Arty married Lily, that's true." I swallowed hard. "But Arty and Lily had an understanding. That they could fool around on the side with other people."

"Really?" Harry frowned, obviously not sure whether to believe that. "Why ...? I don't get it."

"Oh, come on," I said. "This shouldn't surprise you. You wrote Lily a letter shortly before you tossed her off her balcony, telling her that you loved her, asking her to meet you in Cape May. And I'm betting that she did. Only, like you said, poor Lily. Telling her that you loved her was a ruse, wasn't it? A trick to get your hands on the necklace that you gave her cousin, Penny."

Harry narrowed his eyes and glared at me.

My heart jumped into my throat. I couldn't breathe, hyper aware of his gun, and I hoped I hadn't gone too far with my goading. I knew by now that Harry had a hair-trigger temper, and I was playing a dangerous game.

"That package better be on this boat." He shoved me hard toward the kitchen. I fell to my knees.

He grabbed Steve's arm and pressed the gun to Steve's head. "Start looking for it now, blondie. No tricks or your boyfriend dies."

"Okay, okay." I stumbled to my feet. I had to keep stalling. Keep Harry talking.

I went over to a kitchen cabinet and opened it. Stacks of dishes. I lifted one up, then another, then another, making a show of peering behind them while making as much noise as I could to sound earnest. *Clang, clang, clang.*

"Nothing here," I called over my shoulder. "But I'll keep looking."

"Shut up and search," Harry said in a low hiss. "And stop making so much noise while you're at it."

I turned and met Steve's eyes. He looked amused and worried at the same time.

"I bet you're wondering how Story found you, Harry," Steve said. "Well, first, she noticed you at Arty and Lily's party, dressed like a waiter. Then she found your letter to Lily, tucked in her Bible. Pretty smart private eye, don't you think?"

I smiled to myself. Steve was goading Harry, too, to keep him talking. I opened another cabinet and clanged some more dishes.

"Lily loved me," Harry said with haughty pride. "All the girls did."

"But you gave Penny that diamond and emerald necklace," I turned and looked at him. "Why Penny?"

"Impulse." Harry barked a laugh. "At the time, I convinced myself that I loved Penny best of all my girlfriends. But really, I think I just wanted to have someone miss me while I was off fighting the war."

"Liar." Steve smirked at him. "I bet you were just trying to get her into bed."

Harry laughed. A real laugh. Haughty, like he was enjoying the memory. "Yeah, that, too, buddy. Sadly, it didn't work."

He stopped laughing. "Now get cracking, blondie. I'm losing patience with you."

I opened another cabinet, then turned back around. "Penny told me how handsome you were, Harry. She never stopped loving you. I know the war changed you, but you're still a good-looking guy."

His face reddened. "Now I know you're lying."

"No, no, really ... Lily must have thought so because she stole that necklace from Penny to give to you. Just because you asked her to. When you guys met at Congress Hall, I bet she fell right into your arms."

I'd landed on the truth. I could tell by the creepy proud grin on his face.

He chuckled. "You're right. At first my scars and limp shocked and upset her. But she got over it when I convinced her that she'd always been my true love. Convincing her was easy. Because that foolish woman was starved for love. Lily should never have married Arty, the jerk."

"But Arty was your best friend," I said.

Harry shook his head, then impatience sparked in his eyes. "You're not looking for my package, blondie. Keep looking, quit yacking."

I opened another cabinet, then another, then another. Pulled out plates, glasses, mugs, then put them back. It was growing hotter by the minute in the closed cabin and sweat started trickling down my face. How long could I keep up this act?

Would Steve ever find a way to overpower him?

"Why Lily?" I asked after I'd gone through the last cabinet. "Why not write to Penny if all you wanted was that necklace?"

That had always bothered me, but I didn't get an answer.

Instead, Harry went over to the yacht's steering wheel, mounted on a deck above the kitchen. With the hand that wasn't aiming a gun at Steve's head, he started rummaging through a drawer.

He pulled out a large keyring.

Grinning, he held it up, then inserted it in the ignition.

The engine roared to life.

Alarmed, I shouted, "What are you doing?"

"You're taking too long to find my package, sweety." He widened his grin. "Since I'm bored, we're going for a ride while you keep looking."

He left the wheel, lunged at me, grabbed me around my neck, and pressed his gun to my head. "Your boyfriend is going to go out and undo the ropes. If he doesn't come right back, you're dead."

"You got it," Steve said.

He returned in a flash and Harry ordered him to back us out of the slip.

"Me?" Steve protested. "Wouldn't it be better if you—"

"You look like the kind of guy who's driven a boat before," Harry yelled. "Don't pretend you don't know how."

Steve grabbed the wheel and backed out like he'd been operating a yacht all his life.

I made a note to ask him about that later. When we got out of this mess. If we ever got out of this mess.

"Head in the direction of out to sea, then I'll take over," Harry shouted over the sound of the engine.

"Ay, ay, captain," Steve sarcastically shouted back.

Pulling me with him, Harry went over to the windows and slid them open. Fresh cool air blew in with the tangy smell of the sea.

"I need to go over to the shelves in the living room," I said in a strangled voice. Arty's arm around my throat was choking me.

He gave me a shove that sent me flying but this time I managed to stay on my feet. "Go ahead, keep searching," he said. "But if you don't find that package real, real, real soon, you're both going overboard."

He grabbed the wheel from Steve and began steering with one hand while waving his gun in the other.

Okay. This man was totally crazy. He'd totally lost it. He suspected deep down that I was lying about the package. But he still wanted to believe I might be telling the truth.

Only, it no longer mattered. Whether I found the package for him or didn't, I could see what he had planned for us. He was going to shoot us and throw us to the sharks.

Harry had nothing left to lose. But now, neither did I.

"You're the Prince of Pearls, aren't you?" I smirked at him. Why worry about making him mad when he was already mad? He wasn't planning to let us live anyway, so why not goad him to confess?

"Story ...?" Steve raised his eyebrows and shook his head.

I pressed on anyway. "Harry O'Toole and Arty Duncan. My, oh my," I crooned. "You know, I admire you guys. You were a couple of teenage jewel thieves who got away with it. All those extremely lucrative home robberies before the war must have made you rich."

Gripping the wheel, Harry grinned. He clearly enjoyed driving Arty's boat one-handed. And terrorizing us. Steering wildly, he laughed as he watched us stumble again and again as we got tossed about. "Yep, they could never catch us," he shouted. "We were that good."

"There were rumors about the two of you," I said, "but then the war ..."

"Yep, the war came at a good time." He turned the wheel sharply to the right and then to the left, then sped up. "We hid most of the jewels we hadn't yet fenced in a place where no one would ever find them," he shouted. "I didn't completely trust Arty, so I secretly kept some for myself. Only—"

His face darkened. "Only I was hurt bad in the war and Arty wasn't. I was in a coma over in France for a long time. Then, when I woke up, I had to have a bunch of operations to fix my face and my feet. I didn't look like myself anymore."

"That's sad," I said, meaning it despite what he was doing to us.

"Yeah. I thought it would be better to start a new life over there and forget about the jewels. So that's what I did. I truly loved Sophie. Her love for me meant more than money. But then she died." He shook his fist in the air like he was cursing the heavens and screamed, "Why did she have to die?"

He jerked the throttle forward, racing us farther and farther out to sea.

"What are you doing?" I yelled. "Slow down!"

"No way, dolly," he crowed. "I wanna see how fast this ship can go."

This was bad.

"I know how much you loved Sophie," I shouted. "I read your letter to Lily and I'm still curious. If you wanted the necklace, why didn't you just write to Penny? I'm pretty sure Penny would have given it to you. She told me she never stopped loving you. That's why she hired me in the first place, to find the necklace."

Harry stared at me, and something moved in his eyes. Like he was seeing me for the first time. "Don't you get it?" He laughed, turning the boat so sharply I was afraid we'd capsize.

"Revenge, doll," he screamed at the top of his lungs. "I wanted to get my hands on that necklace, to satisfy my deal with Gladys, but I also wanted to get back at Arty."

"For what?" Steve shouted.

Harry cut his eyes to Steve. "Isn't it obvious? When Arty came home from the war and realized I wasn't, he took all our loot for himself. The jewels we'd hidden together and planned to split—he sold them. I know he did. How else could he have become so rich?"

"Good question," Steve murmured.

"When I finally got the courage to come home after ten years in France, I was determined to begin a new life," Harry yelled. "I hid out, ashamed of my appearance. Then, snooping around, I quickly realized what Arty had done." He turned the wheel wildly back and forth. We hit a wave, and sprays of water showered the deck.

"I was right not to trust Arty," he screamed. "He used the money he got from selling the jewels on the black market to buy real estate. Making himself even richer."

"Calm down!" Steve shouted. "Slow down, please, let's not capsize."

Harry ignored him. "I decided to kill his wife in revenge," he yelled. "After I got her to steal her cousin's necklace for me, that is. So that nasty Gladys would tell me where she hid the package. Which is supposed to be on this boat!"

"I'll go search the bedrooms next," I said. "If you slow this boat down. Please."

Harry shook his head. "That package is not on this boat, and you know it, lady. You're lying."

"No, she's not," Steve shouted. "How much is the booty in that package worth, anyway?"

Harry's lips twisted into a cunning smile. "A lot. Since I never trusted Arty, I squirreled away whatever I thought I could get away with. It was my insurance policy. Which it turns out I needed."

"Only ..." His smile turned bitter as he shifted the boat into neutral, slowing our speed. "Only Gladys double-crossed me," he said sharply.

"When I got back, she was the first person I went to see. I assumed she'd be thrilled to see me, even with my good looks gone, because, let's face it, she's no great shakes herself. But no. She tricked me."

"But Lily was thrilled to see you," I said. "She truly loved you."

"Yes. I convinced her that with the money I could get for Penny's necklace, we could start a new life. Together. Lily liked that. She wanted us to run away, just me and her. She was even willing to leave her kids for me."

"But you murdered her instead," I said.

"When she arranged to give me the necklace at the party, I realized I had no choice." He laughed. "I lured her onto the balcony and after she handed it to me, I picked her up and tossed her over the rail."

"And then?" I stared at him, feeling sick. Poor, poor Lily.

He shrugged. "I put the necklace in my pocket and disappeared. Got my necklace, got my revenge."

"But you lost the necklace when you shot Gladys," I said. "It was around Gladys's neck. And now it's in police custody."

"Which is why I was forced to kidnap Arty's kids." Harry glared at me, then Steve. "I needed the ransom money. But you two interfered with that plan when I left to go grab some food. Thanks a lot."

He shifted the boat into reverse, slowing the boat even more. That made me nervous, like he was planning something. "I feel better that we're going slower now," I declared. "I'll go search the bedrooms for the package like you asked."

"Don't bother," he said. "It's over for you two. Payback time now for rescuing Arty's twins. Denying me the ransom money that I desperately needed."

"But how did you know it was us?" I shouted.

Harry smirked. "I'm smart, blondie. I have my ways. And I was thrilled to find you and what's his name—Steve—at Gladys's parents' house."

He slowed the boat, then cut the engine. "Time's up."

"For you!" Steve shouted, lunging at Harry, knocking the gun from his hand.

"Grab it!' Steve shouted to me. But Harry was too fast. He kicked it away, launching it across the slick wooden floor and under the kitchen table.

They wrestled and crashed to the floor.

I dove for the gun, hitting my head on the bottom of the table. Then, raising my chin, I saw it. A rubber swim mask. It was on a storage shelf under the table.

Oh my God. Victor Bravo's warning flashed into my brain. *When you see a swim mask, put it on.*

I grabbed the gun and mask. "Stop!" I screamed, waving the gun as I scrambled to my feet.

But I was too late. Steve and Harry had fought their way out to the edge of the deck.

Ignoring my scream, Harry shoved Steve overboard, then lost his balance and tumbled in after him.

I watched helplessly as the two men wrestled in the choppy water.

"Steve!" I shouted as they disappeared into the dark, murky abyss.

My heart clenched. Steve ... where was Steve?

I dropped the gun and adjusted the mask over my eyes.

Then I took a deep breath and jumped in.

No way was I going to let Steve drown.

Thirty

The cold water swallowed me up. Clawing my way to the surface, I gasped for breath and looked around.

I was alone. Utterly alone.

Panicking, I treaded water and tried to stay calm, focused. Steve … I had to find Steve.

Pressing the mask harder against my face, I went under again. Nothing. Only murky darkness.

No Steve, no Harry. I kicked my way back to the surface, filled my lungs with as much air as I could, and dove back under to look again.

Nothing.

Where could they be? How could they just disappear?

No, not possible, I told myself. Even if they'd managed to strangle each other to death, they wouldn't just sink to the bottom … would they?

Fighting off despair, I stayed under as long as I could, then resurfaced, took another breath and went back.

And this time, I saw something.

Bubbles.

Then flesh. Somebody's arm?

I grabbed the arm and pulled whoever it belonged to up with me.

Gasping for breath, I beamed when I saw who it was.

"Steve," I sobbed. "Steve."

Blood streamed down his face from a gash on his forehead, but he was alive. He wasn't a lifeless corpse splayed out on the bottom of the ocean, fish food. Thank God.

"Story?" he rasped. Coughing, gagging, he spit out water and gaped at me. "What are you doing?"

I grabbed his shoulder. "What does it look like? I'm rescuing you."

"But where'd you get that mask?"

"Never mind, tell you later. Where's Harry?"

"Don't know. He tried to choke me to death, but I got away." Steve pointed to the yacht, bobbing away from us in the waves. "We need to get back on the boat. Hurry."

We began swimming toward it.

But Harry blocked our way, popping up in front of us like a sea monster rising from the deep. An angry sea monster, powered by fury. Gagging for air, he launched himself at me, reaching for my throat.

I planted a foot on his chest, pushed away, then dove under the waves. Thanks to the mask, I could see his body. Eyeing one of his legs, I dug my nails into his thigh. If he wanted to fight, I'd fight.

He thrashed away from me.

I swam up, grinned at him, then went back under, grabbed his foot, and yanked him down, down, down. I was so furious I wasn't thinking straight. I wanted to drown him.

He kicked away.

I resurfaced.

Coughing violently, Harry reached for my arm.

But before he could grab me, Steve punched him in the head. Hard. Then again.

Harry's head snapped back.

Steve slammed a fist into his face.

Harry's eyes closed and his body went limp.

Slipping an arm around Harry's chest, Steve swam him toward the yacht with his free arm. "Come on, Story," he shouted, "follow me."

"What are you doing?" I swam ahead and turned to face him. "Is he dead?"

"No. He deserves to be, but he's just knocked out. We need to get him onto the boat. Tie him up before he comes to. Take him to the cops so they can arrest him. Lock him up."

"Okay." I wanted to argue that it would be impossible to get ourselves and a heavy unconscious man aboard a giant, heaving boat that was slipping away from us. Especially since it was late, and the sun was sinking below the horizon. A storm was brewing, and the waves were growing larger and darker by the minute.

But by then I'd learned that when Steve and I teamed up, nothing was impossible.

I got to the yacht first. Spotting a ladder, I grabbed onto it and yelled to Steve, "Come on, I'll help you get him on board."

It wasn't easy, but we managed, rung by rung. Steve pushing from below, me pulling from above.

When I reached the top, I scrambled onto the deck and pulled Harry onto it as Steve pushed. I looked around for Harry's gun. Not seeing it anywhere, I ran to grab some ropes.

Together, Steve and I tied up Harry up the same way he'd bound me and the twins—hands and feet trussed together. Then Steve grabbed the wheel and turned us back toward the marina.

I left Harry lying face up on the deck and ran to join Steve at the wheel.

The sun had melted down to a sliver of red on the horizon. Thunder rumbled off in the distance. It began to grow windy.

"I think a storm's coming for sure," Steve said, draping an arm around my shoulder, pulling me close.

He was soaking wet. I was soaked and shivering. But we were alive and together.

And I'd never felt warmer in my life.

———

It began to rain. Scattered drops quickly turned into a slashing downpour. "Great," Steve said, squinting into the descending darkness. "Can't hardly see a thing now."

"Harry!" I shouted, pulling away from Steve. "We need to get Harry off the deck. Right now. We don't want him to roll overboard."

"No, we need him alive," Steve agreed. "We need him to testify in court against Arty. Which I'm sure he'll do since there's no honor among jewel thieves."

A dagger of lightning slashed through inky black clouds. Seconds later, thunder boomed.

"We don't want the bastard to get hit by lightning either," Steve yelled. "Grab the steering wheel and I'll go bring him in."

"Hurry," I said, using every muscle in my body to maintain control of the heaving boat.

Steve came back, dragging a still unconscious Harry, and placed him face up next to the kitchen table. Blood streamed from Harry's nose as he snort-breathed through his mouth, exposing a bunch of broken teeth.

"You don't think he'll die here, do you?" I whispered, part of me still wishing he would.

Steve came over and grabbed the wheel. "No. Don't worry. I punched his not-so-pretty face in—but he'll live long enough to see his day in court. For murder, attempted murder, kidnapping, felony theft. If there's any justice in this world, the monster will fry in the electric chair."

Lightning split the sky again. Thunder roared.

Sweet Sailing Two pitched hard to one side, then the other.

I wrapped my arms around Steve's chest from behind and held on as he steered us through waves big enough to capsize us.

I marveled at Steve's calm focus. He couldn't see a thing but was handling the ship like a pro.

"So ... you must have done a lot of boating growing up," I shouted over the roar of the engine and the storm. "You're really good at this."

He nodded. "Grew up with boats. Sailboats, motorboats, a couple of yachts bigger than this. I'm the son of a rich man, remember?"

I could hear the grin in his voice. Steve didn't take his privileges for granted. Few people knew his secret, like I did, about being adopted at birth. I felt privileged that he'd told me. It also made me admire him more—that he acted grateful rather than entitled. Especially because his birth parents were bad people—criminals—which is why his adoption was such a secret.

I'd met his adoptive parents, and they were wonderful folks, who had made me feel welcome at their Fourth of July party. But I couldn't shake feeling self-conscious about our class differences. Steve was raised upper class, while my upbringing was classic middle. We came from different worlds, and—other than in the movies and romance novels—I knew rich boys always ended up with rich girls.

Money attracts money. That's the way it is in real life. Especially when it comes to marriage.

Steve wasn't going to marry *me*.

Sure, he wanted to date me, he wanted me to be his girlfriend. But then what? What would happen after the novelty wore off? Would I be cast aside like the others? Like poor Claudia? Would I be reduced to acting as pathetically broken-hearted as she had at that ill-fated WowWee It's Wednesday party?

The ship pitched back and forth. Waves swamped the deck. Harry would have gone overboard for sure.

"Don't worry, Story, we're going to make it," Steve shouted.

I wanted to believe him. "I hope you're right," I shouted back.

More lightning split the sky. "I am right." He pointed. "Don't you see it? The marina— just ahead."

———

Only fools would venture out in such a storm. So, Steve and I found ourselves alone at the marina when we docked and secured the yacht.

Together, we half-carried, half-dragged Harry off the boat to my T-Bird.

Thank God we'd put the top up. But we still had to deal with squeezing three people into a two-seater car, when one of those people was unconscious.

Who unfortunately began to regain consciousness the minute I turned the key in the ignition.

Thank God I was driving. Steve had insisted on it because Harry was tall and heavy and would have crushed me if I'd tried to hold him on my lap.

Steve had Harry positioned upright against him, facing forward, with Harry's head lolling on his shoulder. When Harry started moaning, Steve turned to me with a grimace. "Drive fast, Story. This isn't going to be fun."

"*Ooooo ... mmmm ...*" Moaning louder, Harry tried to kick his feet, which were pressed to the floorboard but bound tight at the ankles. He opened his eyes and rolled his head to look at me, squinting, confused. "Whoooo ... whaaaa ..."

Holding Harry around his middle, Steve tightened his grip. Not that Harry could do much since his wrists were bound in front of him. "Relax, take it easy, we'll be there soon," Steve told him through clenched teeth.

"Whaaa ...?" Harry butted his head against Steve's shoulder. "Whay rrr ..."

Driving as fast as I dared in the slashing rain, I glanced over at our confused and furious prisoner.

He tried to lift his wrists, but Steve wouldn't let him. Rolling his head back and forth, he stopped and glared at me out of one eye—the other was swollen shut.

He didn't seem to know who I was. Or maybe he'd incurred some brain damage.

Whatever.

I couldn't summon any sympathy for him and concentrated on keeping us on the road. The inside of the car was steaming up and it was hard to see out the windshield.

I glanced back at Harry. Running his tongue over his jagged front teeth, he spit out a dribble of blood. "*Shiiii … taaaa.*"

"Stop cursing, old man, we're almost there," Steve said.

"*Wha … rrr?*"

"The police station." Steve flicked a satisfied grin at me. "Story and I are going to have you arrested for attempted murder, murder, kidnapping—and, oh yeah, burglary."

THIRTY-ONE

Harry played victim.

I don't know how he thought he was going to get away with it, but he sure tried.

As Steve wrestled him out of the car at the Cape May police station, bound and bleeding, he screeched, "Help, help ..."

Nobody came out in the storm to see what his screaming was about—but when Steve and I carted him into the station and deposited him on the floor, face down, he kept up his act.

"These criminals are trying to kill me," he screamed.

That got attention.

A uniformed officer wearing a curious, bewildered grin came out from behind a reception desk, eyed Harry rolling back and forth on the floor like a trussed-up animal. "What have we here?" he asked. "Or should I say, who have we here?"

Two fellow officers joined him to witness the drama.

"This man just tried to kill *us*," Steve said. "You need to arrest him for that and a whole lot more. Is Captain Marino here? He knows us."

"Marino has the day off," the first officer said. "If this guy tried to kill you, then how did he end up like this?"

"Long story," Steve said. "We had to fight him off out at sea, where he took us in a stolen boat. Look at us, we're soaked to the bone, but not just from the storm. He literally tried to drown us in the ocean."

All three cops looked me up and down. At my wet, bedraggled hair, my soaked T-shirt, plastered to my body, at the puddles seeping from my sneakers. Then at Steve, who was in much the same condition, plus his bleeding forehead.

The officers returned their gaze to Harry, now staring up at the ceiling, mouth agape, breathing hard. One officer asked, "What happened to his teeth?"

Harry rasped, "Told you, they tried to kill—"

"No ..." Steve put a hand up. "Truth is, officers, this man is a murderer and a kidnapper and a master thief. If you untie him, please put him in handcuffs because he'll try to run. He's Harry O'Toole, a war hero declared missing and dead since D-Day who's been hiding from the law ever since."

Steve explained that we were private eyes hired to investigate Lily Duncan's murder. And that Harry had confessed to us that he'd killed Lily and kidnapped her children.

"Marino knows all about the kidnapping," Steve said, then explained our role in the recent rescue. "I wish Marino was here."

"This guy also tried to kill another woman named Gladys Jones, presently hospitalized in a coma," I said, pointing down at Harry. "He also confessed that he, along with a friend, was the notorious Prince of Pearls."

"Lies, lies ... all outrageous lies," Harry screamed. "Untie me officers, please ..."

"Wait," I said, suddenly remembering Gladys's parents. We'd left them bound and gagged hours ago. How could I have forgotten them?

"Gladys Jones's parents, Joe and Bertha Jones, can vouch that Steve and I are telling the truth," I said. "Harry tied them up before abducting Steve and me."

I gave the officers their address. "Hurry," I said. "Oh my God, I hope they're okay."

The first officer nodded. "We'll send a squad car there now. Meanwhile ..." he hitched a chin at Steve and me. "We'll get you folks some dry clothes."

He pointed to Harry. "Him, too. Along with some handcuffs."

———

It was way past my bedtime, and I was exhausted by the time the police were ready to question us.

Separately, it turned out, in adjoining interrogation rooms. Which told me they were not ready to believe our version of events over Harry's.

Yet.

They'd given me an orange prison jumpsuit to wear, three sizes too big, and clearly meant for a man, but I didn't give a fig about that. At least it was dry and warm.

I did care about being separated from Steve, though. After all we had been through, it felt as if we were being treated like suspects. Which wasn't quite true. The rational part of me knew that.

A middle-aged dark-haired cop in a suit and tie took a seat across a steel table from where I huddled, alone and angry in a slate-gray windowless interrogation room. "I'm Detective Kenneth St. John," he said. "I'm here to ask you some questions, Miss Smith. We're trying to reach Captain Marino at home, but no one is answering the phone. It's quite late. He's probably getting some much-needed shuteye. So, you have me."

I gave a lips-pressed-together sigh and murmured, "I understand." I wasn't happy about it, but I figured it was in my best interests to act polite. "Ask away. Ask me anything you want."

"The guy you and your partner dragged in here needs medical attention," he said. "He was horribly beaten up." He placed a notebook and pen in front of him, ready to take notes. "Care to explain?"

I pursed my lips, annoyed. "My partner, Steve Evans, already told the other officers that the criminal we dragged in here tried to kill us. It was self-defense."

"He has a broken nose, a broken jaw, missing and broken teeth, and very likely a concussion." The detective leaned across the table toward me. "He is claiming that you and your partner assaulted him. When he tried to stop you from stealing a friend's yacht."

My jaw dropped. "He stole the yacht. Harry O'Toole stole the yacht."

"He claims his name is not Harry O'Toole."

I stared at the detective. Blinked in confusion. "What's he saying his name is?"

"Not Harry O'Toole. He says everybody in Cape May knows Harry O'Toole was killed in the war."

I shook my head. "That's what he wants everyone to believe."

"We're looking into it."

In frustration, I pressed a hand to my forehead. "Joe and Bertha Jones will tell you he's Harry O'Toole. They knew Harry O'Toole."

"Officers have been dispatched to their house."

I closed my eyes. "Good. I'm tired. Can I go?"

"We're waiting for Joe and Bertha Jones to be brought in. To back up your story."

I opened my eyes. "Don't worry, they will."

"Who owned the yacht?" Detective St. John picked up his pen.

I chewed the side of my lip. "A man named Arty Duncan."

"Did he give you permission to use his boat?"

"No."

"So ...?"

"Mr. Duncan is a client of Steve Evans."

"Did he give Mr. Evans permission to take his boat?"

"Not technically."

"What does that mean?"

"We ended up on the boat as part of a murder investigation."

"Your victim says you stole it, and that he tried to stop you."

I blew out a breath. "Ridiculous. Harry O'Toole is no victim. It's the other way around. He stole the boat, then forced us out to sea at gunpoint."

"Where's the gun?"

"I don't know. It's probably on the bottom of the ocean right now."

"The man you are calling Harry O'Toole claims his name is Charles Harrington."

That was so ridiculous, I had to laugh. "Are you kidding?"

"What's funny, Miss Smith?"

"Trust me, the man Steve and I dragged in here is not Charles Harrington."

"He claims that he is a friend of Mr. Arty Duncan. And that Mr. Duncan was letting him and his wife, Renee, use the yacht for the weekend."

I scoffed. I had to give Harry credit for his creative cleverness. "Arty does have a friend named Charles Harrington, who does have a wife named Renee. But Charles and Renee are probably at home in bed right now. Well ... not necessarily in bed together ... Uhm ..."

"You know the Harringtons, then?"

"Yes. And Harry O'Toole is not Charles Harrington. That should be easy enough to prove. Everything Harry told you is a lie. Everything." I could not believe this was happening—not after the day I'd been through. But I wasn't surprised. Harry O'Toole was quite good at what he did.

"Please," I said. "Let me go for now. Let Mr. Evans go for now. We'll come back in the morning. I promise."

The door to the interrogation room opened and an officer poked his head in. "Joe and Bertha Jones are here," he said, then looked at me. "They were tied up and gagged, just like this lady and her friend said. By a guy named Harry O'Toole."

Detective St. John nodded. He stood up and met my gaze. "Okay, Miss Smith, you and Mr. Evans may go. We'll give you your clothes back. But do not leave town, I'm warning you, do not leave town. And be back here in the morning by ten."

———

"Geez, that was a close call," Steve said as we left the station and headed to my car. "For a minute there I thought they were going to lock us up for the night with Harry."

"You sound like you think that's funny," I said, fighting back tears. I reached for his hand and pulled him to a stop. I couldn't read his expression in the dark, but I couldn't miss the amusement in his voice.

And I saw nothing funny about our situation. The rain had stopped but my mood was as black as the night.

"Lighten up, Story," Steve said, softly. "They let us go."

"But we can't leave town. So, what do we do now?"

He put my hand to his lips and kissed it. "We make the best of it. We spend the night at Congress Hall, the best hotel in Cape May. My favorite, anyway."

My heart skittered. "Congress Hall ...?" I took back my hand. "Steve, I can't afford ..."

"Relax, I'm paying for it."

"Not again. I can't let you keep paying my way. It's not right."

"It's fine. Separate rooms, if that's what you're worried about. Come on."

I shrugged and followed him to my car. He helped me in, went around, and jumped in the driver's seat. I was in no mood to argue about where we were going. Again, I had little money on me. And no place else to go. And I was back in my still-damp shorts and T-shirt since I couldn't exactly go back out into the world wearing prison scrubs.

All I wanted to do was strip my clothes off and crawl into a warm bed.

But not alone.

I suddenly realized I did not want to be alone, and I couldn't fight the feeling. I wanted to be with Steve. My heart wanted to spend the night in his arms, while my head was screaming *no ... no ... no ... bad idea.*

He glanced over at me as we drove through dark, puddled streets. "You're quiet. That's not like you. Are you okay?"

I was far from it. I'd narrowly escaped death more than once that day. But I couldn't tell him the real reason for my fraught silence. Didn't dare.

He glanced at me again. "Are you shaking?"

"I'll be alright."

"You cold?"

"My clothes are still wet."

"I know, mine, too. Don't worry, they'll give us guest robes at the hotel. Our clothes will dry by morning."

A nice, dry, fluffy robe sounded like heaven, but ... "Congress Hall is expensive," I said. "Are you sure you want to do this?" My voice sounded tight and squeaky, and I hated not having the money to pay my own way. Like not having enough money was some kind of moral failing on my part.

"Stop worrying about the money," Steve said.

"What if they don't have any rooms available?" I sniffed. "It's almost midnight. It's July. The peak of the summer season ..." And God forbid ... what if they only had one room available?

Steve chuckled. "Relax. We have reservations. I called and made them from the police station. The cops insisted that I give them the name of the place where we'd be staying and lucky for us Congress Hall happened to have two adjacent rooms. Something about a cancellation."

"Oh, okay."

"You didn't want to spend the night in a cell next to Harry, did you? Don't think we would have gotten much sleep. Didn't you hear him howling for a doctor when we left?"

"Yeah ..." I didn't think I would be getting much sleep in any case. Thinking about Steve in the next room ... longing to be in his bed. Oh, no, oh, no, oh, no. What was wrong with me?

I didn't say anything else. Couldn't. My mouth was suddenly so dry I couldn't move my tongue.

Steve shot me a puzzled look but didn't try to make any more conversation as we turned into the hotel parking lot.

My shaking got worse. I opened my door and jumped out before he could come around and help me. I didn't want him to take my hand or put his arm around my shoulder because ...

My face went hot. I couldn't even look at him.

I hurried ahead to the lobby and waited for him to catch up. As if sensing my mood, he didn't question me.

The clerk behind the counter gave us a curious look as we stepped forward to check in. "Any luggage?"

"No," Steve said stiffly, reaching for the keys to both rooms. "We're just here for the night. But we will need robes."

"They're in your rooms, sir."

"Thank you."

I followed Steve up the stairs to the second floor. He unlocked and opened my door for me. "Oceanfront room for you, my dear." He flicked me a questioning smile when I just stared at him, then dropped the key in my outstretched palm.

Our eyes locked.

He wasn't touching me. But I knew he wanted to. He was

pressing his lips together and standing uncharacteristically still, like he didn't know what to do next, like he was holding himself back.

Like he wanted to kiss me—but wasn't sure what would happen if he did—and wasn't willing to take the chance that it would go badly.

I wanted him to kiss me. I really, really, really wanted him to kiss me. But I knew what would happen if I let him. We'd kissed before, but not in a situation like this. If he kissed me now, I wouldn't be going into my oceanfront room alone.

"Good night, Story," he whispered, his voice husky with desire.

"Good night, Steve," I whispered back. But I didn't move. I wanted to move. I wanted my legs to move. But I couldn't seem to make them move.

His lips twitched into a smile, that smile of his that always grabbed my heart and wouldn't let it go. That one-sided quirky grin that twinkled his eyes and shot desire into my soul. "Story?" he whispered.

"Steve ..."

"What do you want?"

"I want you to kiss me."

That smile deepened. "If I kiss you," he whispered, "I might not stop."

"Kiss me then. And don't stop."

"Are you sure?"

"Yes ..."

He pulled me to him and pressed his lips to mine.

Sizzling hot desire surged through me as I wrapped my arms around him and kissed him back, not caring what happened next.

To hell with what happened next. My world was spinning, spinning, spinning out of control—and I didn't care. Kissing Steve was exciting, not scary, thrilling, not shameful. All that mattered was that he was holding me and kissing me in that hallway, and I didn't want the raging, burning bliss of it to ever stop.

Passion was setting fire to all my doubts and inhibitions, burning them up and melting them away.

I don't know how long we stood there with our lips locked, pressing our bodies together like we were one. Then he drew back and looked into my eyes with a yearning that left me breathless. Cradling my face in his hands, he showered it with kisses.

I'd never felt so loved. I'd never felt such lust.

His hands slid down my cheeks, then down my neck, to my breasts.

I kicked the door open and backed into the room, pulling Steve with me.

He pulled away. "No, wait ... we can't do this."

I blinked at him, confused. "What ...?"

"We can't do this," he said, breathing hard. "Believe me, I want to ... I really do ...but you're not ready."

My jaw dropped. What did he mean—I wasn't ready? I was ready.

"I'm ready," I said.

"No. You're not. You'll hate yourself in the morning. And you'll hate me."

I gaped at him.

The door was half open and Steve was backing out of it.

I reached for him. "No, don't go."

He took my hand and squeezed it. "Someday this will be right for us, but not now. We have too much going on, you and me. With our businesses, with our case. And you're a virgin, aren't you?"

I widened my eyes and swallowed. "How do you know?"

That smile of his returned, magnified. "Believe me, I know."

I stared at him and realized I'd been wrong to judge him as a womanizer, a player, as someone who would love me and leave me. I wanted him more than ever. But he was right. I would hate myself in the morning. Not him. I'd never hate him. But I would hate myself.

I pulled my hand away. Gave him a shy smile. "You're right. I'm not ready. I mean, I am …but I'm not. We do have too much going on to ruin our partnership with lust."

"And our friendship." He grinned. "Which is what it needs to stay for now. Although you know and I know this is more than lust."

My heart slowly sank to the floor. He loved me but was leaving me. I felt abandoned and confused and ridiculously relieved all at once. "Good night, Steve," I whispered.

"Good night, Story." He blew me a kiss. "See you in the morning."

THIRTY-TWO

My fear that sleep would elude me that night proved true. Not because of Steve, but because I dreamed about Dean. Nightmarish dreams which kept waking me with a pounding heart and overwhelming guilt.

I'd been worried that Steve would keep me awake, keenly aware of his presence in the room next to mine. There was a connecting door between us that I knew I could open and step through at any time.

And that door beckoned me to do just that as I stripped off my clammy clothes and wrapped my naked body in the fluffy white robe laying neatly across my bed.

In my imagination I watched a brazen version of myself slip into Steve's bed, delighting him with my sudden surprise presence.

But the wiser version of me shut that vision down, wrestling those imagined wonton thoughts out of my head as I turned off the lights.

It wasn't long after finally falling asleep that I dreamed about Dean. Who had loved me, too.

"I miss you Story," he murmured, smiling at me the way he always used to, a thatch of his sandy hair falling onto his forehead. Pushing it back, away from his eyes, he held my gaze and asked, "What happened to us?"

Speechless, I stared at him. He looked good. Happy and healthy, just the way he'd looked on our last day together—right before I broke his heart. Before I ripped it out of his chest and tore it to shreds.

"You died," I cried, then woke up, my heart pounding so hard I thought I'd have a heart attack. Which is what I deserved because of what I'd done to him.

I threw off the sheets, stumbled to the window, and gazed down at the dark beach below. White capped waves rolled onto shore. I hugged myself and shivered.

I glanced over at the door to Steve's room and longed to run to him. I wanted to, badly. I wanted him to comfort me, enfold me in his arms, kiss me, tell me he loved me.

But I didn't deserve that. I didn't deserve Steve's love. Because I was the reason Dean had died. Dean was a good man, and I didn't deserve the love of another one.

Numb, I stumbled back to bed and crawled back between the sheets and cried myself to sleep.

And that's when Dean came to me again. "I loved you," he said, waving a ring with a diamond as big as a coconut in my face.

He grabbed my left hand and tried to slip it on my ring finger. I jerked away, crying, "No, please, no."

"But you said you'd marry me," he whimpered, then grabbed my hand again and forced the ring on. It was too tight, and my hand caught fire, and I screamed so loudly I woke myself up.

I sat up, hoping I hadn't screamed for real. What if Steve heard me? He would come to see what was wrong and what would I tell him?

I stared at our connecting door and held my breath, willing it to stay closed.

It did.

With a shaky sigh, I laid back down and tried once more to fall asleep. But I could not stop thinking about Dean.

I'd met him at a friend's party while in my junior year at Bryn Mawr College, and we hit it off. He was nice and he was fun. He became my boyfriend because I was supposed to have a boyfriend at that point in my life, at least according to society and everybody I knew.

Unlike my friends, I had not obsessed about landing a cute boyfriend in high school and getting married and having babies. No, I wanted to be the 1950s equivalent of Nellie Bly, a female Victorian journalist who traveled the world and wrote about her adventures. I did not want any guy holding me back and sabotaging my goals.

Dean was so accommodating and easy going that I never worried about him doing that. He loved me, a love I took for granted as something I just deserved, but I wasn't sure I loved him back because I had no idea what romantic love was supposed to feel like.

People said we looked good together, and making out with him was fun. Not all the way of course, because good girls didn't do that, and I was a good girl. I felt safe with him. He allowed me to focus my true passions on my English classes and my career goals. My life was good.

Until the day he asked me to marry him. And I couldn't find a way to say no. I'd played the game too well, assuming I could keep playing it forever.

Wrong.

"Great, wonderful, fantastic!" Dean beamed at me after I'd accepted his proposal with an awkward "yes." He reached for my hand and kissed it.

It was early summer, and we were in his father's 1948 Buick, parked by a lake with the windows down. "When can we get married?" he asked. The birds in the trees went silent, as if listening for my answer.

I didn't know what to say. What was I doing? I wasn't ready to marry him, or anyone. I had only graduated from college the week before and was eagerly hunting for my first job as a newspaper reporter. "Uh, I don't know ..." I stammered. "I have an interview lined up next week for my dream job and right now I can't think about anything else."

"Oh." He nervously cleared his throat. "Well, after we get married, you won't have to work."

"Oh." I eyed him with surprise. "But I want to work. I thought you knew that."

"But I'm going to be President of the United States one day." He flicked me a confident, you-already-knew-that grin. "A politician's wife can't work. It would look bad."

He was a political science major at the University of Pennsylvania, trying to get into law school. While he'd boasted about his future goals, I had never taken him seriously.

I had my out then—and should have taken it. I didn't want to marry him. It would have been the fair and honest thing to do to decline his proposal right then. But he was looking at me with such eager little-boy eyes that I just said, "Can we talk about this later?"

"So, you will marry me?"

"Uh...yes ... but we can't set a date ... yet ..." Swallowing hard, I looked down at my left hand. "Because I don't have a ring."

"Oh—that." His eyes danced. "That's easy, let's go pick one out."

My head was spinning. "What? When?"

"Today? Tomorrow? As soon as possible."

It was too much, too fast. I had to stall. "After my job interview," I blurted. "I really do want that job and if they see that I'm engaged they might think I'm not serious about a long-term career."

He sighed. "Okay ..."

"Let's keep our engagement a secret," I said. "I insist. We can tell nobody until I have that ring on my finger. Promise?"

He groaned. "Okay, I promise."

But when the time came, I couldn't do it. When we pulled up to the jewelry store, I went numb with fear. I felt like a wild bird being forced into a cage, and I knew that a ring would lock me in that cage forever.

"I can't do this," I whispered. "I'm sorry. I can't marry you. I'm sorry."

"What?" The stricken look on his face went from confusion to shock. From disbelief to despair. "What, why?"

"I'm not ready to get married," I whispered. "I can't marry you. Not now. Not ever."

"What ... but ..."

"Please just take me home."

"But I thought you loved me," he pleaded, the agony in his voice jabbing a knife into my heart.

"I *thought* I loved you. But I don't think I do. Because I don't think I really know what true love is."

He didn't say anything else then. His face drained of all color, pressing his lips together as if to hold back tears, he did what I'd asked and drove me home. In complete silence. Like he had nothing else to say. Truthfully, what was there to say?

I wanted him to be angry. I wanted him to call me a liar. That's what I deserved.

But he said nothing, and his strained silence made it so much worse.

"I'm sorry," I cried when we pulled up to my parent's house. Feeling horrible, just wanting to get away from him, I said, "Goodbye, Dean."

No goodbye, either.

I ran up to my room and flung myself onto my bed because I didn't want my parents or my brother to see me. I needed to be alone.

Staring up at the ceiling with teary eyes, I felt ashamed but also relieved. I'd set myself free, but I could never forgive myself.

In a stupor, I don't know how long I laid there. But at some point, I heard a knock on the front door.

Heard my mother answer it. Heard her sharp cry. Heard her call my name.

I ran down, alarmed. A policeman was in our living room, holding his hat to his chest, looking like he'd rather be anywhere else.

"Dean's dead," my mother cried. "His mother sent this nice officer to tell you because you and Dean were practically engaged. And she thought you should know."

My mother's voice sounded hollow and far away. I couldn't take in what she was saying. It didn't make sense. I'd just seen Dean a few hours before. I squinted at her, confused. "What?"

"He shot himself in the head," the officer said. "His mother found him on the floor of his room. With his father's gun in his hand."

I clapped a hand to my mouth, trying not to throw up. Dean was dead because of me. I'd killed him.

"It's possible he was just examining the gun or getting ready to clean it," the officer said. "But it looks like he intended to end his life."

I dropped to my knees and began to sob.

My mother knelt next to me and put her arm around me to comfort me. "I know you loved him," she crooned. "He had his whole life ahead of him, with you. It doesn't make sense."

Sobs wracked my body. Dean had been facing the rest of his life without me. Our engagement had been a secret, and I had not told anyone we'd broken up. Now I felt like his death was my fault.

I had not deserved his love. And now I would not deserve any man's love. I'd wanted a life as a career woman—and now I was going to get it. My punishment would be to live life alone. That would be my fate because that is what I deserved. I certainly didn't deserve Steve.

Friends flocked to Dean's funeral. His parents and siblings hugged me. No one blamed me, but I blamed myself, feeling like a complete fraud.

And ... I never told anyone the truth about Dean's death. Until I'd told Steve, during a recent unguarded moment when we were working together. He was the only person on the planet who knew.

I didn't get any more sleep that night. I didn't dare close my eyes because I didn't want to see Dean again.

Lying in the dark, I stared at the door to Steve's room, knowing I had no right to even think about opening it. Because Dean had come to remind me of what I'd done.

To remind me that I had no right to Steve's love.

THIRTY-THREE

"You look like crap," Steve told me the next morning when I joined him for breakfast in the Congress Hall dining room.

Detecting a mischievous, teasing gleam in his eye, I didn't find my situation amusing. "Gee, thanks," I said, plopping myself down in the chair across from him. I gave him a weak smile. "You look well rested, must be nice. I see you've already ordered."

Eyeing me with concern, he took a bite of egg, followed it with a sip of coffee, waved a waitress over to our table, then turned back to me. "You have dark circles under your eyes, and I don't think I've ever seen you wear your hair like that. What's wrong?"

I sighed. I'd jammed my hair into a sloppy ponytail that was probably sticking out all over and was so tired I didn't care. "Couldn't sleep." I yawned. No use pretending.

Steve flicked me a slow, flirty, suggestive grin. "Because of me I hope?"

Frowning, I shook my head.

"Oh. Bad dreams about our case?"

I shook my head again. "Nightmares. About Dean."

His grin faded. "Oh ... that guy. Again."

The waitress stepped up to our table. I had no appetite but knew I had to eat something, so I ordered toast and coffee.

"She needs more than that," Steve smiled at the waitress, then eyed me sternly. "Bring her some eggs, sunny side up, with bacon and orange juice, too."

"I don't know if I'll be able to eat all that," I protested after she hurried off to complete his order. "I'm not hungry."

"Because of Dean?" Steve didn't try to hide his impatience. "Forget about him. I've told you before that his death was not your fault. You need to stop blaming yourself."

"It's not that easy."

"Then you need to try harder."

"I didn't want to dream about him, I just did. And then I couldn't go back to sleep. I'm sorry, I'm going to be a mess today."

Steve's frown softened. "You should have dreamt about me instead. I dreamed about you. About those kisses ..."

Those kisses. How could I ever forget those kisses? But I didn't want to talk about them, so I didn't say anything. I didn't want to lead Steve on the way I'd led Dean on, thinking we had a future together. Although, now with Steve, I knew what being in love felt like. And denying it was agony.

The waitress brought my food. I dug in so I didn't have to talk.

"You have an appetite all of the sudden," Steve remarked as he watched me eat. "Good girl, we have a long day ahead of us. Starting with the police, who are expecting us back at the station soon."

"Right," I said, happy to change the subject. "Don't know what more we can tell them. Let's just hope Harry has changed his mind and confessed."

———

We showed up at the station a few minutes early to keep the cops happy.

With a decent breakfast in my belly, I was feeling somewhat better and was grateful to Steve for that.

Joe and Bertha Jones were at the station when we arrived, also raising my spirits. They didn't appear to have suffered any lasting harm from being tied up and gagged by Harry O'Toole—a huge relief.

Marino was there and said hi. As was Detective St. John, who gave us the good news that Harry had broken down and confessed.

Ushering the Joneses and Steve and me into an interrogation room, St. John shut the door and told us that Harry has confessed to not only being the Prince of Pearls, but also to murder, attempted murder, and kidnapping.

Then he handed Steve his pistol. "We recovered this from the Jones residence. Right where you said you'd dropped it in the fight with O'Toole. Thought you might want it back."

"Thanks." Steve smiled. "But how'd you get O'Toole to confess to everything? Last night he was denying it all, insisting that Story and I were the liars."

St. John's lips formed a crafty grin. "He kept yelling from his cell that he wanted to see a doctor and a dentist. So ... we promised to send for a doctor and a dentist when and if he told us the truth. He caved. Oh, what a little pain will do."

"So ... Steve's not going to be charged with assault, right?" I met Steve's gaze and smiled. "That's great."

"No, Mr. Evans inflicted injuries on Mr. O'Toole in self-defense," St. John said. "Mr. O'Toole made that clear, but he also made it clear that he wants his former friend, Arty Duncan, to be arrested as soon as possible for being his partner in crime as the Prince of Pearls. Says *Princes* of Pearls is more like it. As I suppose you know, he's bitter about Mr. Duncan ending up with all their loot."

"So bitter that he took revenge by murdering Arty's wife and kidnapping his kids," Steve said. "Arty did not deserve that but he does deserve to pay for robbing people."

"Not so fast," the detective said. "We have one problem. We have only Harry O'Toole's word for it that Arty Duncan helped him steal those jewels, which Mr. Duncan will undoubtedly deny. We have no other proof."

"Gladys ..." Bertha Jones said. "Gladys knows the truth, I'm sure of it. She was Harry's lover and believed she was his fiancé. There's a good chance that Harry told her everything—that he and Arty were partners—when he gave her that package."

"If only she could talk," Joe Jones muttered. "I'm sure she'd testify to everything she knows in court."

"If only," I agreed. "Gladys is a key witness. And the only one who can tell us where she hid the package, which still needs to be explained."

Bertha Jones squirmed in her chair. "Gladys will probably fear getting arrested, too, if she spills the beans."

"Don't worry about that," Detective St. John told her. "If she helps put master criminals away, I'm sure the law will give her leniency. In any case, she needs to do the right thing."

"If she lives—and if she wakes up." I met Steve's eye and knew he was thinking what I was thinking. "When we leave here," I said, "we need to go see Gladys in the hospital."

The Joneses exchanged meaningful glances and Joe said, "We're coming with you."

————

The sound of her mother's voice pleading for her to wake up brought Gladys out of her long coma at last.

Bertha Jones gasped when her daughter opened one eye, then the other, and stared at her in bleary confusion.

"Mother ...?" Gladys's voice was so weak that I thought I might have imagined it. Her lips barely moved, as if uttering just that one word took a great deal of effort.

"Baby ..." Bertha put a hand on her daughter's forehead. "Thank God ... you're coming back to us, honey."

Gladys blinked her eyes, then let them close, as if keeping them open was too difficult.

But this was good. Very good. She was waking up. Hope fluttered like butterfly wings in my chest.

"We need to tell her police guard," Steve said, turning to fetch the uniformed officer stationed outside her room. "He needs to hear whatever she might say."

"Gladys ..." Her mother leaned over Gladys's still body, covered by a thin gray hospital blanket, her bony hands lying limp on her chest. Even covered by the blanket, I could detect that Gladys had lost a great deal of weight. I don't know much about medical procedures, but I knew that the tubes running fluid into her arms had been keeping her alive.

"Hmmm ..." Gladys's low moan made all of us surrounding her smile—me, Steve, her parents, her police guard, and a nurse who announced she was going to go get the doctor.

"You've got a lot of company, honey," her father told her. "You're a popular gal. Open your eyes again and you'll see."

Gladys's eyes opened again, and I wondered how well she could see and what she would think of me standing there, looking down at her. Would she remember me? Why we'd met? Remember what we'd been discussing before she was shot?

Moving her eyes from her mother to her father and then to Steve and to me, she kept her gaze on me and slowly moved a trembling hand to her neck. "The necklace ...?" she croaked.

"The police have it," I said. "Do you remember me?"

"Yes." She closed her eyes again and keeping them closed, murmured, "What happened?"

"He shot you," I said. "Harry O'Toole shot—"

"Please," the police guard stepped between Steve and me to get closer to the bed. "Let me ask the questions now. This is important."

Nodding, I pressed my lips together, anxious to find out everything Gladys knew.

"Miss Jones," the officer said, "do you remember who shot you?"

"Yes." Her eyes fluttered open. "Harry O'Toole."

"Are you sure it was him?"

"Positive."

"Do you know why he shot you?"

"Yes." She focused her eyes on me. "He wanted my necklace."

I knew that was only part of the truth. He'd also wanted his package, and since she'd lied to him about its whereabouts, he'd taken revenge. Harry was big on revenge. He also didn't want Gladys talking to me.

And now she was.

"Where did you hide Harry's package?" I asked her. "That's what—"

"Let me ask the questions," the officer said, turning to glare at me.

"What package?" Closing her eyes again, Gladys murmured, "I don't know ..."

"Harry has—" I swallowed the rest of my words when Steve grabbed my arm in warning. It was frustrating not to be able to ask questions because I knew far more than the officer. I shot Steve a just-trying look and clamped my mouth shut.

"It's alright, Gladys," her father said. "You need to come clean and tell the truth because they caught Harry. He's in jail and he's confessed to everything."

"Sir!" The officer snapped at him. "Let me—"

"Harry gave you a package to hide before he shipped off to war." Joe Jones said, ignoring the officer's order to shut up. "No use trying to lie about it now."

"Not lying." Gladys muttered, keeping her eyes tightly closed.

"Where is the package?" the officer asked. "Where is it now?"

No answer.

"What was in it?" the officer pressed. "We have reason to believe it was stolen jewelry."

No answer.

"Where is it, honey?" Bertha Jones pleaded. She picked up her daughter's hand and squeezed it. "Come on, tell us, because you're going to get arrested if you don't."

Gladys opened her eyes. "Arrested?" she whispered.

"For helping Harry O'Toole get away with being the Prince of Pearls," I blurted out, no longer caring if I got in trouble for helping with this bedside interrogation. "Harry told us what was in that package and that he gave it to you to hide and we need to know where it is now. Please, tell us, please."

Gladys stared at me unblinking—for so long I was afraid she wasn't going to say anything else. Finally, with a sigh, she attempted a smile. Her chapped, pale lips quivered up. "Okay … okay. I sold it. To Arty Duncan. Long, long time ago."

I wrinkled my forehead. "Arty? How? Why?"

"I knew Harry wasn't coming home. That he wasn't ever going to marry me. So … I sold it. To Arty, his partner in crime. I needed the money."

Pow. That was bombshell news. But before anyone could say anything else, the nurse came back with a red-faced, white-coated doctor who eyed everybody crowding around Gladys's bed with extreme displeasure.

"Please, please, everyone needs to leave the room this minute. All of you, go wait in the hallway," he ordered. "I need to examine my patient—and she cannot be subjected to any more stress."

Out in the hall, Steve pulled me aside. "They're probably going to order an arrest warrant for Arty. He's my client, and to be fair to him I would like to get back to Philly, pronto."

I nodded. "At least he should be happy to hear that you accomplished what he hired you to do." I gave a wry smile. "You found out who murdered his wife. You got the perpetrator arrested."

"Yeah," Steve said. "But he's not going to like the rest of it."

THIRTY-FOUR

The police arrived at Arty 's house before we did.

When we pulled up to his mansion that afternoon, a half dozen Philadelphia Police Department squad cars, lights flashing red, were parked by the front door.

"Great," Steve muttered, drumming his fingers on the steering wheel as he eyed the scene.

Great was right. Here we'd made the trip from Cape May in record time, without going home to change out the clothes we'd been wearing for days.

I chewed the side of my lip. "Well, what do we do now?" I asked, exhausted from lack of sleep and feeling horribly grungy and grouchy. All I wanted to do was go home and get some sleep. Let the police take Arty in and do with him whatever they wanted.

Steve blew out a breath. "Guess I'm just going to have to talk to Arty at the station."

But that wasn't going to be that easy. Because many minutes went by as we waited in the car, with the top down, for Arty to be brought out in handcuffs.

Finally, a swarm of police officers came out the front door without Arty. One of them came over to us. Squinting at Steve, he asked, "You a friend of Mr. Duncan?"

Steve glanced at me, then back at the officer. "I'm his private investigator and this is my associate. We were hoping to speak to Arty, but it doesn't seem like a good time."

"Welp, apparently, he's not here." Pursing his lips sarcastically, the officer stroked his chin. "His mother-in-law says he took off with the nanny for parts unknown."

Oh brother. Why did that not surprise me? Still ... "Arty took off with Stella?" I furrowed my brow. "What about his little girls?"

The officer hitched his chin at the house. "Left them with Grandma. Don't know how, but he must have got word we were headed his way, so he took off with his teenage babysitter."

"With his mistress, you mean." I pushed a loose strand of hair away from my eyes. "His mother-in-law, Anna Ash, must be fit to be tied. We need to speak to her."

"Be my guest," the officer said. "She claims to have no idea where Mr. Duncan went but maybe you can get more out of her than we've been able to. She's one angry old lady, I can tell you that."

Angry didn't begin to describe Anna Ash. Her face was flushed and her eyes snapped fury when she greeted Steve and me at the door, then waved for us to follow her into the living room, her high heels clicking furiously against the hardwood floor.

Her gray hair neatly pulled into a bun, she was dressed in a tailored blouse and skirt, as if she had planned to spend the day taking tea with friends. Not dealing with police officers who had come to arrest her son-in-law.

"I could strangle Arty," she said. "I would, too, if it wasn't for Janey and Jeannie. Somebody's got to take care of them."

Wow, what a difference a few days had made. Anna had projected a noble, quiet pride in the face of grief the last time I'd been in her presence. She was still steely now, but also steaming, like a tea kettle ready to explode. And who could blame the poor woman?

"Where are the children?" Steve asked.

She pointed a finger up. "In the playroom. I sent them up there, promising to take them for ice cream this afternoon if they did as Granny asked. Poor things were scared to death when the police came pounding on the door, demanding to see their daddy."

She scrunched up her nose in disgust. "He wasn't here of course. Because he'd run off with Stella, who he'd refused to fire after the kidnapping incident, despite my pleading. Of all the ..."

"Any idea where Arty and Stella went?" Steve walked over and took a seat on the sofa.

"No."

I sat down next to Steve. "How did Arty know the police were coming?"

Anna sat down in a chair by the fireplace and smoothed her skirt over her knees. "I have no idea," she said, her voice tight. "I wasn't even aware that he and Stella had left until the police arrived. I was in the kitchen with the twins. They'd been outside playing, and I was preparing them a snack when we heard the commotion at the door."

Steve nodded. "What happened next?"

"When I couldn't find Arty, the police searched the house, I suppose to see if he was hiding in a closet or something. Then when I couldn't find Stella either, I ran to the garage and discovered one of his automobiles was missing. His Bentley Continental." She rolled her eyes. "How many people own a Bentley? It won't exactly blend in on the road."

"What color is it?" I asked.

"Dark red. Almost maroon."

"Hmmm," Steve said, "I agree, that vehicle should be easy to spot. Unless he has it parked in a garage somewhere. Do you have *any* idea where he might have gone?"

"No. I already told police that." She fixed her gaze on me. "Tell me, Miss Smith, what is this all about, anyway? What exactly do they want with Arty? The police would not tell me. Just that he was wanted for questioning and that they needed to take him downtown. Were they going to arrest him?"

I hated to be the one to tell her. "Apparently, he was one of the Princes of Pearls. Have you heard of them?"

She sniffed, pulling a hanky out of her skirt pocket, and dabbing her nose with it. "I'm sorry, I've heard of the Prince of Pearls. Jewel thief. I thought there was just one."

"Story and I just learned that apparently there were two," Steve said. "Arty was one of them and the other was his high school buddy, Harry O'Toole."

"Who, though reportedly killed in the war, is still alive." I filled her in on how Steve and I had caught the supposedly dead war hero. I left out that Harry had confessed to killing her daughter, Lily, and all the rest of it, knowing she would find that out soon enough. The poor lady was already reeling.

Her face had gone alarmingly white, and I was glad she was sitting down because she looked in danger of fainting. She opened her mouth and gaped at me, as if she wanted to say something, but couldn't put the words together.

"Grannie-Annie?"

Anna turned toward the staircase. "Oh, hi, Janey," she said, her voice shaky. "Are you alright, dear?"

Janey, dressed in pink shorts and a striped pink-and-white T-shirt, crept down the stairs with fear in her eyes, as if a scary monster might be waiting to grab her. "Can me and Jeannie come down now?" she whimpered. "We're tired of playing."

Jeannie, dressed in a purple version of her sister's outfit, trailed behind her, looking equally frightened.

Poor things. My heart broke for them. They'd lost their mother, and now their father had run off with their poor excuse for a nanny.

Lucky for them they had a strong, loving grandmother. "Of course you may come down now," she called, holding out her arms. They ran to her, jumped onto her lap, and snuggled close.

"Don't worry, everything is going to be okay, my darlings," she said murmured. "The police are going to find your daddy and Miss Stella, and Grannie-Annie is going to take care of you."

Steve stood and flashed the girls a sympathetic smile. "You know what? Miss Smith and I are going to go help the police find your daddy. Do you have any idea where he could have gone? Do you know if he has any secret places where he likes to go?"

Janey's eyes lit up at the word secret. She leaned across her grandmother's bosom and cupped a hand around her sister's ear. Jeannie grinned and whispered something back.

"Daddy has another house," Janey declared, then clapped a hand over her mouth, as if telling might get her in trouble.

"Yeah. It looks like a little castle." Jeannie grinned. "Daddy said it's his fairy princess house. He took us there once."

I shot Steve an oh-wow look. Of course. Leave it to Arty to have a secret house. He was a real estate investor and developer and probably owned quite a few houses. Why not keep one for his own private use? As a place to bring women who were not his wife.

My eyes cut to Anna. If her shocked expression was any indication, she had known nothing about Arty's secret castle. Neither had Lily, I was willing to bet.

"And ... where is this fairy princess house?" Steve asked with cool curiosity, as if he was inquiring about a castle in a nursery rhyme. "Is it far away?"

"Not far," Janey said. "It's in a park. In the middle of a big, big park."

Steve's eyes met mine. "There are a lot of parks in Philly. I wonder which one?"

"There's a sign," Jeannie said. "A big sign on the gate. With a giant lion on it."

"Lion Gate Park." I smiled grimly. "I know where that is. It has flower gardens ... and ponds ... and a caretaker cottage that ..."

"Resembles a castle ..." Steve jumped to his feet and held out a hand to help me up. "Come on, let's go."

———

Lion Gate Park was a short drive south from Chestnut Hill, so it didn't take us long to get there.

Just north of the larger and more well-known Fairmount Park, it was smaller—about 1,000 acres—but just as beautiful, with rolling hills, meandering trails, shady woodlands, and pretty duck ponds.

Arty's fairy princess castle—more like a fairy princess cottage—faced one of the ponds. And lucky for us, did not include a garage for automobiles because Arty's Bentley was parked at the rear of the building.

"Gotcha, Arty." Steve grinned. "Now all we have to do is talk you into giving yourself up."

"Right." I stared at the two-story stone building, rounded in the front with a wide, wooden front door, slate roof, and narrow windows. Two soaring chimneys with a roof-top widow's walk did sort of make the place look like a castle—if you used your imagination.

Under the circumstances, it looked like a fortress to me. Pursing my lips, I turned to Steve. "You don't think Arty's just going to surrender, do you?"

He winced. "Maybe if we just go up and knock on the door and ask nice?"

"He might shoot you, Steve. Then what?"

"I don't think he owns a gun."

"But what if he does?"

"Then you'll need to drive off and get help."

I shook my head. "Nice try, ace. If he does have a gun, he'll probably shoot my tires out."

Steve opened his door and got out. "Don't worry, if Arty even owns a gun he probably doesn't know how to use it. Anyway, I've got mine on me. Just stay—"

Bang. Crack. A bullet hit the trunk of a big oak tree near our car, not more than twenty feet to my right.

I ducked down below the windshield, my heart racing a million miles an hour. Arty owned a gun, alright.

Steve dove back into the driver's seat and ducked down, too. "Great. It doesn't look like Arty's going to go willingly. Not willingly at all."

"Looks like he's trying to kill us," I hiss-whispered. "What now?"

Steve raked his fingers through his hair. "We should not have let him see us. As soon as we saw his car was here, we should have turned around and gone straight to the cops. This is my fault, I'm the experienced P.I. Should have known ... Damn. Now I'm going to have to keep him here while you go get help, Story. We can't let him take off and he will if we both leave."

I pressed a hand to my chest to calm my wildly beating heart. What was Steve saying? "Wait," I whispered. "You want me to take off without you?"

"I have a gun, Story. You don't. I'm going to take up position behind that tree that just got hit and shoot it out with Arty if he tries to leave."

"Steve ... no!"

"Don't think we have a choice," he said grimly as he got out of the car.

Bang. A bullet whizzed past Steve. He threw himself to the ground and scramble-crawled over to the tree.

Bang, bang, bang. More bullets hit the wide trunk, sending pieces of bark flying. Using the tree for cover, Steve fired back.

I watched in horror. Too frozen with fear to even move. My brain was screaming at me to jump into the driver's seat, take off, go get the cops.

Instead, I watched Steve and Arty take turns shooting at each other, turning the once peaceful park into a war zone.

Suddenly, the screeching of police sirens added to the chaos. Seconds later a swarm of police cruisers pulled up next to me and officers jumped out, with semi-automatic rifles ready.

"It's Arty Duncan," I shouted. "The guy you're looking for. He's in there with the teenage nanny. At least I think the nanny's in there, too."

From his position behind the tree, Steve nodded in confirmation.

One of the officers had a bullhorn. "Arty Duncan—come out now—hands up! *Now.*"

Silence.

My eyes darted back and forth between Steve and the massive front door. What was Arty thinking? Surely, he wasn't stupid enough to risk a shoot-out with police.

"Come out now—or we're coming in," the officer with the bullhorn shouted.

I held my breath. Would Arty risk his life—and Stella's? Did he care for Stella at all? If he did, he would do the right thing.

Silence. Except for the blood pounding in my ears.

Finally, after many long minutes, the door opened and Arty walked out, hands up, followed by Stella, pale and trembling.

Two officers ran over, cuffed them, and led them to separate patrol cars.

Steve ran over to me. "Let's go," he shouted, turning the key in the ignition and gunning the engine. "We need to follow the police. My idiot client just added attempted murder and resisting arrest to his troubles and I want to be in on his interrogation."

"Me, too," I said, but I was suddenly overwhelmed with guilt and shame. Because I had just sat there, huddled in my car, unarmed, because after losing my gun, I'd never replaced it. Immobilized by fear, I'd done nothing but watch Steve and the police do it all.

"I'm sorry, Steve," I cried. "I'm sorry that I didn't go for help like you wanted me to. I couldn't move. I was scared—scared out of my mind that you were going to be killed."

He floored the gas pedal, keeping the parade of flashing-light police cars in sight as they left the park. "Don't worry." He glanced over at me with a grim smile. "Things were happening too fast—besides, if you get into a shootout in a quiet city park, you're bound to get the cop's attention." He patted my arm. "The important thing is that I'm still alive."

"Thank God." I closed my eyes and took deep breaths as we sped toward the police station. I could not stop shaking. Every part of my body shook, and my mind raced as I kept thinking about what had just happened.

Steve could have been killed. Right in front of me. Taken a bullet to the head. Or the heart. As I just sat there, watching.

A big part of me would have died with him.

Wait, that wasn't true. All of me would have died with him. Because I would have run to him and cradled his bloody body in my arms as Arty pumped bullets into me, too. I would not have cared if I lived or died. I would have wanted to die with Steve.

I stifled a moan. What did these crazy musings say about me? As a woman? As a private eye? What did they say about my feelings for Steve? They said I would rather die with him than live without him.

I opened my eyes and looked over at Steve, filled with gratitude that he was alive.

"We're here. Police headquarters." He pointed to a large gray building ahead and made a right into the parking lot. "You ready to go in and hear Arty confess to being one of the Princes of Pearls?"

"Oh, I'm ready," I said. "And he better damn well confess." I gave Steve my best gutsy-girl-gumshoe grin, but I don't think he was fooled.

Because my grin and my voice were as shaky as the rest of me.

THIRTY-FIVE

I'd never felt so in need of a shower and a change of clothes, but that didn't matter now as I followed Steve into the headquarters. Clean clothes would have to wait. As would taking a nap.

As would planting a big kiss on Steve's cheek, which I had a crazy, overwhelming desire to do.

Focus, Story, focus, I told myself. Arty's interrogation was too important, and I needed to keep my wits about me.

We entered a huge lobby where many of the officers from the shootout were gathering. The one with the bullhorn saw us and came over. "You guys need to follow me," he said, pointing to a large glass door on the other side of the reception desk. "They're waiting for you."

Steve gave a tight smile. "That's why we're here. Lead the way."

We were ushered into a long hallway and then into a gray, windowless interrogation room where Arty sat at a long steel table, guarded by two policemen. Staring straight ahead, his face stone-cold expressionless, he didn't look at us when we took seats across from him.

A gray-haired man in a suit and tie entered and closed the door. "I'm Detective Jed Burke," he said, shaking Steve's hand, then mine before taking a seat at the head of the table. "I understand that Mr. Duncan is your client," he told Steve as he placed a notebook on the table and pulled a pen from his jacket pocket. "Care to fill me in, starting with your name and the name of your lady friend?"

"He's fired!" Arty shook a finger at Steve. "Get him out of here— and ..." He turned his furious gaze on me. "He can take Miss Full of Herself Troublemaker P.I. with him."

"I'm Steve Evans and this is Miss Story Smith," Steve said calmly, ignoring Arty's outburst. "Mr. Duncan hired me to find out who killed his wife, and since I succeeded with the help of Miss Smith, who was hired by another party, he cannot fire me." Steve planted his elbows on the table, leaned toward Arty, and stared him square in the eye. "In any case, I quit because I don't work for people who try to kill me."

"A cousin of Mr. Duncan's wife hired me," I said, "to solve what has been a complicated case that involved tracking down a man who had been presumed dead in the war."

Arty slammed his fist on the table. "Get this woman out of here."

"Please continue, miss," the detective told me. "If Mr. Duncan continues to try to disrupt this interrogation, he is going to make things much worse for himself."

"Harry O'Toole was the man." I narrowed my eyes at Arty, daring him to interrupt me again. "Harry, currently in police custody in Cape May, was a buddy of Mr. Duncan's from their school days. In addition to admitting to murdering Mr. Duncan's wife, Harry has also confessed to being the notorious Prince of Pearls jewel thief and claims that Mr. Duncan was his partner in crime."

"Which is why, after being contacted by the Cape May police, I sent officers to your home, Mr. Duncan," Detective Burke said, his tone dry. "We wanted to question you about your friend Harry's assertions, but you fled with your children's nanny when you learned we were on our way—and then got into a shootout in a public park, of all places, with your private eye. Explain, sir."

Arty pressed his lips together hard and stared off into space, unblinking. For a minute I thought he might ask to call a lawyer. But he didn't. His breathing grew slower, his face paler, and then something in him changed.

The stubborn anger vanished, replaced by sad surrender, then defensive arrogance. As if he realized it was pointless to continue lying about what he'd done and was proud that he'd gotten away with it for so long.

"They never caught us." His lips curled up in a proud smirk. "We were that good."

"Good at what?" Detective Burke pressed.

"Robbing houses. Stealing money and jewelry. Mostly jewelry." Arty gave a crafty grin. "It was fun. And profitable. And nobody ever got hurt. We just snuck in, grabbed what we could, and snuck out. House after house, year after year." He heaved a sad sigh. "Until the war."

"So ..." Detective Burke looked up from jotting notes in his notebook, "Does this mean you are confessing to being the thief known as the Prince of Pearls?"

"One of them. There were two princes, me and Harry. But it was all Harry's idea. He talked me into it."

"But you ended up with all the loot," Steve said. "Harry got nothing."

"Harry got nothing because he died in the war. Or so we thought." Arty sniffed. "At first, I was sad about losing my friend. But then I pulled myself together and started selling stuff on the black market, one ring, one bracelet, one watch, one necklace at a time. With the money I made, I started buying and selling real estate and before I knew it, I was rich."

I leaned toward him. "Did you know that Harry squirreled some of the stolen goods away for himself?"

Arty scoffed. "Yeah. Found that out a couple years after the war when Gladys Jones offered to sell me a package that Harry had left with her. She figured he wasn't coming back, and I gave her a good price. She was happy, I was happy."

"But Harry was not happy when he finally did make it home," Steve said. "And since he'd been a suspect before the war, and since he couldn't exactly go to the police, he decided to get revenge on you for becoming so wildly successful. By killing your wife."

"The bastard. Don't know why he didn't just come to me and ask for money." Arty pounded his fist on the table. "I would have given him some."

"Some wouldn't have been good enough," Steve said. "And anyway, he was mortified by his appearance and bitter that his life was a mess while yours was going great."

I was feeling great about Arty confessing. The case was wrapping up nicely, with all the puzzle pieces falling into place. Except ...

"Arty, did you know that Harry gave Penny Ash one of the stolen necklaces?" I asked.

He shrugged. "Sure. He told me. Right after he did it. Thought he was in love with her or so he claimed. I told him it was a bad idea but we were shipping off to war so what could I say?"

"Why that particular necklace, out of all the ones you stole?" I asked.

He snickered. "You know, it was the first piece of jewelry we stole on our first heist. He kept it for himself since the whole jewel thief thing was his idea. And I didn't argue. There were plenty of other necklaces after that."

"Do you remember the address of that first house?" I found myself holding my breath, hoping it might be the one mentioned in the newspaper article I had read in the newspaper archives. I wanted, needed, closure on that necklace. For myself and for Penny.

My face must have given me away. Realizing how much the address meant to me, Arty slanted a grin at the detective. "Hey, where's Stella? I want to know where Stella is."

Detective Burke raised his eyebrows. "She's in another interrogation room. Why?"

"I don't want any charges filed against her in all this. She's a sweet innocent girl."

I met Steve's gaze and started coughing. His raised eyebrows matched the detective's.

"She's obviously too young to have been part of your Prince of Pearls capers," the detective said dryly. "So, what are you getting at?"

"I talked her into coming with me when I left the house this morning. She was not involved in the shootout in any way. She didn't even know I owned a gun."

The detective jotted something in his notebook, then looked up. "What I hear you saying is that you don't want us to charge her as an accessory to evading arrest?"

Arty nodded. "Right."

"Noted." The detective smiled. "Alright, then. Give us the address of that first house you robbed."

Arty raked a hand through his hair. "Sure. It was on Beach Avenue."

He gave the house number and Detective Burke wrote it down, then looked back at Arty. "For your information, we were planning on sending Miss Stella Murphy back to Iowa in any case. We've been in touch with her parents and will be putting her on a plane to them tonight."

Arty gave a relieved nod, which turned into an anxious frown when Detective Burke stood up and gestured for one of the officers to bring him handcuffs.

Motioning for Arty to get up, he went over and cuffed him behind his back. "You, sir, are under arrest," he said, "and you won't be going anywhere for a long, long time."

———

Victory. It had never felt so sweet.

Not only had I found Penny's lost necklace—with Steve's help— together we'd solved her cousin's murder and unraveled a years-long mystery involving stolen jewels.

In truth, though, the victory didn't feel entirely sweet. Two little girls would now grow up without a mother or a father. Luckily, their grandmother would see to it that they had a good life, but they would always live under the scandalous cloud of having a father who was a convicted felon.

There was also the sad fact that Penny would not be getting her necklace back, not that she would want it after I confirmed the full truth about Harry.

It was time to go see her and Jonathan at their home.

Only visiting them was going to have to wait because going home to shower and change my clothes came first.

"I wholeheartedly agree," Steve said as we walked out of the police station, and I told him my plans. He ruffled my hair and grinned. "You've looked better my dear and you are beginning to smell."

"What?!" I slapped his hand away, then caught his teasing grin and laughed. "If I'm stinky, then you're stinky, sir. We're quite the team."

He took my hand in his as we walked toward my T-Bird. "My Mercedes is at your office," he reminded me as he led me to the passenger side and opened the door for me. "I need to go home and change, too. I can meet you at Penny and Jonathan's later if you want."

I hesitated. We'd done so much together. Maybe I needed to do this alone. Only together felt so much better than alone.

He gazed into my eyes. "Or maybe you should wait—we should wait—until tomorrow to go see the Millers. It's getting late and you didn't sleep well last night ... and ..." His finger brushed my cheek. "Those dark circles under your eyes are rather concerning ..."

"I don't want to wait," I whispered. "But I do want to kiss you."

"Here?" He grinned. "In the parking lot of Philadelphia police headquarters?"

"Why not?" I grinned back. "You're alive and that's a glorious thing, and I've finally realized that if I have the courage to die with you, I should have the courage to live with you. Starting here and now."

"No better time," he whispered softly, then gathered me in his arms and kissed me passionately without a care for who saw us or what they might think.

Then he helped me into my car and went around and got behind the wheel and turned to me with a happy but puzzled expression on his face. "I hate to bring this up, Story, but what about Dean? You're still dealing with his ghost."

"Oh." I suppressed an inward groan. That burst my pretty balloon, but Steve was right. "Oh," I said. "Yeah. Dean."

"He's always going to be there, getting between us, unless you do something about it, Story."

I sighed. "Yeah ... but how do I deal with a ghost?"

We looked at each other and laughed.

"Victor Bravo," I said.

"Victor Bravo," Steve said.

———

I ended up visiting Penny and Jonathan that evening alone.

I realized I would get a better night's sleep if I went to see them solo and Steve agreed, with the understanding that he and I would go see Victor Bravo together in the morning.

Penny and Jonathan were surprised to see me when I showed up at their house so late, wearing my favorite blue dress, with clean hair, and a fresh-faced grin. But they were also pleased to see me because they could tell by my grin that I had good news.

"I have great news," I told Penny as she led me into her living room, bid me to take a seat on the sofa, then called for Jonathan to join us. "Or at least most of it is good," I cautioned. "Some is rather sad."

"Oh ..." Penny said as she and her husband settled themselves in armchairs facing me. Her expression was hopeful but guarded. "Go on."

I brought them up to date, telling them that Penny's long-lost love, Harry O'Toole, had been arrested for murdering Lily. That Arty and Harry had both confessed to being the jewel thieves behind the Cape May Capers. And that Arty's girls were safe with their grandmother while Stella had been sent packing.

"I know it's a lot to take in," I said to break the stunned silence in the room. "All of this must come as a horrible shock, but you hired me to find Lily's killer and with Steve's help, I did. I also found your necklace, Penny. Which unfortunately you will not get back because we need to return it to its rightful owner now that we know where it came from."

"But of course I don't want that necklace back," Penny cried. "Especially now that I know it was stolen by the man who gave it to me. Who I loved and trusted, whose memory I cherished. Who it turns out was in cahoots with my beloved cousin's husband. No, no, no."

She pressed a hand to her forehead. "All I want is my Lily back," she whispered brokenly. "I want Lily back."

"Penny, dear," Jonathan said. "You know that is not possible."

"But I loved her," Penny wailed. "She was like a sister to me. She was my best friend. Who cares about that stupid necklace? I never should have accused her of stealing it from me."

"But she did," I said. "You were right about that part. It was just far more complicated than anyone knew."

"None of this is your fault, Penny," Jonathan said. "The truth is distressing but it's important that we know it, as ugly as it is, and that justice will be served."

I wanted to do something to soften Penny's remorse and grief. "I have an idea," I said. "When the Cape May police return the necklace to its owner, do you want to go with them? I know I would like to."

Penny's eyes lit up at that. "Yes. Yes, I would very much like to be part of that."

Jonathan nodded in agreement.

"It's settled, then." Penny smiled. "Let us know when the police are ready, and we'll join them. It will be a good way for me to bid farewell to that chapter in my life."

THIRTY-SIX

I wanted to believe Victor Bravo could communicate with the dead. I really did.

For one, it would mean there was an afterlife, and that at least some of us would end up in heaven.

It would also mean that those who did make it to paradise maintained some interest in the lives of the loved ones they'd left behind on earth—and could offer some words of advice or wisdom through psychic mediums like Victor.

Who was delighted to see me and Steve the next afternoon when we showed up unannounced at his door. Flamboyantly dressed as usual, he sported a lime-green turban on his head that of course went smashingly with his billowy white shirt and flared green pants, made of a thin, gauze-like fabric that looked wonderfully cool on that hot July afternoon.

"My favorite couple, come in, come in," he said, ushering us into his small living room, where three big floor fans blew hot air around.

The windows were open, but it was still stinking hot in there. The fans at least gave an illusion of coolness, helped in part by the droning whirl of the blades.

My eyes were drawn to the psychic medium's bare feet. I couldn't help it. Today, each toenail was painted a different color, which made me smile. Victor was so Victor. Whether or not his supernatural gifts were real, the guy was fun to be around.

Waving for Steve and me to take seats on the sofa, he plopped himself down in a chair across from us and met my gaze with twinkling eyes. "You look well, my dear. I bet you found that swim mask, didn't you?"

I grinned. "Yes, thank you so much. It probably did save my life."

"The mask on the boat?" Steve glanced at me, confused.

"During my last visit to Victor he saw a vision of me under water, wearing a swim mask," I explained. "He predicted that I was about to face great danger, and he told me that if I saw a swim mask, to put it on. His prediction came true."

"Amazing," Steve said.

Victor squinted at me. "I see good vibrations around you now, nothing threatening on the horizon, which is wonderful, wonderful news. In fact ..." He widened his eyes as they bore into mine. "In fact, you seem to be radiating incredible love energy right now."

"What?" I whispered.

Victor shot Steve a sly smile, then turned back to me. "You two didn't get hitched, did you? I was hoping to get an invite to the wedding."

Too shocked to answer, I felt myself blush.

"Or maybe you just got engaged?" Victor jumped up and grabbed my left hand. "Let me see your ring—*oh, ow!*"

Dropping my hand, he backed away, his eyes bulging in disbelief. "Your hand is burning hot. Like it's on fire." He reached for my right hand. "This hand feels normal. Meaning you don't have a fever. This is strange, so strange."

Oh. My. Lord. My dream. My dream about Dean. In my dream, my left hand had burst into flames when he'd tried to jam a ring on my finger. "Uh ... uh, maybe this is not so strange," I squeaked.

I held my hands up in front of my face and stared at them. Was I dreaming now? No, I couldn't be. My left hand was not on fire. It looked fine. "I had a dream," I told Victor. "More like a nightmare. And that's why I'm here."

Then I told him about Dean and the cruel way I had broken off our secret engagement and how he had ended his life and how I'd blamed myself ever since. And then I told him about the dream.

"Your hand caught fire in the dream?" Steve stared at me. "Wow."

"And you would like to speak to this man, Dean." Victor nodded as if now everything made sense.

"Yes," I whispered. "Please. I want to ask for his forgiveness."

Nodding sagely, Victor raised his hands in the air. Gazing up at the ceiling, he lowered his hands and placed them palms down on his thighs as he closed his eyes.

He stayed that way for many minutes.

I was afraid to move. Afraid to look at Steve. Afraid to do anything but keep my eyes fixed on Victor, alert for any sign that something supernatural was happening.

"He is here," Victor said, finally, his voice low and soft. He waited a beat, keeping his eyes closed, then said, "Dean is here."

My heart stopped. My lungs froze. I couldn't get any words to come out of my mouth. What could I say, except forgive me, but I couldn't even manage that.

"He says you look good," Victor said. "That you are as beautiful as ever."

Guilt flooded my veins. I didn't deserve that. I didn't deserve his kindness. "I'm sorry," I finally managed to blubber. "I'm sorry, Dean. I was mean to you. The way I broke up with you. It was cruel and I'm sorry."

Victor opened his eyes. He tilted his head and stared up at the ceiling, then lowered it and looked at me. "You have nothing to be sorry for, he says. He does not blame you. He says what he did was his choice alone."

"Damn straight," Steve whispered. "That's what I've been—"

"Shhh," I hissed.

Victor closed his eyes again. He waited, then crooned, "Peace. He wishes you only peace. As he is at peace."

"Dean," I said, "please tell me you forgive me. Please."

Victor waited, with eyes closed, then said, "He says you did nothing wrong. That the person you must forgive is yourself." He popped his eyes open. "That is all."

"All?" I widened my eyes and waited. "That's *it*?"

"Yes. He has left."

I couldn't believe it. I could not believe what had just happened.

I turned to Steve.

He smiled at me. "Nice guy," he said. "I think I would have liked him."

THIRTY-SEVEN

It was time to bring the missing necklace case full circle. A case that was supposed to have been simple, that had ended up being anything but.

It was time to deliver the diamond and emerald necklace to its rightful owner.

I'd learned a lot in the process, personally and professionally, and while I was proud of my success, I needed to remember those hard-won lessons.

Beginning with how important it is to expect nothing, be open to everything, and to be prepared for anything.

I shouldn't have expected that sneaking away from a party unnoticed would be easy. I shouldn't have believed that I was too clever to be caught. And I shouldn't have assumed that a presumed dead war hero really was dead, much less a hero.

I also shouldn't have assumed that rumors about a handsome private eye with a reputation for being a womanizer were true. Or, that if there was some truth to them, that he couldn't change—or turn out to be the man for me.

I'd learned that I needed to be open to believing that I needed such a man. And that I deserved his love.

I also realized that if I was going to succeed in this private investigation business, I really, *really* needed to get a new gun. And that I needed to keep an overnight bag with a change of clothes, pajamas, toiletries, makeup, and a toothbrush in the trunk of my car.

Because I had to be prepared for anything.

"Well, hello, Story." Wendy greeted me at the office the next morning when I arrived bright and early, before eight o'clock, eager to a get a jump on the day.

She came around her desk to give me a big hug. "Congratulations on a job well done. Jonathan filled me in on everything you've been up to. I'm impressed. And so is he."

"Thank you," I said. "Do you know if he's on his way here?"

"He is, and so is Penny. I understand you guys are going to Cape May?"

"Yes, to return Penny's necklace to its original owner, a woman named Violet Cunningham. I spoke with Cape May police last night and they told me she still lives at the address Arty provided and that she's excited about getting her necklace back."

"Wow, that's wonderful," Wendy said.

"At the time of the robbery, in 1938, the *Philadelphia Inquirer* published an article about it. Sadly, poor Mrs. Cunningham has been grieving the loss of her beloved necklace all these years because it was a gift from her husband, who was killed in the war."

"Oh, dear."

"I can't wait to meet her," I said. "Neither can Steve." I wiggled my eyebrows, grinning, because I knew how much Wendy liked him. "He's coming, too."

"Oh, yay. Just looking at Steve makes my day." She gave me a saucy wink. "If you don't want him, Story, I do."

"Very funny, Wendy." I turned to head to my office because I had reports to type for the Millers before we left for the Shore. Suddenly I did not want to talk about my love life. It was too confusing and scary to contemplate. "Got to get to work," I told her. "Talk to you later."

Only I didn't get much work done because later turned out to be about thirty minutes later.

Wendy's squeal announced Steve's arrival and then he was at my door with Jonathan and Penny.

"Ready to go?" Jonathan asked. "We can all go in my New Yorker."

"Thanks, but we'll follow you," Steve said. "It'll give us more flexibility and ..." He smiled at me. "For a change, we can take my Mercedes instead of your T-Bird."

"Okay." I smiled back. "But what do you mean by flexibility?"

His smile turned teasing. "You ask too many questions, Story."

"Steve, I'm a private eye." I grinned. "Asking questions is what I do."

"You also need to stay open to surprises," he said. "We have a necklace to deliver, so, let's go."

I liked surprises. And I was in a celebratory mood, so I shrugged and agreed.

We arrived at the Cape May police station two hours later, where Detective Kenneth St. John was waiting for us. He ushered us into his office, opened the top drawer of his desk, and handed Penny the necklace.

Cupping it in her hands as if she was holding a small, wounded bird, she gazed at it with wonder. "I was so worried I'd never see this again," she said softly. "And now I cannot wait to give it away. Isn't it strange how time and circumstances can change your perspective on something—and how wrong you can be about something that you were certain was true?"

I asked, "You mean about Harry?"

"Yes." Running a finger along the diamonds and emeralds, the way she must have done so many times while grieving his memory, she sighed. "The love I felt for Harry and from Harry turned out to be something that existed entirely in my imagination. It was all a lie."

"Maybe it wasn't *all* a lie," I said. "Maybe a tiny part of it was true."

"Harry must have had some feelings for you, or he wouldn't have given you such a beautiful gift," Steve said. "He might have done it impulsively, and it's true that he had stolen it. But he didn't have to give it to you. And he did."

"The jerk," Jonathan said. "What a creep."

Detective St. John cleared his throat. "The owner is expecting us. Shall we go?"

Penny nodded and handed the necklace back to him. He wrapped it in a tissue, put it in the pocket of his dress shirt, and we followed him out the door and into his police van to make the short trip to Beach Avenue.

Violet Cunningham's home was magnificent. A four-story Victorian mansion with many windows and turrets, several porches, and a stained-glass front door, the place proclaimed wealth and taste.

It was easy to see why the Princes of Pearls had chosen the Cunningham home for their first Cape May caper.

We walked up to the front porch and Violet opened the door before we could knock. She was younger than I'd expected, maybe only several years older than Penny, and her eager smile warmed my heart.

"Come in, please," she said, nervously smoothing her shoulder-length auburn hair. "I can't tell you how grateful I am that you've come to return my necklace to me after all these years. All of you ..."

Detective St. John introduced us and explained why we had all come along for the ride. Then he pulled the tissue-wrapped necklace from his pocket, unwrapped it, and handed it to Violet. "Are you certain this is yours?"

A slow smile formed on her lips, lighting up her face. "Yes, yes," she cried.

Her eyes brimming with tears, she held it out in front of her and swung it back and forth. Sunlight spilling in from the front window made the jewels sparkle. I was glad to be there to witness her heartfelt gratitude. To witness something good coming from something so awful.

"Thank you," she said, moving her gaze to Penny. "Thank you for taking such good care of my precious necklace. My husband, Franklin, gave it to me on our first anniversary. God rest his soul—his plane was shot down during a bombing raid over Germany. He was a pilot for the Army Airforce. A true gentleman and a wonderful husband and a hero who died for our country."

"It must have been a shock to discover your house had been robbed," I said. "And that your necklace was gone."

"It was horrible." She shuddered. "They also took money that my husband had hidden in a drawer, along with my entire jewelry box and his watch. We were out and came home late and the police determined that they had forced open a ground floor window and snuck in."

"The first of many such robberies," Detective St. John said. "Unfortunately, Mrs. Cunningham, your necklace has to date been the only piece of jewelry recovered." He nodded at me and Steve. "Thanks to these private investigators and their hard work."

"Thank you," she whispered.

"We might need you to testify in court, Mrs. Cunningham. And to bring the necklace with you as evidence," the detective added. "Both of the thieves have confessed, but you never know—one or both could change their minds and retract their confession. Although not likely, a court trial might be necessary."

He turned to me and Steve. "You'll be glad to know that Gladys Jones has already agreed to testify. She's been discharged from the hospital and is recovering under the care of her parents. We've decided not to press charges against her due to her willingness to cooperate with us."

Violet Cunningham kissed her necklace. "I am ready and willing to do what I can do to see that justice is served," she said. "Just let me know if and when I am needed."

THIRTY-EIGHT

"Congratulations on a job well done, Miss Story Smith," Jonathan told me after Detective St. John brought us back to the police station. "I sure did get a good deal when I agreed to let Wendy work for you in exchange for your investigative services."

"Thanks," I said. "I'm glad it's worked out for both of us."

He turned to Steve. "Congratulations to you, too. What a team you guys make."

"I agree," Steve said as the four of us headed to our cars in the station parking lot.

"Jonathan and I are going to head back to Philly now," Penny said. "What are you guys going to do? Something fun to celebrate? Steve, didn't you tell Story you had a surprise for her?"

"Sure did." Steve raised his eyebrows at me. "I'm not in any hurry to leave Cape May, and I don't know about you, Story, but I thought we could start with lunch—since it's lunch time—and then maybe go to the beach."

I gaped at him. The beach? "Lunch sounds great," I said, "but I didn't bring a bathing suit." Oh boy, there I went again, not thinking things through in advance. Should have packed a suit. Darn.

He shrugged. "I'll buy you a bathing—"

"No, Steve ..." I shot him a look. "I can't keep expecting you to buy me clothes."

"Hey," Penny said. "I have an idea. Remember, Story, when I told you that my parents and Lily's parents owned adjacent cottages on Beach Avenue?"

I nodded, wondering where she was going with this. "Sure."

"And that I told you that the cottages are still in the family?"

"Mansions, you mean." I smiled. "Like Violet Cunningham's."

"Well, yes, not far from her on Beach Avenue. My Aunt Anna will probably be spending a lot more time at her place now that she's raising Janey and Jeannie. My mother only comes down to stay occasionally, when the mood strikes, and right now, the house is empty."

Penny reached into her purse and pulled out a key ring. She slid a large key off and handed it to me.

"What's this?" I asked.

"Wow," Steve said, "is that what I think it is?"

"It's the key to Mother's house." Penny winked at him. "Stay as many days as you like. You two deserve it. The address is engraved on the key."

"What?" I felt my face blush. "What are you saying? Just me and Steve? An entire mansion to ourselves? But ... but ... I still don't have a bathing suit—and I didn't pack a suitcase."

"Penny and I have a bedroom on the second floor," Jonathan said.

"We keep summer clothes there for when we visit, including swimsuits. Help yourselves. I think our sizes are comparable."

Holy cow. What were the Millers thinking? It wasn't as if Steve and I were married. "Uhm ..." I swallowed down the huge lump gagging my throat. "Uh ..."

"Oh." Penny laughed when she saw my expression. "Oh. Don't worry. There are many bedrooms. Seven, I think." She tapped a finger to her chin. "And maybe one on the fourth floor ... that would make eight. Anyway, you'll have a choice of guest bedrooms to pick from. Story, you can have one and Steve, you can have one." She stopped, looking as uncomfortable as I felt about where this conversation was heading.

But Steve didn't appear the slightest bit uncomfortable.

He was clearly delighted. "I think this is a marvelous idea." He flashed me that grin. The one I couldn't resist. "Thank you so much, Penny and Jonathan. Thank you, thank you."

———

Penny's mother's house was as impressive as Violet Cunningham's, if not more so. Painted a cheerful summery red and white, the massive mansion had a wide front porch lined with wicker rocking chairs, large floor-to-ceiling windows that faced the ocean, and a front yard that was mostly a rose garden, tucked behind a white iron fence and gate.

Steve and I pushed open the gate and walked up to the porch. Nervous and heart-poundingly giddy, I watched Steve insert the key in the door and held my breath. What was I doing?

This would be no overnight stay in a hotel with adjacent rooms.

This was to be a several-day-stay in a palace with many rooms ... and many beds ... and oh, my God ... I tried to banish the image from my mind but couldn't.

Steve pushed the door open, and a heavenly scented sweet mixture of sun, sea, salt, and suntan lotion greeted us as we entered.

I slipped off my sandals and left them by the door as I followed Steve across the cool hardwood floor into the living room.

The bright, open-air beauty of that room made me smile despite my nervousness. All the furniture was white. Sofas, ottomans, easy chairs. All the rugs on the hardwood floor were either seafoam green or sunny sky blue. All the paintings on the walls were seascapes.

And all the windows were framed by filmy white curtains.

Steve went over and, pushing aside the curtains, opened the windows facing the sea. A salty soft breeze blew in, a welcome relief from the heat of the day and the heat of my heart.

"Heavenly," I said.

"I feel like I've died—and that this is heaven," Steve said. Stretching out his arms, he moved toward me and took my hands in his. His eyes widened. "You're shaking. What's wrong?"

"You could have died, Steve," I said. "You almost did. When Arty pushed you off that boat. And then in the shootout in the park." There was grief and panic in my voice even though we were safe now. Cocooned in our own, cozy, just-the-two-of-us paradise.

"You came close to dying yourself, Story," he said. "Too many times for my comfort."

"When we leave here, can you help me buy another gun?" I squeezed his hands. Too hard, but I couldn't help it.

"Of course I'll help you." He gazed into my eyes. "You're scared, I can see that. But there's something else. Is it me?"

"It's not you, it's me," I whispered. "I don't want to be alone. I've learned together is a powerful thing."

He grinned. "I like the sound of that."

"But it scares me."

Steve led me over to one of the sofas. He sat down and looked up at me with a gentle expectancy, his eyes saying, "trust me."

I sat down next to him.

He put an arm around me and pulled me close.

I relaxed and put my head on his shoulder.

"You're afraid to be in this big house with me, all alone. Just us," he murmured. "Am I right?"

I nodded.

"Don't be afraid."

"I'm trying not to be."

"Are you still concerned about my so-called reputation with women?"

"I'm trying not to be."

"I'm not going to love you and leave you, Story."

I whispered, "But how do I know?"

He pulled back and met my anxious gaze. "Because we're going to pick out separate rooms in this house and we're going to spend several days getting to know each other." He smiled. "We're going to talk and go for walks on the beach and swim in the ocean and go out to eat and have fun, like tourists. We've never had that kind of time together and we need that."

He was right. But ... "Just talking?" I looked at him teasingly, scrunching up my nose. "What about kissing?"

"Oh, plenty of kissing." He grinned. "Plenty of that."

"Okay ... good."

"But there will be no hopping from bed to bed here, even though we could, and even though I'd very much like to," he said. "Because in all seriousness, I'm going to prove to you that I'm not that kind of man."

"Okay." My heart was beating so fast that I thought it would burst through my chest. But in a good way. A happy way.

Steve was a good guy. I could trust him. Not only with my life, but with my heart, too.

Gazing into my eyes with an intense love that I'd never believed was possible, he took me in his arms and kissed me. "The first of many kisses to come," he promised, his voice husky with desire. "But first ..."

Giving me that too sexy grin of his, he ran a finger lightly across my lower lip. "Let's go get lunch."

Acknowledgments

Thank you to my readers for loving my books and letting me know in so many ways.

Thank you to my fantastic editor, Caren Burmeister. You've been with me on my fiction writing journey since the beginning and I couldn't have done it without your encouragement and expertise.

Thank you to my cover designer, Robin Johnson of Florida Girl Design. You have also been with me since my first novel, and I am amazed and grateful at how skillfully you illustrate the essence of my stories with your art.

Thank you to my husband, Jim, and to my family and friends for being my biggest, enthusiastic fans.

And thank you to my friends and fellow writers from First Coast Romance Writers. I love how we continue to support each other and learn together. Writing can be a hard, lonely business, but with you guys I never feel alone.

Maggie FitzRoy writes historical romance, romantic suspense, and romantic mystery thrillers.

A former journalist who grew up loving Nancy Drew books, Maggie always liked the idea of becoming a private investigator but ultimately decided that writing a mystery series about a female detective would be safer—and with romance woven in, pure fun.

Since she's also a history buff, the Story Smith Mysteries are set in the 1950s. The first book in the series, Never on Monday, was a First Coast Romance Writers National Excellence of Romance Fiction Awards Finalist.

Maggie lives in Ponte Vedra Beach, Florida with her husband and beloved pets. When she is not writing, she enjoys pickleball, swimming, walking on the beach, and choral singing. You can learn more about all her books and her upcoming Story Smith adventure, Thrill Me Thursday, by visiting her website and signing up for her newsletter at http://maggiefitzroy.com.

Read More by Maggie FitzRoy

A STORY SMITH MYSTERY SERIES

Never on Monday

Tuesday Means Trouble

Woe is Wednesday

Coming next: Thrill Me Thursday

HISTORICAL ROMANCE

Mercy's Way

Beacon Beach

His Haven